CITY OF
SPARROWS

CITY OF SPARROWS

Eva Nour

MELVILLE HOUSE
BROOKLYN • LONDON

Melville House Publishing

46 John Street

Brooklyn, NY 11201

and

Melville House UK

Suite 2000

16/18 Woodford Road

London E7 0HA

mhpbooks.com

@melvillehouse

ISBN: 978-1-61219-852-1
ISBN: 978-1-61219-853-8 (eBook)

Library of Congress Control Number: 2020934622

Printed in the United States of America

1 3 5 7 9 10 8 6 4 2

A catalog record for this book is available from
the Library of Congress

For Sami

CITY OF
SPARROWS

I

It wasn't because they might be diseased, though many of them likely were. No, it was because they lived under the siege, just like you. The cats were as innocent and as thirsty, as emaciated and starving as you. 'It would be like eating your neighbour,' you said.

A cat has seven souls in Arabic. In English cats have nine lives. You probably have both nine lives and seven souls, because otherwise I don't know how you've made it this far.

What determines whether you survive or not? Chance. But chance doesn't inspire hope. Instead, you say there are strategies, two strategies to be precise. The first piece of advice came from a friend in the Syrian army, who said that imagined freedom is a kind of freedom.

'When they wake us up in the middle of the night and pour ice water over our naked backs, convince yourself that you are choosing this, that it's your own choice.'

The second piece of advice, and you can't remember who gave you this, is to never look back and never feel regret. Not even about the things you do regret.

When you tell me about your childhood, I think about the Russian-American author Masha Gessen's words. 'Do not be taken in by small signs of normality,' she writes, on how to survive in totalitarian times. Your childhood was bathed in light and sunshine, in safety and love. All the small signs of normality.

1

IT WAS HIS older sister's idea to fetch a kitchen knife to save the sparrow. The little bird sat stock still, chirping urgently, in the glue their parents had smeared across a couple of flattened cardboard boxes on the roof terrace. The glue was meant to catch mice but the sparrow had got stuck instead. Down below, the streets and square courtyards of Homs shimmered in the heat. The air was thick with exhaust fumes and the sweet fragrance of jasmine, which climbed over stone walls and iron gates, but the occasional refreshing breeze reached seven-year-old Sami and his nine-year-old sister.

They leaned over the bird. Hiba gently cut away the glue from under its claws as though she were a top surgeon from Damascus and not a schoolgirl with a short attention span. But they soon realized there was glue in the bird's feathers and it wouldn't be able to fly. Sami carried it in cupped hands down the stairs to the bathroom, careful not to trip – take it slow, his sister told him – and they rinsed and washed the sparrow in the sink, making sure the water was neither too hot nor too cold, the jet neither too powerful nor too gentle. The light brown ball of fluff rested in his hands while Hiba softly dabbed the trembling body with the green towel.

'What are you doing?' their mum asked from the kitchen.

Their parents, Samira and Nabil, would sit in there on the weekends, discussing matters relating to the children and the house, listening to Fairuz' soft songs on the radio. Sami heard the clinking of their cups, black coffee in which cardamom pods rose and sank, and the sound of his father clearing his throat as he wiped crumbs out of his moustache, the part of his appearance he was proudest of.

'Saving a bird,' Sami replied.

'No more animals,' Nabil said.

'No, we're going to release it now,' Hiba promised, in the same tone she used to tell her teacher she hadn't glanced at her classmate's answers on the test.

They reached the top of the stairs and opened the terrace door. The sun loomed high above their heads like a mirage, impossible to look straight at. Hiba took the sparrow and held her hands up. Fly, little bird, fly! But the bird sat still, curled up and without emitting so much as a peep.

'It's because its wings aren't dry yet,' his sister said.

So they sat down on the sun-warmed roof, under a sky as blue as the pools in Latakia, to wait for the last of the moisture to evaporate. The kitchen knife glinted. Hiba held up the newly sharpened edge and the light that bounced off it blinded the two chickens and drove them clucking back into their coop.

The heat made Sami drowsy and happy at the same time. It reminded him of a similar day the week before, which, in spite of its simplicity and unpredictability – or maybe because of the randomness of the moment – made him feel warm inside. Sami had lost his balance on a bicycle. Perhaps there had been a small rock in his path. Whatever the reason, he had taken a tumble. For a split second, he had been weightless, alone and insignificant, like a cloud of dust swirling through the white morning light. Nothing could stop him. No one knew where he was. No one except for Hiba, who ran inside and told on him, saying he had borrowed the bike, even though he wasn't allowed, and ridden it out on the main road, even though there were cars there. Then the moment had ended and everything returned to normal. But for an instant, he was sure of it, he had experienced absolute freedom.

The guilt he felt at taking the bike without asking made him keep quiet about his little finger. It hurt more than anything he had ever felt before, and stuck straight out like a bent feather on an injured bird. He tried to hold back his tears but Grandma Fatima noticed. She noticed the scrape on his right knee, where blood was beading, and him trying to hide his hand behind his back.

'Let me see,' Fatima said, and closed her wrinkled hand around his little finger.

She recited an elaborate chant, a monotonous half-singing that breathed tenderness and solemnity. Words that ran like a red thread through his childhood.

'There,' his grandma said and opened her hand. 'It will be fine tomorrow.'

He went to bed and tried to think of the pain as a cloud hovering above him. The cloud was still there in the morning, now edged with rain. His sheets were wet too. When Samira found out, her face changed colour and she scolded both her son and her mother.

'Why didn't you go to the doctor? Your finger's broken.'

His chest burned again. Because he had fallen on the bike, because he had wet his bed, because he had believed in his grandmother's stupid chants. If her words of wisdom couldn't be trusted, what was safe and unchanging? Nothing seemed to last for ever. Soon even their sparrow would leave them.

Their sparrow. That was how Sami thought of it, even though it had only been in their possession for a short while. For an hour or two, their rescue operation had been so exhilarating they'd lost track of time. He felt a bond with the bird, as though a connection had been created simply by watching its dark pinhead eyes. By touching its downy feather coat. Feeling its light weight in his hand. He felt responsibility and love for it; no, he didn't think those words were too big. He would miss it when it spread its wings and disappeared across the sky.

His thoughts were interrupted by the sound of inane whistling and he felt a shudder run down his spine, despite the heat. When he looked over the roof ridge, he saw the neighbour's daughter ambling about their courtyard.

'Don't worry, I'll protect you, little sparrow,' Sami whispered.

The girl always popped up when you least expected it. Behind the bins or in a doorway, or she would drop out of a tree. She wore glasses and had two stiff plaits and was a head taller than him. Why did she pick on him? Possibly because he offered no resistance. There was a methodical stubbornness about the blows. He lay on the ground and tried to curl up and protect his face. It was widely known the girl's mother was a secret drinker and that her daughter probably took as many beatings as she handed out. But in that moment, he felt no compassion. Such injustice, that someone could lay into a body so small and insignificant without God, fate, a passing neighbour or the world at large intervening.

Hiba distractedly twirled the knife on the cardboard. Sami grew more sleepy. He couldn't put it into words, not then. It was a dizzying feeling, amplified by the bright light, like the feeling of being thrown off the bike. The thought solidified later in life: perhaps there was no fate to control him, perhaps he was completely and utterly free. When you took a step in any direction, you immediately faced a choice and then another one. Time forced you to move. Every second was a new start in which you had to act.

But that was a dangerous thought that went against everything he had been taught. You were supposed to trust in fate and the higher powers. God, first and foremost, then the leader of their country. Or was it the other way around? Hafez al-Assad first and God second.

Sami and his sister were sitting on the roof terrace with the knife and the bird, almost dry now, between them. The sparrow's heart was beating rapidly in its chest. Afterwards, you might regret it and ask what might have happened if you had done this or that, if you hadn't cycled on the main road, if you had put up a fight the very first time you met the girl next door, if you had listened a little bit less to what other people thought and said, like your older sister, for instance. But by then, it was too late.

'You have to throw it,' Hiba said, interrupting Sami's contemplation.

'What do you mean, throw?'

She showed him how he should lift his cupped hands up and out, to give the bird momentum and make it understand it had to unfurl its wings.

'That's how they learn to fly, their mums push them out of the nest,' his sister said.

'But our bird already knows how to fly.'

'Exactly, it just needs to be reminded.'

They each kissed the bird's beak and stroked its back. In that moment, he regretted not giving it a name. If it had had a name, it would stay with them, a name would anchor his love for it. Instead he whispered, *teer ya tair*: fly, bird.

He raised his hands and hurled the sparrow into the air and, for a moment, it looked like it was flying in a wide arc out across the rooftops and courtyards of Homs, through the shimmering blue sky, before it plummeted towards the asphalt three floors down, broke its neck and died.

2

HE IMAGINED A quilt and that it was his country. Sami's mother used to collect patches of fabric, from ragged jeans to old curtains and torn tablecloths, and sew them together on her shiny black Singer. Their country looked like one of her quilts, made out of fourteen pieces. Some edges were as straight as if cut out with a pair of scissors. Homs' governorate was the largest part, occupying the middle – most of it was camel-wool, the colour of sand, and showed Palmyra, whose Roman ruins attracted pilgrims and tourists. At the other end of the cloth, a blue thread seemed to wander, surrounded by orchards and cotton farms. The stitches became more sprawling in that part, more broken and colourful. A silk blue patch of water, a cross-stitch of roads and hills.

In that corner was Sami's hometown, Homs, which gave its name to the province. Looking more closely at the blue thread – the Orontes river – it divided the city in two. To the east was the centre and the most important neighbourhoods, and to the west, the new and modern al-Waer suburb.

Yes, both the country and the city resembled the quilt Samira held in her hands: an incongruous collection of pieces, which she patiently sewed together with equal parts frustration and love.

◆

Homs was the country's third biggest city and home to about a million inhabitants, situated on the river banks near the Crusader castle Krak de Chevaliers. There was the old clocktower, the Saint Mary Church of the Holy Girdle and the Khalid ibn al-Walid Mosque, but the city didn't attract as many tourists as the capital Damascus or the commercial centre Aleppo. Homs was primarily a city for the people who already lived in it, an unassuming place. No one was particularly rich and no one was particularly poor; everyone ate the same kind of food, as the saying went.

Sami's home was in al-Hamidiyah, in the Old Town, the most condensed part of the city. Several of the houses had shops and cafés at street level while the owners lived upstairs. Sami could recognize his home streets from the smell: fresh coffee, roasted almonds and diesel steam. Their house, like the neighbouring houses, was striped, built with dark and bright stone. When Sami was born his father had had a small shop to make ends meet but it had been closed down long ago and made into a garage. They reached the apartment from an outside staircase. It had two levels, three if you counted the roof terrace.

The house had originally been built with a square courtyard, which an orange tree brightened during the day and a starry sky illuminated at night. But as the family grew, floors had been added and the courtyard built over. Now the pride of the house was the children it contained, not to mention all the animals. Sami and his mother would place bowls of leftovers on the stone steps for the neighbourhood cats. From time to time, a cat or two would move in, and they were usually allowed to stay so long as they didn't get pregnant or pee on the Persian rug. Two hens lived in a mesh-encircled coop on the roof terrace, alongside a turtle on a water-filled silver tray.

The white duck, however, that had been Sami's special pet, had vanished without a trace. His parents had told him it was sick and they had taken it to the vet. That night, they had meat for dinner. When his mum leaned across the table and asked if he liked it – pulling a face as though trying to stifle a giggle, and then she coughed and

Nabil handed her a glass of water – his sister said they were eating his duck. Sami didn't want to believe it. Besides, only half of what his sister said normally turned out to be true. But they wouldn't tell him where the white duck had gone. The meat on his plate was light and tender and had tasted juicy up until that point, but afterwards he wasn't really hungry any more.

After dinner, Sami went to the biscuit jar and comfort-ate some of the sweet pistachio rolls in it. He was not allowed to do so and to emphasize the point his mother had placed a note at the top of the jar that read *God sees you.* Samira was the only one in the family who turned to Mecca five times a day and fasted during Ramadan. Sometimes the others joined her so as not to make her sad. She was the heart of the family, tall, imposing, with a thick braid that swung far down her back when they were at home. Like many women of her generation, she didn't work, aside from the work required to bring up three children, twenty-four hours a day, seven days a week.

Sometimes, however, Samira made tablecloths that she sold in the market. She had started sewing at the same time she started wearing a hijab. It was a few years before, not because she had to, but because people around her were. Samira wore it on special occasions and with her fringe visible, more in the style of early Hollywood starlets. She made her first headscarf out of one of her mother's polka-dotted 1950s dresses. When she had the sewing machine out anyway, she also took the time to make things for Sami and his siblings. A skirt for Hiba, a pair of sweatpants for their big brother Ali, a jumper for him.

The jumper was yellow and black with two penguins on the front. Sami wore it every day, until he went to a classmate's birthday party and someone called him an egg yolk. That made the jumper lose some of its charm, but the penguins still captivated him. His dream was to one day travel to a permanently cold place with snow and ice – his older brother talked about exotic places like Svalbard and Antarctica. He imagined the cold did something to the people there, that it created a silent mutual understanding. They dressed in thick jackets and blew smoke rings and had a common enemy, namely the biting winds. He figured there would exist a deep bond between humans and animals there. So long as you respected each other's habits and didn't act unpredictably, you could live side by side. Penguins would waddle about, polar bears would hunt seals, seals would dive into their holes in the ice in search of fish. And he for his part would live in an igloo, staring himself blind at the white landscape.

'Hey, egg yolk, what are you staring at?'

The girl next door pulled his jumper. She pulled so hard the sleeve ripped. Samira offered to fix it but Sami said there was no point. The fabric had faded after many years of use anyway. By this time his mother was wearing a headscarf every day, careful to push in any stray wisps of chestnut hair. Like Sami with his yellow jumper, she never explained why she stopped wearing it the way she had before. She only said it felt more comfortable.

His mother seemed to feel guilty about the white duck and gave Sami a calligraphy set. The sharpened edge of the wooden pen was dipped in black ink and scratched across the paper. He slowly moved from right to left, letter by letter. His siblings each received a sign with their name on to put on the door of their room.

First, he wrote his brother's name, Ali, who was the oldest and tallest of the three. Sami looked up to him. When he walked, his tanned arms were in constant motion, as though he were restless or on his way somewhere important. Ali didn't like being told what to do. He was sociable, well-liked and always surrounded by friends, who didn't even seem to notice he had a stutter. He did well in school but it was not his first priority. That was why he got into so many arguments with their father. Nabil believed people should apply themselves and work hard, and, for some mysterious reason, that precluded spending a lot of time with friends.

Sami wrote Hiba's name in smaller script on his own sign because they shared a room. They played and fought almost all the time. He didn't think of her as different but was aware something separated them. He could tell from the way their father gave Hiba, but not his sons, little presents, like jewellery and sweets. When Sami pointed that out, Nabil asked if he was a girl. It was the same thing when Hiba was allowed an extra hour of computer games.

'Are you a girl? No, well, there you go then.'

The computer had been a compromise in the family. Their father had also agreed to have a TV, so long as they put the remote in a plastic case to protect it from dust. For Nabil, the radio would have been enough. He listened with his chair turned to face the set, claiming he could hear better when he saw where the sound was coming from. Their father worked at the train station and had little time for new-fangled things. The railroad was a remnant of another era. Most people drove between cities; tourists and the odd commuter were the only ones who chose the train. Sometimes Sami went with his father to work. A white-haired man with a watch chain in his waistcoat would cycle up to the rails and turn the tracks when a train was approaching. Automated switches and the internet, what were those things? Nothing but a fad.

In the end, their father let them talk him into buying a computer. He had grown up in less affluent circumstances and wanted his children to have what he hadn't. Samira sided with the children and was used to having her way. Her strong will had come in useful when she and Nabil had first met and fallen in love. Her family were better off and considered more cultured, and required a good deal of convincing before they approved the marriage.

Not long after the wedding – perhaps not long enough – Ali was born. A couple of years later, Hiba arrived. His parents had grown blasé with two children before Sami, their relatives would say, and that was why there were no baby pictures of him. In his first photograph, he was six and dressed in the black-and-yellow penguin jumper.

'That's because our parents found you in the street,' Hiba said at the dinner table once.

Sami ran into his room and pulled his quilt cover over his head, pretending he was hiding underneath all the rivers and deserts and hills his country contained. He knew Hiba was lying but he couldn't be completely sure. Maybe something about him was different, maybe he didn't belong? A corner of the cover was lifted and Hiba's cat-like eyes squinted down at him.

'I was just kidding, you're my brother.' She pointed to three white dots next to the thumb on his left hand. 'Look, this is where I bit you when you were little.'

Sami followed his sister back into the kitchen so as not to miss dessert. When they gathered around the table, their father said they needed him to write one more sign. Samira stroked Nabil's back, and he returned her smile and gently put a hand on her belly.

'Is it true?' Hiba gasped. 'Are we getting a little brother?'

Sami muttered silently, looked down and scratched his spoon against the plate.

3

A COOL BREEZE wafted around his ankles when Sami put his feet down on the floor. He checked that the envelope was in the outer pocket of his new backpack, a gift from when he turned twelve last month, and felt a thrill of anticipation in the pit of his stomach. He even beat Hiba into the shower and didn't have to worry about the hot water.

No one seemed to notice that Sami wasn't touching his breakfast. Samira was busy pitting black olives, asking Hiba about her chemistry homework and reminding Ali to pick up the chocolate cake on his way home from school. It was 1999 and that evening they were celebrating Malik's first birthday. Malik, who was at that moment smearing hummus all over the kitchen table while screaming for attention, his cheeks a deep red. Sami felt he resembled a pet more than a new sibling.

Sami crept into the hallway and noticed that his grandpa Faris was already standing in front of the oval gold-framed mirror next to the mahogany chest of drawers. Half of him was in shadow; a ray of sunlight across his face lit up one cheek, his strong nose, a thick moustache that hid his top lip and his wavy raven hair, similar to Nabil's, which made him look like one of the Roman statues at the national museum. He spent at least fifteen minutes in front of the mirror every morning in the quest for a perfect side-parting.

'Would you like a couple of drops?'

Sami's friends used hair gel but he preferred hair oil. It was fragrance-free and smooth to the touch and had an aura of elegance, which probably sprang more from Grandpa Faris than the oil itself. He was wearing pressed suit trousers, a snow-white shirt and patent leather shoes. His cane was made of walnut and specially ordered from Aleppo. Walking with Grandpa Faris was like being out with a celebrity. He said hello to his neighbours, asked about sick relatives, girlfriends and newborn babies, smiled at clever anecdotes, dispensed advice to people who found themselves in a pickle and listened whenever anyone needed to vent.

'You should run for parliament,' people would tell him.

Grandpa Faris would laugh and raise his hand in self-deprecation, which inevitably made his admirer insist.

'You should. I would vote for you!'

Grandpa Faris would resist making any sarcastic response about the so-called voting procedure, the kind of comment he sometimes made when they were alone, just the two of them.

'When you're older, you'll see how it's done. They give you a ballot with two boxes, yes or no, to the sitting president Hafez al-Assad. Because our leader is a generous man who listens to the will of the people, they are given a completely free choice . . . yes or no . . .'

Sometimes Sami accompanied Grandpa Faris in the evenings, at the hour when the moon rose through the sky. The walk took them to the famous *souk*, the old market in the city centre, where the winding alleys opened into food stands and small shops that sold everything between heaven and earth. That was when Grandpa Faris would tell him about the French company he had worked for in the 1940s, when Syria was under French rule. Granted, the French had been no angels, and a lot of people had been killed back then, but they were respectful, according to Grandpa Faris. Like if the French soldiers were chasing a suspected rebel and he ran into a church or a mosque, well, they wouldn't run after him and shoot him in there. Some things had been sacred, even to the French occupiers.

'Besides, it's thanks to the French we eat *croissants*,' he said. 'And some of the words you use are from the French, like *canapé* and *chauffage*.'

Now they were standing side by side in front of the mirror, each applying oil to a dark swirl of hair. Grandpa Faris tilted Sami's chin up, adjusted an out-of-place strand and asked if there was something special happening that day. It couldn't be helped; Sami's cheeks flushed.

'It's just a theatre play at school.'

'Then maybe you'd like to try a bit of perfume?'

Sami studied the result in the mirror. Newly ironed khaki shirt, oil-combed hair and a cloud of oud around him. Then he passed the kitchen, where Malik had moved on to throwing olives on the floor, and hurried out the door.

His best friend Muhammed was already waiting at the corner, his freckly face hidden beneath a bird's nest of curly hair. Sami was jealous because his friend was taller than him, but he was also proud because everyone believed that Muhammed was in high school already, which made Sami feel mature by association.

'Wow, what's that smell?' Muhammed asked, sniffing the air.

His friend had recently started wearing spectacles and the thick glass made his eyes look bigger, like he was in constant surprise.

'Nothing,' Sami said. 'Come on. Let's see who gets to Nassim first.'

The street had flooded after the night's spring rain and they zig-zagged between pools that looked like drops of the sky had fallen on the asphalt. There was the rattling sound of metal shutters being pulled up, the chirping from small birds, the cries of mothers who shouted at their children to hurry up for school. Muhammed seemed to win the race but slowed down at the end to give Sami a chance to catch up.

'It's not fair,' Sami panted. 'Your legs are too long.'

'Too long! Your legs are too short.'

They walked into Nassim's store, which was similar to many of the small shops on the street. All owned by old men who spent their days listening to the radio channel Monte Carlo, talking to customers and filling the shelves with goods from floor to ceiling.

'You are lucky, boys, the bread car just came.'

Sami bought them a croissant each, and Muhammed promised to pay him the next day, which he rarely did, but it didn't matter. Muhammed had lived with just his mother and three siblings since their father was imprisoned when Muhammed was little. It wasn't something they talked about. Like Sami never mentioned that Muhammed's school uniform was slightly outgrown, the colours faded and the sleeves frayed. Sami's mum usually put an extra apple or banana in his backpack to give to his friend at lunchtime.

'Bye, Abu Nassim, see you tomorrow.'

'Bye, boys, be good and study well.'

On the street they greeted a teacher, and when they passed an all-girls school, they slowed down and peeked silently through the fence. Their school was mixed, with boys and girls, but there was something special about that place. At least, up until recently, when Sami had found a new interest in his own school.

Their school was built out of basalt – Homs was known as the city of black stones – and surrounded by high walls and fences. Songs with zealous choruses echoed across the schoolyard from speakers. A lot of them were about the invisible enemy just down the road: Israel, waiting for a chance to destroy them. Back then, he didn't connect the songs with a real country with real inhabitants. It was just part of the school day, like maths, art and military studies.

Sami lined up with his classmates and waited for the morning lecture, delivered by their headmistress, an older woman with candyfloss hair gathered in a tight bun at the nape of her neck. First the Syrian flag was raised, then the flag of the Baath Party.

'Repeat after me,' the headmistress said as feedback surged through the speakers. 'With our soul, with our blood, we submit to al-Assad.'

'With our soul, with our blood, we submit to al-Assad!'

'And what do we fight for? Unity, freedom and socialism.'

'Unity, freedom and socialism!'

She inspected the rows of khaki school uniforms over her rimless glasses. The morning assembly continued with her scolding the students, one by one or in groups, while thwacking the ground with a switch. Sami had never seen her use the switch on anyone but even so it was a relief when, after repeating her phrases about the almighty father of their country, the eternal and wonderful, they were allowed to march into their classrooms. Especially since this term he had been sitting behind a girl he had only recently noticed.

Yasmin never raised her hand if she could help it, but if she was asked a question she always knew the answer. Sami studied the back of her neck during English class until she turned around and he looked down at his notebook. He wondered how it would be to run his hand through her dark hair, gathered in a ponytail, and feel the gentle curve of her head under his fingertips.

A few months earlier, while he was lost in thought at his desk, a crumpled-up note had hit his cheek. Sami saw Muhammed's crooked grin on the opposite side of the classroom. His best friend had a way of butting into situations that were none of his business. Sometimes in an attempt to come to the rescue, like by taking the blame if Sami forgot his homework, or, like this time, by throwing a note to set things in motion. $1 + 1 = 69$. He wasn't sure what it meant but he sensed it referred to something adults did in secret.

'Can I borrow your pen?' Yasmin asked.

'This one?'

'Yes, it's a pen, isn't it?'

He gave it to her and the note accidentally slipped from his hand. 'Oh, I guess I wrote that wrong . . .' he mumbled when she read it.

'I guess you did. It's actually two,' she said and drew a 2. 'Which is also good.'

After that, Yasmin always greeted him with an *ahlain* or *marhabtain*, two hellos or double hi. If Sami grabbed a juice box in the canteen,

Yasmin would appear behind him. *Shouldn't you be grabbing two?* When they were sitting on a stone bench in the schoolyard and someone asked if there was room for them, she said, *Sorry, this is a bench for two.* They lay down on their backs with their heads close together and looked for shapes and signs in the clouds. When he quickly kissed her on the way home, under a tree with low-hanging oranges, she said: *Two.* Everything was better doubled.

Yasmin and he spent all their time together, just the two of them, for a while. Then a new boy started in their class. Haydar. He wore the same school uniform as the rest of them, but it looked more ironed, and he had a silver wristwatch as well. The school guard wasn't supposed to accept jewellery but she only smiled and let him pass at the gate. Both the guard and their teachers were delighted at Haydar's politeness and sarcastic jokes, little knowing that during break-time he swore more than all the other students put together. Worst of all was that the new boy was good-looking. Handsome, even. High cheekbones and dark eyes under thick, blond hair. Yasmin invited Haydar to join their games and let him sit with them at lunch. *There's only room for two,* Sami wanted to say, but heard how silly it would have sounded.

He noticed how Yasmin changed when Haydar was around. Before, she loved asking him to crack his knuckles. Now she said it sounded gross. Before, they would compare comic books, but since Haydar didn't bother with reading, now Yasmin didn't either.

This particular day, during lunch break, the envelope was burning in his breast pocket as the students gathered around the kiosk to buy croissants and *manakish*, a sort of mini pizza with thyme and sesame seed. Sami looked out for Yasmin but just as he spotted her among a group of girls playing basketball, the bell rang.

Military class was next. Their usual teacher was ill and there were no substitutes, so their religious studies teacher filled in. She wore a silver cross around her neck and balanced her short and stout body on a pair of black heels. She was a mild woman who took the time to answer their questions, and sometimes her eyes would wander to the orange trees outside the classroom as she took off on philosophical flights of fancy. In the schoolyard, however, she underwent a personality transformation before their very eyes.

Clouds hid the sun, plunging the schoolyard into shadow, when she called out for everyone to line up. The first fifteen minutes was theory. She held up a Kalashnikov, described the various parts – the wooden butt, the magazine, the adjustable iron sight – and where to insert the cartridges.

'This is the setting for fully automatic, and this is for semi-automatic, in other words, for firing one bullet at a time.'

A student raised his hand.

'Miss, how fast can you shoot?'

'Well, it depends on the model, but this could probably do six hundred rounds a minute.'

Then it was time for practical exercises, but not with the rifle. Their teacher ordered them to do gymnastics and formations. Dressed in their school uniforms, they obeyed her commands. When Yasmin fell and scraped her knee, she was told to do ten extra push-ups. When she was done, Haydar held his hand out to her and the silver watch shone in the shade.

'Straight line!'

The teacher asked Sami to stay after class was over. Why had he looked so distracted? She leaned forward and sniffed the air. He was afraid she would comment on the perfume, even though she herself walked around in a cloud of artificial lavender, but she pointed to his oil-combed hair.

'Ask your mother to take you to the hairdresser. Your hair is getting long.'

He had not managed to talk to Yasmin yet, but then he saw her waiting for him on the front steps. There she sat, with a beaming smile and sparkling braces. Haydar sat next to her.

'Hello, hi,' Sami said.

'Hello,' Yasmin replied.

Haydar rummaged around in his bag and said there they were, the theatre tickets.

'Great, what are we seeing?' Sami said.

He tried to sound normal, as though his heart was not in his mouth. The envelope he had brought from home, which had been sitting in his breast pocket all day, contained exactly that, theatre tickets. He would have preferred to take Yasmin to the cinema, but Homs had only old cinemas that showed black and white films and were rumoured to be places where criminals went to strike deals.

'We only bought two,' Yasmin said, shifting uncomfortably. 'They're for *Romeo and Juliet*, and you don't like it.'

Granted, he didn't, but he could have liked it if they had asked. The tickets he had bought were for a comedy that Yasmin would probably find childish, he realized now.

'All right,' Sami said. 'I hope you have a good time, then.'

'I'm sure we will.'

Sami rocked back and forth on his heels and grabbed the straps of his backpack. Yasmin moved closer to Haydar, who smiled and laid an arm around her shoulders.

'I think I'm going to stay here for a while,' Yasmin said. 'But I'll see you tomorrow, right?'

She said it breezily and naturally, as though there were a tomorrow.

An oily strand of hair fell into Sami's face. When he walked across the schoolyard and out through the gates, he felt both more watched and more invisible than before. From that day on, three was apparently a crowd, the answer to all questions was two, and one felt lonelier than ever.

4

ONE TIME IN school, when they were hiding from the rain under the tin roof of the cafeteria, Haydar told them about a girl at the school he'd gone to before. The girl had snuck into the headmaster's office one morning and taken over the PA system. Instead of the usual chorus, a phrase like 'death to the enemy' or the Baath Party slogan, she had sung a song she had composed herself about the will of the people. An informer must have reported it because the next day the secret police, the *Mukhabarat*, came to their school to talk to the girl's teacher. The teacher was fired the same day.

'That's terrible,' Sami said.

It reminded him of a time in first grade when his dad had realized that Sami had doodled on the portrait of al-Assad in his school book. The slap came without warning, a searing pain that left a red mark on his cheek. It was a moment that split reality in two: one half in which his dad never flew off the handle, and another in which his dad could get upset, frightened even, by doodles in a school book. It was the first and only time Nabil hit him. It was also the first time Sami truly sensed the power of the president. He secretly began hating the pictures of the serious-looking man in military uniform.

'I think it was fair,' Yasmin said about the dismissed teacher. 'They watch us because they love us.'

Sami was willing to agree that love was about being seen, but he felt it was also about acceptance, whatever one's flaws. Their country would not tolerate any defects or mistakes. He watched the pouring rain, how it formed gutters and ponds on the schoolyard. Yasmin sat between the boys and Sami felt the warmth from her body.

'Want to borrow my jacket?' Haydar said, and Sami regretted that he hadn't asked first.

'Nah, it's OK.'

There were informants and members of the secret police everywhere, that much they knew, but Haydar had more detailed insight into how they moved and behaved. Taxi drivers were almost always members of the secret police, he claimed. They might say something along the lines of 'Isn't al-Assad just terrible for this country?' and if you agreed, you were in trouble.

Informers were ordinary people with no conscience. They were rarely recompensed directly, but they gained contacts that might be useful in the future. Your best friend might have been an informer for years without you suspecting. Neighbours, colleagues, relatives – you could never be sure.

Aside from the secret police and informers, there was the *Shabiha*, a criminal syndicate headed by members of the al-Assad clan. Blackmail and the smuggling of luxury cars, drugs and weapons were their specialities, according to Haydar.

'Isn't it weird how he knows all that stuff?' Sami said, which made Yasmin inexplicably angry. 'What? I just said it was weird.'

After that rainy day, Yasmin became even more meticulous about following the rules. Even when they were alone, she would hush him and say, 'The walls have ears.'

It was safer to follow the rules, Sami agreed with her on that. But what if you didn't know the rules? Sometimes you thought you knew something was true and it turned out to be false. Just take all the things grownups knew and passed on like truths. That watching too much TV would make your eyes square. That you could drown if you swam straight after eating. And then there were the truths passed between students in the schoolyard, often about dangers so dire you couldn't ask the grownups about them.

Like the man with the goatee and the cane. All the children in the area knew he was a sorcerer. Unsuspecting young boys were invited into the man's house, hypnotized, then sliced into ribbons. The gate to the low house was usually wide open. The man would sit alone by a table in the courtyard, next to a babbling fountain, cutting thick, fatty pieces of meat.

One day, they were kicking a ball around after school and Haydar took a long-range shot. They watched the ball sail in an arc from the tip of Haydar's shoe, up over the rooftops and down into the old man's courtyard. They stood in silence, Yasmin's the deadliest of them all. Within seconds, they were fighting about who should ring the gate and fetch the ball.

'I'll do it,' someone said.

They all stopped and looked around. Who was going to do it?

'I will,' Sami heard himself say again. 'I'll ring the bell.'

When he pressed his finger against the doorbell, it didn't feel too bad at first. The old man stepped aside and showed him the way in. At that point, his legs started trembling and it grew worse with each step. It was like moving through quicksand, as though he might at any moment sink through the stone floor into an underground cave. He pictured a dark cavern with bats, damp walls and long shadows.

When he stepped back out into the sunny street with the ball under his arm and his belly full of hot tea, the others surrounded him and cheered. He looked for Yasmin but she seemed to have left. Haydar was gone too.

'What happened, what did he do? Why were you in there so long?'

Sami smiled and threw the ball in the air. The old man's air of mystery seemed to have rubbed off on him and, for the rest of the week, everyone wanted him on their team.

Being in the know could be an advantage, but there were things he wished he had never found out. Like how there had been a catastrophe in Hama five years before he was born.

Hama was a neighbouring city, further north on the Orontes river, known for its beautiful norias used for watering the gardens. However, as it turned out, the flowery front hid a dark secret. The catastrophe, or the event, as it was usually referred to, was not talked about. Not at home and definitely not at school. Sami caught on anyway, because certain topics and words opened up a black hole of silence in which all conversation died.

'It never happened,' Nabil said.

Samira, who was pouring a glass of water, spilled half the pitcher over the table.

'We don't need to talk loudly and protest,' she said. 'But at least don't lie.'

'What never happened?' Sami asked.

'You'll understand when you're older,' his father said.

He nagged his older brother Ali until he told him, but it was so unfathomable it couldn't be true. He then asked a classmate from Hama, who punched him on the nose and ran away with wet cheeks. When their teacher wanted to know what was wrong, they both sat in silence, unsure what would happen if they revealed anything.

'I'm sorry, I didn't know,' Sami mumbled to his classmate.

'Didn't know what?' the teacher said.

Neither he nor the classmate replied. What he knew but would never utter aloud outside the home or conversations with close friends – since the walls had ears – was that a long time ago, the army had gone into Hama in search of enemies.

'Is it true?' he asked his mother after school. 'What happened in Hama?'

She was making one of his favourite meals, vine leaves stuffed with silky rice. Samira dried her hands on her apron and pulled him in tight.

'I know your father doesn't want me to tell you, but sometimes it's safer to know what you shouldn't know.'

Her braid rested on her shoulder; her big hands were warm.

'It was in 1982,' she said, lowering her voice.

Certain Islamist groups who had previously supported the Syrian regime formed a united resistance, and President Hafez al-Assad decided the rebellion had to be put down. The army was sent into Hama to identify dissenters. During two weeks in February, the streets were black with regime soldiers and tanks. It was a bloodbath. At least ten thousand people were killed, probably tens of thousands more. It was not the first or last massacre by the regime, but it was the most violent.

Samira told this to Sami, but chose other words.

'After the events in Hama, there were school classes where all the children had lost their fathers.'

It struck Sami then – an insignificant detail, but still – that their religious studies teacher, who when stepping out into the schoolyard in full view of all those blind windows had transformed into someone else and shouted commands at them, had probably felt as alone and watched as everyone else.

5

THE BLUE NIGHTS were long and fragrant in the late spring, with gentle breezes cooling the outdoor serving areas, which were full of people drinking tea and smoking *shisha*. But their father Nabil rarely stayed out late. He often went to bed around eight, never later than nine, in order to get to the train station before the first commuters arrived in the morning.

In the early evenings he liked to watch a black and white western, preferably alone and in silence. His children, however, interpreted his solitude as loneliness he should be saved from.

'Could you at least be quiet?' Nabil sighed from the black leather sofa as he reached for the remote control. 'And stay away from the TV screen.'

'We just want to keep you company, Dad.' Malik's bright four-year-old voice was muffled by the chocolate candy he was eating.

Sami took the right-hand corner of the sofa and leaned back, unconsciously imitating his father, who sat with his arms crossed and his long legs spread, like one of the cowboys in the movie.

'The one who finishes his candy first, wins,' Sami said, glancing at his little brother. His voice had just started to get deeper but sometimes made involuntary high sounds.

Malik immediately ate all his sweets like a hungry puppy, and afterwards looked jealously at Sami eating his one by one. Meanwhile Hiba had entered the room, still dressed in her high school uniform, and pushed herself in between Nabil and Sami.

'Why are you so mean to him?' Hiba said.

'What? You did the same to me.'

'My sweetheart Malik, you have to stop listening to your stupid older brother.'

Malik frowned and reached over his father and sister, trying to steal some chocolate, but Sami pulled it away.

'Sami. Just give him a piece,' Nabil said tiredly.

'But they're mine.'

'Be kind to your little brother. If you are big, you have to be extra kind.'

On the TV, a cowboy was chewing on a straw and peering at the horizon, where the desert continued into infinity. Sami thought the movie was too dramatic but his father loved everything about it, as did Malik. His little brother wanted a Stetson hat like that. A vest like that. A neckerchief bandana. And, of course, those high boots with spurs. The camera zoomed out until a shining dark horse was visible. The animal breathed heavily, widened its large nostrils and stood up on its strong hind legs.

'Oh, Dad, I also want a horse like that,' Malik whispered.

'What have we said about getting more animals? How do we get it up on the roof?'

'It can be parked outside on the street.'

'Parked?' Sami snorted.

'Quiet now. All of you.' Nabil hushed them.

A stranger showed up in the scene and challenged the lonesome hero to a quick-draw duel. Malik hid his face in his hands and peered between his fingers.

'Dad . . .'

Nabil sighed. 'Yes?'

'How do you know which of the cowboys is the good one?'

'Whoever wins,' Nabil said. 'The good ones always win.'

'That's not true,' Hiba said, and laughed. 'If the good always won, Sami would never win in chess.'

'Shut up!' Sami dug an elbow in her side.

'Come on, move your legs.'

'Do. Not. Fight. What happened to all the kind children I used to have?'

Malik looked up with big eyes. 'I'm here, Dad. I'm kind. Do I get a horse if I'm really kind?'

'Maybe if you are all silent and let me finish the movie . . .'

The scene changed and now showed a young woman stepping out of a saloon. She had a well-defined nose and dark freckles and deep, serious eyes that showed she had seen too much already, and she just wanted some peace and quiet without cowboy duels in her backyard. This was their father's favourite part, Sami could tell, because Nabil smiled and leaned forward with his elbows on his knees.

'That's how your mother looked when I met her. Proud and beautiful.'

'Where did you meet her?' Hiba pulled her feet up in the sofa.

'Well, I came by on a white horse and saw her carrying a stack of books, and I asked if she wanted a ride.'

Malik looked thoughtful. 'Where did you park it?'

'Outside school,' Samira said, who had appeared in the doorway. 'And it was not a horse, but a motorcycle.'

'It was white though?' Nabil raised his eyebrows.

'Once upon a time, maybe. Your sweet dad followed me for several days in a row, as if I wouldn't notice. The rusty motorcycle was as quiet as a coffee maker on the boil.'

'What time is it? Nine already! Time to go to bed . . .'

Samira crossed her arms and smiled, and Nabil stood up and kissed her gently on the cheeks, while Hiba rolled her eyes.

'Please, get a room.'

◆

Their older brother Ali still lived at home but he was mostly out at work, or in his room until late evening. As soon as Nabil's gentle snores could be heard, Ali crept into the hallway and stuck his hand in their father's coat pocket. Within minutes, the engine of the grey Volvo rumbled to life. From his bedroom window, Sami watched the car roll out of the garage and disappear down the illuminated street.

His mother, sister and little brother were still sitting on the leather sofas in front of the TV – too absorbed in reruns of *Kassandra* to notice Ali's nocturnal excursions. The theme song of the Venezuelan soap opera had sent the entire population into a trance when it aired in the 1990s. If you missed an episode, you were hopelessly excluded from conversation the next day. It was even said burglars used the *Kassandra* hour to break into houses.

The first time Sami asked his brother if he could ride with him in the car, the answer was clear.

'Not a chance,' Ali said.

But after nagging and threatening to tell on him for using their father's work car, Ali gave in. The spheres of light around the streetlights were sucked up by the darkness like lumps of sugar in a cup of coffee. But the surroundings were not particularly interesting to Sami. Instead, he watched how smoothly Ali shifted from first to second, then into third and fourth on the main road into the city centre. When they ended up behind a lorry, Ali gently pushed the brakes, leaned out the window and took a drag on his Alhamraa cigarette, which made the glow crackle and creep closer to the filter. The packet of cigarettes had been another find in their father's coat pocket.

When Sami had turned eleven, he was allowed to sit in the driver's seat and start the engine. The first few times, he just started the car and touched the buttons and switches, and at one point Nabil mentioned how clean the windscreen always was. When he was twelve, he tried the different gears. When he was thirteen, he slowly drove forward and reversed inside the garage. When he was fourteen, he rolled out into the driveway, continued down the street, turned and drove back. And now, at fifteen, he was a confident driver.

When Ali finally bought a car of his own, Sami took his place at the steering wheel of their dad's Volvo. As soon as the *Kassandra* theme music came on, Sami got up and went into the hallway. Rumour spread among his friends and they all asked for a ride. They rarely had anywhere to go so they drove into the city centre, talked to some girls who worked at an ice cream café and drove back.

One day after returning the car to the garage, Sami noticed a scratch all along the back. After dialling the wrong number a couple of times out of panic, he heard Muhammed's drowsy voice.

'What shade of grey?' Muhammed said, as though he were waiting in his teenage room with a palette of greys, poised and ready to swoop in and buff up unexpected scratches on people's fathers' cars.

'How should I know? Do you have more than one?'

'No.'

'*Khalas*, then why are you asking?'

Within the hour, Muhammed knocked on the garage door. He let out a low whistle, shoved his hands in his pockets and studied the scratch. In that pose, he looked thin and lanky like a weathervane, aside from his mop of curls. He hunched down, licked his finger and pulled it over the scuffed paint.

'What are you doing?'

'Prepping. The water has a healing effect.' Muhammed stood up straight, pushing his glasses up his freckled nose. 'It'll cost you,' he said.

'I'll let you drive it,' Sami replied. 'And as a bonus, I'll buy you Pepsi.'

'I prefer Coca-Cola,' Muhammed said.

'Deal.'

They shook on it and Muhammed opened the jar of paint. He was the one who usually found them a way out of trouble. The one thing

33

Muhammed didn't like was being stressed, so Sami kept a few steps back, listening for footsteps at the garage door. Only when Muhammed had finished and wiped away a couple of paint splashes from his glasses was Sami allowed to examine the result.

Sami slept fitfully that night. In his dreams, grey, viscous raindrops started falling. The sky rumbled with thunder and the ground shook. Sami opened his eyes and realized it was his dad, shaking him.

'My son, what have you done?'

'I was sleeping.'

'You know what I mean. Yesterday I had an accident with the car. I drove too close to our neighbour's mailbox and scratched the back. But now the scratch is gone!'

'I don't know what you are talking about.'

'Are you sure? Maybe I'm just getting old and forgetful . . .'

That settled it. His dad still didn't suspect that Sami borrowed his car, and so he continued to use it. To keep his promise to his friend, Muhammed was given the chance to drive, but he frowned and said the city traffic stressed him out. Instead he sat in the passenger seat and picked the music, usually American rock or metal.

At the time, in 2002, they didn't know that metal would be banned a few years later. Maybe it had always been illegal, prohibited by some lurking legislative paragraph, but if so, the law had never been enforced before. It wasn't only listening to or owning the music that was forbidden, just looking as though you liked rock was suspicious. A guy in their school was arrested for having an earring, unwashed hair down to his shoulders and a tattered denim vest.

Was it that the lyrics were considered subversive and likely to instigate civil unrest? Who knew.

The concerts might have been the problem. Gathering in groups was only allowed under certain circumstances, such as during the annual manifestation in support of President Bashar al-Assad, who had taken over at the turn of the millennium after his father died. People got signed attendance sheets to prove they had participated, and were given pictures of the father of the nation. Many praised the new president, not least Sami's dad.

'Things are going to change for the better now,' Nabil said.

'I thought you were happy with things the way they were,' Sami said.

'Yes, but now they are going to be even better.'

Sami's teenage years were about walking a fine line between different sets of expectations. Because he did well in tests in school, he was expected to raise his hand and choose the advanced courses. He won the calligraphy competition in their district, writing excerpts from the Quran and other poetic verses in different, ornate styles. Afterwards, all the teachers recognized him in the hallways, said hello and told him he should sign up for future calligraphy competitions.

Instead, he joined a boxing club. He punched mitts and sandbags for a couple of months, until his coach suggested he start competing. That made him quit boxing, too.

When Muhammed asked if he wanted to split a bottle of wine, he usually said yes. Before going home, he chewed a couple of coffee beans.

'What's that?' Samira said when she kissed his cheek at the door.

'Just a new kind of gum.'

'Is that right?'

Sami engaged in other everyday protests too. For the most part, it was enough that he knew about them. The challenge lay in exuding enough confidence and compliance to get away with overstepping certain boundaries. In creating a pocket of freedom in the unfreedom. Like keeping a rock album under your mattress. Like borrowing your dad's car without asking.

6

HE LONGED TO be older, but the growing itself was an unpleasant process. His body shot up, his voice made involuntary backflips and he slept like a hibernating animal. In the mornings, he borrowed Hiba's concealer to cover the worst spots on his face. At least until his father caught him in the act.

'Are you putting on makeup, my son?'

Makeup was on the long list of products that were not suitable for men. So was moisturizer, and electric razors.

'Real men use straight razors,' Nabil said.

'You've seen too many cowboy movies, Dad.'

'What did you say?'

'Nothing. Can I borrow yours?'

Samira exploited Sami's new height in her weekly cleaning. They began every Sunday morning by turning off the power. Then the furniture was carried outside and the rooms doused with water. Walls, ceilings and floors, everything was washed and scrubbed. Afterwards the water was poured away down the floor drain, but only once it had cooled down, so as not to awaken the evil spirits. Hiba teased their mother for believing in *jinn*, but at the same time it did seem stupid to risk it. Especially since it was said the spirits could take any shape they wanted: trees, animals or humans. How would you be able to tell where they might be?

Sami was responsible for the crystal chandelier in the living room. It was a balancing act that took at least a full hour to complete, standing atop a rickety ladder. Every crystal had to be polished individually. His older brother Ali was too heavy for the ladder, his younger brother Malik too short and Hiba had her hands full with other things.

'What's this? Ew . . . disgusting.'

Sami turned to see his sister holding up a flimsy piece of cloth and making a face.

'Hey, they are not disgusting. They are perfectly clean.'

'Could we please not use Sami's underwear to dust the shelves? Or any other underwear.'

'Why? You don't use them any longer,' Samira said. 'What should we do with them, throw them in the bin?'

'Well, yeah.'

'Do you know how much water a cotton bush needs? Do you know what it would cost to buy cleaning towels every week? Do you want me and your father to grow old and poor?'

'Mum.'

'Would you and your brothers prefer if I use them in the quilt and sell it at the market?'

'OK, OK.'

But before Hiba had time to dip the boxers in water, Malik snatched them from her hand and put them on his head.

'Guess who I am? An evil jinn who has come to eat you . . .'

Sami's little brother walked with his arms out, like a sleepwalking ghost, and before Sami had time to stop him – *Hey, careful!* – Malik had bumped into the ladder, which swayed dangerously but stayed put.

Around one, they turned the power back on. Sometimes, Sami turned the chandelier on too quickly, to check if he'd missed any spots, and was rewarded with a shock from the damp switch.

'See, I told you.'

Samira smiled triumphantly, one hand on her hip and the other on the scrubbing brush.

'Seriously,' Hiba said. 'If you're a spirit and you can live wherever you want, wouldn't there be better places than drains and electrical outlets?'

At night, Sami was afflicted with another kind of electricity, which had him waking up in the mornings with stains on his sheets. It was as though something took over his body at night, as though it were possessed. His older brother laughed when Sami, mortified, asked if a jinn might be behind it.

'My brother, you are growing up, that's all.'

Yes, he grew taller and older, and one day he was offered his first job. He and Muhammed frequented a restaurant where they ate *shish tawook*, grilled chicken. The big windows had a view of the mosque and a small square with palm trees and water features. Sami's father was good friends with the owner, Abu Karim, who would sometimes stop by their house for a cup of coffee in the evenings.

Abu Karim always came in a suit, unless it was the weekend, when he wore a long and expensive-looking *djellaba* under the jacket. He always brought sweets or fruit with him, and praised their well-kept home. Sami didn't know how his father met Abu Karim, other than that they were colleagues in a state-owned factory in their youth. Nabil had been responsible for clocking in the workers and had covered for Abu Karim when he was late in the mornings.

'Who would have thought that one day that sleepy boy would become the owner of his own restaurant?' Nabil joked.

'But that's precisely why,' Abu Karim said. 'I don't have to get up early any more – my employees do.'

Samira had tried to get Nabil to think about his health but he couldn't resist Abu Karim's baklava from the best bakery in town, baked with thin dough and fresh butter and lovely layers of crushed pistachio and auburn-coloured honey and – Nabil stretched for another one.

'Take one more, my friend.'

'Well, if you insist . . .'

On one occasion they were discussing the restaurant's finances. Abu Karim told Nabil he had all his papers in order, well, near enough anyway, but that the authorities still weren't satisfied.

'Maybe I could help?' Sami said.

Nabil laughed at his impudence, but let Abu Karim ask him some questions to test his knowledge. At first, his father was flipping through a magazine and stroking his silver moustache, but by and by he started listening attentively, leaning forward in his leather armchair.

'Where did you learn that?' Nabil said.

'School,' Sami replied.

It was almost true, but he had also had a peek at the books of Ali's computer shop, which had just opened in the city centre. Overnight, it seemed, his older brother had grown into a mature adult who wore a shirt and tie and talked with Dad about business. Sami felt like it was his turn to step up.

'Would you like to help me out after school one day a week or so?' Abu Karim asked.

His father leaned his elbows on the worn knees of his trousers and Sami thought he would say no, that his son was only sixteen and needed to focus on his schoolwork. Instead, he shrugged and smiled at him.

'So long as your grades don't suffer.'

The next day, Sami went straight to the restaurant. Downstairs, a magical world of steam, clatter and loud voices opened up. A number of men were moving between hobs and counters. They roasted and fried meat, rinsed lettuce and sliced tomatoes, sifted egg whites through their fingers to save the yolk for mayonnaise. Abu Karim put an arm around Sami's shoulders and gave him a tour.

When they reached the office, the sounds became muted but the smell of food lingered. The room was sparsely decorated: a huge desk in dark wood, an espresso machine in the corner, and a TV screen showing pictures from the surveillance cameras in the kitchen. Sami thought something was missing, and then realized there was no portrait of the leader on the wall.

The clutter was all hidden under the surface. In the desk drawers, that is. From the top drawer, Abu Karim pulled out a thick wad of receipts from the lunch service. He just had to put the numbers in the columns, here and here. Questions?

When Abu Karim left him alone, Sami realized this was serious. His shirt clung to him and his mouth went dry, then he picked up the topmost receipt and read it. There was a knock on the door and a stranger put his head round.

'What are you doing?'

'Accounting,' Sami said.

The stranger laughed and disappeared. He picked the receipts up one at a time and wrote down what dishes and drinks the customers had bought in one column, the price in the other. As he worked through the pile, he discovered that some receipts were invalid – usually due to the wrong dishes having been entered – so he put them into a separate pile.

By his second day in Abu Karim's office, he already felt like part of the team. It was not unusual for the restaurant to have a call from a company ordering two hundred chicken sandwiches in one go. Could they deliver in two hours? They always could. If they weren't fast enough, someone else would be. Sami was responsible for keeping the books on a day-to-day basis, under the supervision of Abu Karim's oldest son. A couple of hours after school, on the weekends and more in the summer. Before long, the other employees got used to Sami being around.

'Hey, bookkeeper boy, want a sandwich?' Anwar, one of the more experienced chefs, would say.

Anwar was wide and tall and had what people used to call 'good health'. His starched apron was stretched tight over his stomach, and the sleeves of his white shirt were neatly rolled up around his thick arms. He kept his hair in a tight knot and wore a black bandana that gave him the look of a martial arts trainer. Despite his size, Anwar was the smoothest operator in the kitchen. No one could roll sandwiches like him. He moved between benches and bowls and juggled bread and chopped vegetables as smoothly as a professional karate coach.

Sami watched in awe as Anwar squirted on sauce and clamped the sandwich shut in one motion. He made Sami feel like he was one of them. Sami, who made his own money and was free, a grownup, at least in his own eyes.

Winter and spring blended together. Sami worked at the restaurant and tried to keep his grades up. He regularly visited Ali's computer shop but barely ever saw Hiba, who spent all her time at the music school where she had just been accepted. It was at this time their mother was taken to the hospital with a lump in her breast. It was benign, but even so, it did something to her. Samira said the sunlight was too strong. She pulled the curtains shut and often stayed in bed until almost noon.

Meanwhile, their youngest brother grew increasingly neglected. When Malik came home with the wrong school books or a scraped knee, Sami scolded his little brother and told him he had to do better. Malik would put in an effort for a while, but would often be distracted by what was in front of him in the moment, a comic book or a friend to play with.

Being siblings was supposed to be uncomplicated, a love that was a given. But that was not how it was for Sami and Malik. Perhaps it was because his little brother was so much younger that he didn't feel like a real person, more like a dog who was always demanding attention and following him around. Never a moment's peace. But Sami had promised to help with bedtime and it was on one of these nights that Malik whispered to him.

'You know what, I have an idea about how to cheer Mum up.'

The next day, Malik brought home a puppy that he claimed a friend of his had asked him to look after. The little mutt had tangled fur and ears that flapped when it shook its head. It was like Malik himself, with a dark, unkempt fringe and big, soft eyes, playful and naive. Was his little brother insane, bringing home a stray dog? But when Malik scratched the dog's ear, it rolled over and licked his fingers.

'Aw,' Samira exclaimed and put her hand on its pink belly like a star.

'It can live on the roof,' their dad said.

Memories can change shape over time, but later in life, when Sami thought about his little brother, one moment always came to him first. It was when Malik took his hand on the roof terrace and pointed to a hunk of green shell next to a heap of black, raggedy fur. The turtle squinted as they approached. The puppy languidly wagged its tail. There they lay, the dog and the turtle, dozing next to each other, as though they were sprung from the same womb.

7

NABIL DIDN'T SAY in so many words that Sami ought to choose one thing or the other. Instead there were unobtrusive comments: I always hoped your older brother would become a doctor. Or, imagine having an officer in the family, the advantages you'd get.

It wasn't just education and careers that had to be chosen. When Sami turned eighteen, a voting card arrived in the post. His first instinct was to tear it up but Nabil stopped him.

'It's never going to get better than it is with the Baath Party,' his father told him.

Baath means renaissance, and what was to be born anew was Arabic nationalism. The Baath Party advocated a united Arab state, since it was said that the division of the Middle East into different states and peoples was made up – artificial lines and borders drawn by colonial powers.

When Sami thought of belonging, he felt more like a resident of Homs than anything else. Syrian, sure. Arab, why not? But he didn't understand the pompous speeches and parades. Did his father really think there would never be a better party? Sami didn't know. All he knew was that his parents, in fact most of their generation, thought differently than he did. It wasn't just that they supported the regime. Some even seemed in love with the military uniform gazing back at them from school books, office posters and long televised speeches.

Or perhaps the aftershocks of previous massacres were still reverberating, a quiet quake manifesting as silence.

'Fuck the Hafez generation,' said Muhammed, one of the few times Sami heard his friend swear.

There was an imbalance in their society. It was like tiny tears in silk cloth, growing and multiplying until the fabric was unable to conceal what lay behind it. The knowledge of the massacre in Hama was one tear, and the militaristic school uniform and the propaganda songs were another. At the same time, living in their country was fine, so long as you stayed on the right side of the curtain. On the surface, nothing was wrong or lacking. There were hospitals, schools, holiday resorts, churches and mosques. There were malls, gardens, theatres and libraries. The problem was the arbitrariness, that you could never know when the fabric would rip in two and reveal the other side.

'There's no point bothering with politics,' Nabil said. 'So long as you have nothing to hide and you keep your nose clean, they leave you alone.'

Sami used to think that way, too. It was a banal, inconsequential event that made him change his mind.

What happened was that Sami went to the state bank to cash a cheque and the teller asked him for a bribe. A bribe! Sami knew it had happened to other people but hadn't thought it would happen to him. Naturally, he wouldn't pay someone under the table for a service he was entitled to.

'Is it true, did he really ask you for money?' the bank manager said.

Sami described the course of events again and explained his surprise. Gave a matter-of-fact account, curbing his anger, to make sure the teller would be reprimanded. The bank manager nodded several times. He was leaning forward in his chair, his elbows on the polished teak table, a confidence-inspiring pose that made it seem he was both listening intently and not listening at all. When Sami was done, silence fell and the bank manager took a sip from a dainty porcelain coffee cup. Then he dabbed his lips with a napkin, folded it four times and put it in his breast pocket. The only sound was the ticking of the clock on the wall.

'Was that all?'

That was all.

The bank manager slowly turned to his colleague and opened his mouth and from his throat came a rumbling, almost inhuman sound. He was laughing. The bank manager was laughing and his colleague was laughing with him, and it was so absurd Sami joined in, too. They sat in the bank manager's office, laughing. Their laughter grew and echoed and bounced between the walls, filling the room until they almost ran out of air. It was a good feeling. How stupid of him to have even worried about drawing attention to the corruption! Sami leaned back in his chair and considered asking for a cup of coffee.

The laughter died down and the bank manager straightened a stack of papers. He said not to worry about the bribe. Sami was welcome to pay it to him directly.

Sami paid and left. He decided to file the event away with others of the same kind. Gather them in a pile, in case one day he needed to draw energy from past injustices. If you could even call it an injustice. The bribe was a pawn that fitted very nicely into the rules of their society's game. It would, in fact, have been an injustice if the bank manager hadn't asked for money, since that would have constituted an exception, giving Sami an advantage relative to the rest of the population.

For Nabil, the bank incident was an argument for why Sami should join the army. The bank manager was an Alawite, a member of a religious minority with their own interpretation of Shiite Islam. Under the French mandate, they were given more power in Syria, and now the ruling élite in the country was primarily Alawite. The military was no exception.

That his father wanted at least one of his sons to join the army was natural. You never knew when you might need connections, a *wasta*, a person who could help out with bureaucratic tangles.

But Sami had no appetite for such a career. The mandatory military service awaiting him after graduation was bad enough. Sami couldn't understand those of his friends who were looking forward to shooting rifles and sleeping in muddy trenches. More than anything, he didn't want to lose time. Not now, when he had just had a first taste of the freedom of adulthood.

Military service seemed to unite people, but it also seemed a thoroughly unpleasant part of life. His friend Muhammed preferred to do it before going to university rather than after. He would be gone for almost two years, aside from the occasional home leave.

Already on his first leave, he had changed, Sami noticed. His curly hair cropped, his back straight, hardened somehow. Muhammed had a new look in his eyes but shrugged when Sami asked him what it had been like.

'There's nothing to be done about it. Best to get it over with.'

It wasn't until that evening, over a bottle of arak, that Muhammed could be drawn on the details. Three conscripts in his division had died during training, he told Sami. Another had lost a couple of cartridges for his Kalashnikov and was sent to prison in Palmyra; the boy was nineteen years old and was never heard from again.

'Military service is the closest most of us will ever get to the regime,' Muhammed said, 'so you have to be on your guard at all times. Stay on the good side of the right people and watch what you say. It does make you a bit paranoid in the end.'

His older brother Ali had told similar stories, but he had done his service long ago, and Sami had almost forgotten that the same thing awaited him.

'Want some more?' Muhammed asked and held up the bottle.

'No, you take it.'

'To friendship,' he said and raised the glass.

◆

At night, Sami helped out with repairs and orders in his brother's computer shop. That meant he had to quit his job at Abu Karim's. Even though Sami liked it in the restaurant – in his office that reeked of cooking, right in the middle of the well-oiled machinery of chopping, peeling, slicing and more or less creative curses and insults – he felt more at home with technical stuff. A broken computer was a rational riddle. The only cure was patience, calmly and systematically searching for, then fixing, the problem. There were no shortcuts to the solution and no way of talking your way to it or out of it.

'And here I was, hoping one of my sons would become a doctor,' Nabil said.

'But, Dad, I can't stand the sight of blood.'

'An army officer then.'

'I don't think that's for me.'

'Engineering is a respectable career.'

'But that's what I'm going to study – computer engineering.'

'I mean a real engineer, who builds houses, something I could be proud to tell my friends about. And what's wrong with being a doctor?'

There was nothing wrong with being a doctor but it wasn't what he wanted to do. Against his father's wishes, Sami applied to the IT programme at the university in Homs.

Attending university was going to change everything, but not in the way he thought it would.

8

YOU MIGHT THINK it is the major choices that are the turning points, the crucial moments that change your life for ever, but it can be as simple as what you choose for dessert.

It was the beginning of the university term and the late summer heat remained. The sand-coloured buildings looked as though they were inspired by Roman times, with pillars and gold writing over the entrance, and a huge statue of the former president overlooking the sea of new students as they caught up with old friends or made new ones.

Sami had finished his first class and was standing in the university cafeteria with the plastic tray in his hand, feeling the soft coolness from the open fridge. There were two kinds of mousse left, vanilla and chocolate, and he hesitated for a second. He liked both, but there was only one chocolate left, which made it feel like the more exclusive choice. He picked the brown cup and put it on the tray.

'Oh, I hate vanilla,' someone said behind him. 'Could you please take the other one?'

He turned to see a girl about his height, wearing distressed jeans and a short denim jacket – finally, no school uniforms – with red hair tumbling down her back.

Sami smiled. 'Hate seems a bit strong,' he said, 'but sure, you can have the chocolate.'

If he had chosen vanilla from the start, she would never have talked to him. Everything that happened from then on would have been different.

'Is it OK if I sit here? I'm Sarah, by the way.'

He didn't notice that she hadn't found a place until she stood right next to him. Sarah sat down and took out the earplugs from her phone before he had time to nod. He felt warm even though he was only wearing T-shirt and jeans.

'I'm Sami. What are you listening to?'

She mentioned the singer's name and when Sami said he didn't know about her, Sarah let him listen.

'Her voice is like candyfloss,' she said.

It was true. The song was sweet and soothing yet crispy and clear, and closed out the sound from the other students.

'She's from Damascus, like me,' Sarah continued and leaned forward over the table as if to tell him a secret. 'I convinced my parents that Homs had the best university for my master's, so I could live away from home.'

She smiled and Sami noticed a dimple in her right cheek, the most perfect shape he had ever seen.

'So, what are you studying?'

'Modern Arabic literature and English literary history.' She leaned back. 'And you?'

'IT. You know, computers and stuff.'

He kept his eyes on the food and only glanced at Sarah now and then, trying to come up with a question that would make him seem smart and interesting.

'You read . . . quite a lot then?'

He blushed and felt like biting his tongue, but she didn't seem to notice.

'Yeah, I like to read. When everything is dull around you, at least you can escape somewhere between the covers of a book.'

Her leg grazed his and it was probably a mistake, but still a minor electrical shock went through Sami's body, like touching the damp light switch after cleaning the chandelier.

'You don't seem to lead a dull life.'

'What do you know? I wouldn't mind some more adventure,' she said.

The following day they met in the library after class and studied together.

'See you tomorrow then,' Sarah said, filling her bag with books. 'Same time and place?'

He watched her leave, her hair swaying as she walked, the backpack bouncing on her shoulder, and by the door she turned and raised a hand. He waved back and then something struck him.

'Sarah, wait!'

The librarian gave Sami a look from across the room. He ran up to Sarah, who smiled with raised eyebrows, and there was the dimple, and what was it he had intended to say?

'Maybe I can have your phone number? I mean, if something happens and I'm late tomorrow . . .'

'Sure,' she said. 'You can have my number.'

He texted her the same evening.

Messah alkheer. Kifik?

She said everything was good, but wrote nothing more. He asked for the name of the singer with the candyfloss voice.

Lena Chamamyan, she replied.

Sami searched for her music and found a photo of the singer, and realized Sarah looked a lot like her: round cheeks and dark eyes and red hair, only less curly. A few months after the life-changing choice over a dessert, they were a couple.

To be in love was to gather each other's peculiarities and habits as treasures. Sarah said Sami wasn't as serious as everyone thought he was and that his portion sizes were curiously large for someone so slim. Sami noticed that Sarah started speaking faster when she talked about books she was reading, and bit her nails when she got stressed or nervous.

His lips were large and dry, hers were soft and tasted fruity from her lip balm. When they were together, it was like drowning and free-falling at the same time.

Sarah came from a Christian family in Eastern Ghouta, a suburb of Damascus. Sami noticed every detail in her student room: the stacks of books on her windowsill, from Jane Austen to Ahlam Mosteghanemi. Three over-watered mini cacti drooping in their tiny flower-pots. The collection of trainers under her bed. The hairs in her brush on the nightstand, the condoms under a pile of magazines. The glass where her lips had left a shiny imprint on the edge.

Sarah lent him her copy of *Chaos of the Senses* and he soaked up every word, at first because it was Sarah's book and then because of the language. The Algerian author Ahlam Mosteghanemi wrote about a woman whose husband was a senior officer. The main character was writing a novel, while the novel wrote her life. Reality and fiction were woven together. Sami started doubting everything that was visible in the world. Were there undercurrents that followed different laws? He took out a pad and paper and wrote a paragraph but was unable to capture the feeling. Instead, he penned a love letter to Sarah. Later she embraced him and reached for what lay under the stack of magazines on the nightstand. Golden sunbeams streaked her hair as it spread out across the pillow.

Homs was a major city but slightly more conservative than Damascus or Aleppo. Homs was like their prim and proper older sister, confident and unafraid to live life, but never truly overstepping since her parents and siblings were watching. You would routinely find kissing couples in the shade of trees and in hidden corners of the campus, but cohabiting before marriage was rare, and usually carried out in secret. Even more secretly, men who wanted to meet other men sought out special bathing houses.

Sami staying in Sarah's room overnight was out of the question. Instead they snatched brief moments of kissing and pleasure. It sounded romantic in theory, the foreplay extended by furtive looks and ambiguous text messages, but their intimacy often felt hurried and insufficient.

A few times Sarah did sneak him into her room during daytime. They lay in her bed and she read from one of her favourite writers, Nizar Qabbani. The Syrian poet rose to fame in the middle of the previous century when he sought to rebel against the shameful silence surrounding sex and relationships. In Qabbani's love poetry, the woman was the focus, her body and pleasure.

'I'd never come across a man who knew women so well before,' Sarah said.

'Hey, what about me?'

'You're learning,' she teased and stroked his back.

Writing so openly about passion and politics, with heat and intensity, was revolutionary for their parents' generation, Sarah said. There was room for all women in Qabbani's poems: the ones who fell in love with each other, the ones who had extramarital relationships and the ones who chose not to have children.

'When Nizar Qabbani was fifteen, his older sister killed herself,' Sarah told him. 'It was after she had refused to marry a man she didn't love. That's what made him want to write about social injustice.'

His rebellious streak seemed to be a family trait. Qabbani's father owned a chocolate factory and had supported the rebels during the French rule, a stance that landed him in prison several times. And his grandfather's brother, the famous dramatist, caused protests when he staged a performance criticizing Caliph Harun al-Rashid – who was not only immortalized as a character in *Arabian Nights* but was also infamous for his brutality.

Scheherazade, Sami wrote in black ink on Sarah's arm.

'Does that mean you'll cut off my head if I don't keep telling you stories?'

He kissed her wrists and held her close under the cover.

'No, tell me more.'

'So, Nizar's second marriage was to an Iraqi woman called Balqis.' Sarah lowered her voice. 'She was the love of his life.'

During the civil war in Lebanon, however, she was killed in a bomb attack at the Iraqi embassy in Beirut. Nizar never fully recovered from Balqis' death. He wrote a poem to express his grief and anger, a furious accusation hurled at the entire Arab world, which the poet felt was to blame for her death.

'Will you write a poem if something happens to me?' Sami asked.

'Don't be silly. The civil war is long gone. We'll have a peaceful life with lots of kissing and reading and . . .'

'Let's put the book away.'

When Sami heard Sarah talking, he realized poetry didn't have to have anything to do with words. It was a way of viewing the world, a way of creating patterns and meaning. Of making visible what was hidden. In this way, it was what he felt for Sarah: as if the world had more colours and sharper contours, and the air was clearer to breathe.

9

THE SNOW WAS melting on the streets and showed traces of the New Year's celebrations. The first holiday from university had passed and Sami lingered in the kitchen, waiting for his siblings to leave.

'By the way,' Sami said when he was alone with Samira, 'I'm bringing a friend here tomorrow.'

'Oh lovely. Who is it? Someone I know?'

'Oh, just a friend. I study with her sometimes.'

'I understand,' Samira said and dried her hands on a towel.

'It's not like that. Don't make a big deal of it,' he said and grabbed his backpack.

'Of course not. No big deal. Tell your friend she is very welcome.'

The next day, Sami and Sarah walked home together, sometimes crossing each other's steps to get the other one to trip. As they approached al-Hamidiyah, he pointed out Nassim's store and told her about the bird he and his sister had tried to save on the roof terrace.

'Watch out for the bowls,' Sami said as they walked up the stairs. 'Mum likes to feed the cats.'

He hadn't been nervous before, but when he opened the door he understood that it wouldn't be as relaxed as he hoped. Samira must have heard their voices from the open window and was already waiting in the hall. Because they were at home, she had taken off her hijab and braided her hair. She had also put on the gold earrings, bracelet and necklace Nabil had given her as wedding gifts – not that she thought her son would notice the subtle gesture.

Samira embraced Sarah and kissed her three times, as if they were good friends who hadn't seen each other for a long time. Behind his mum stood his sister.

'Hiba. I didn't think you would be home today.'

'Well, surprise.' His sister turned to Sarah with a broad smile. 'So nice to finally meet you. My brother has talked so warmly about his good friend.'

Sami gave his sister a look but she pretended not to notice.

'Thank you. He's talked a lot about you as well.'

'Only good things, I hope. What dialect is that? You're not from Homs, are you?'

'No, I'm from Damascus,' Sarah admitted.

'The city or the countryside?' Samira asked.

And with that, the hearing had begun.

'What's your surname? Do you come from a big family? What do your parents do? Any sisters and brothers?'

The women led Sarah into the living room and left Sami in the hallway, and he felt bad that he hadn't warned her.

'You do plan to finish university, don't you? Education is so important for any young woman of today . . .'

One hour later, Samira held out the plate with cookies and Sarah said she had had enough, which made Sami's mum insist a second and then a third time, until she finally gave in. Samira looked pleased and said that maybe the young friends wanted to spend some time alone.

'That was terrible,' Sami sighed when they got into his room and closed the door. 'Sorry you had to go through that. How do you feel?'

'They were very kind and caring,' Sarah said.

'A bit too caring, no? If it's not the regime spying and prying, it's our own family.'

'Really, that was nothing. Wait till you meet my mum and dad.'

She sat down on his bed and looked around his room.

'Want to watch a movie?' he asked.

They got themselves comfortable on the bed and Sarah chose a movie on his computer. But they only got as far as the opening credits when there was a light knock on the door, and there was Malik.

'What are you watching? Please can I watch too?'

And before Sami had time to answer, his little brother had squeezed himself in between them. His mum had surely sent him – the sticky lollipop in his mouth was a bribe.

University meant the beginning of something new, and not only thanks to Sarah. Sami realized that computers, like poetry, were also a way of organizing the world. Together with his friend Rasheed, Sami decided to start his own business. The idea was simple: they would set up their own ADSL network in Homs. Granted, the government had a monopoly on the internet, but they were going to start small enough not to draw any attention.

Rasheed was Syrian but had grown up in Germany and moved back to Homs a few years earlier. To do business, he said. He dressed in a pale linen suit and made sure they had a modern office with green plants, an ice machine and air-conditioning. They complemented each other. Where Sami preferred solving the technical challenges, Rasheed was the extrovert who talked to customers and made business contacts. He had a round friendly face and a good way with people. It worked well most of the time, but Rasheed, who had wanted to escape German bureaucracy, hadn't yet grasped the hidden bureaucracy of his home country.

'Why do we have to pay those two people at the electrical state office?' Rasheed asked once again. 'My mum has good enough contacts.'

'Just trust me on this,' Sami said.

They only advertised once, by handing out flyers Sami made on the university's photocopier. They had barely signed up their first two customers – Ali's computer shop and a nearby internet café – when word about their network began to spread. It was both cheaper and faster than the state-provided one. They laid cable after cable from their tiny server hall in the city centre. People offered Sami and Rasheed tea and biscuits to show their appreciation. People he didn't know said hello in shops and cafés. It was like when he was little, walking down the street with Grandpa Faris. He pictured the company growing, providing internet to the entire city, even the entire country. A Syria where everyone was online and connected. Where you could pay bills, look for work and do admin digitally, without a single bribe.

Their first profit was invested in hiring an electrician. Younes was five years older than Sami but his street-style clothes made him seem younger. He had a shaved head and wore baggy jeans and a checked sweater with the sleeves rolled up to show the tattoo on his left upper arm. *Esther*. His girlfriend in Tel Aviv, whom he talked to and texted several times a day.

'My mum got mad when she saw it.' He grinned. ' "My son, why ruin your body with ink? When you die and God sees your unclean skin, you will burn in hell." '

Younes held out his mobile and showed a picture of Esther wearing dark sunglasses and standing in front of the Eiffel tower.

'She's pretty. But that's not Tel Aviv?'

'She's half French, so she travels to Paris sometimes.'

'Have your family met her?'

'Let's put it like this. Mum says: if you had to make a bloody-hell tattoo, why not choose your own dear mother's name? Why a girl you've known shorter than a blink of an eye?'

Sami laughed and Younes shook his head. He was certainly good at talking away the time, but he was efficient when he worked.

The business did so well that they were even able to pay themselves modest salaries. Sami used his to buy his first car or, rather, half a car. Muhammed agreed to pitch in the other half, saved from the small amount he had earned during military service. Especially when he saw the colour.

'We have to name her the Pink Panther!'

The car was certainly pink – bubble-gum pink – but there was nothing panther-like about it. It didn't matter. The car was a beauty, with its curved bonnet and classic outline: a 1952 Volkswagen Beetle.

Not a day went by without heads turning in the street. Police officers asked to see their licences just for a chance of a closer look. The Pink Panther sounded like a retired old lady with a racking smoker's cough and didn't have enough horsepower to get up steep inclines. But Sarah loved it, and on the weekends they drove to Damascus and hung out in cafés, sipping mint lemonade and sharing meze.

Sarah was drawn to everything that alleviated the feeling of dreary everyday life. Aside from reading and going for drives, she liked horror films and TV soap operas. The highpoint was during Ramadan, when several new TV shows were always introduced, since people generally slowed down during the fasting period and spent more time in front of the TV. Sami said it was a waste of time. She said he was the one wasting time, what with all the late nights he was spending at the office.

University seemed less and less important. Sami was often ahead of his course mates and he found it more stimulating to work on concrete tasks. Two of his teachers knew about his business and offered conflicting advice. One warned Sami about the consequences if the government ever found out what he and Rasheed were doing. The other teacher helped solve the various technical problems that cropped up.

As it was, Sami was concerned about more immediate perils, like laying cable in a nine-storey building in Homs' business district. Using a safety harness never crossed his mind. He and Younes gave the janitors a small financial incentive to let them into the apartment buildings, and they climbed out on to the roofs and laid the cables down as best they could. Sami was untroubled by vertigo, so long as he didn't look down. But the sun and the blue sky could make the world start spinning, and brought to mind what had happened once to a sparrow that couldn't fly.

Their cables stretched like a spiderweb through the streets of Homs. On one occasion, during the annual festival in the desert city of Palmyra, which tempted the crowds with concerts, horse racing, craft fairs and car races, they were even praised by senior politicians. Take a look at these ambitious entrepreneurs, one minister said, providing our country's third-biggest city with reliable internet!

Poetry or not, apparently, computers can be as radical as words. If he and Rasheed had contented themselves with their original network, with what they had already achieved, then perhaps nothing would have gone wrong.

10

AS TIME WENT on, they were ready to take the next step. Sami had been working at the company alongside his university studies for almost three years, and now he and Rasheed wanted to put their money into wireless internet.

But one February morning in 2009, their network unexpectedly shut down. Sami's phone started ringing around lunchtime and continued nonstop until evening. Only then did people realize it wasn't just their network that was down. Friends and relatives in other cities told them they were offline too. In fact, all of Syria seemed to have gone offline.

Since they were unable to work, and since he and Rasheed felt on the verge of burning out – 'Don't overdo it,' Nabil had told him every time they had talked to each other in the past year – they decided to drive the pink Beetle to Latakia and spend a day by the sea. The weather was warmer by the coast and the breeze would clear their heads and do them good. They planned to bring pierogi, parsley salad and arak and have a quiet time playing cards to the sound of the waves.

Sami packed a cooler and arrived at the office before lunch to pick up Rasheed. He parked and opened the car door, which gave a displeased sigh. That was when he saw them: a group of about ten men, dressed in civilian clothes and armed with Kalashnikovs, standing around the entrance. Sami assumed it was the secret police's monthly visit to Rasheed's mother's company next door. She ran an agency

placing nannies and maids from other countries, primarily the Philip-
pines. Working with foreign countries always aroused suspicion that
you were handling smuggled goods or even spying, but in the case of
Rasheed's mother it was more likely that her venture was so profitable
the secret police were asking to have their palms greased. They certainly showed no signs of caring about the nannies who worked under
slave conditions or had their passports confiscated.

Sami considered turning around, but the pink car had attracted
attention.

'Hey, you, show me your ID.'

Sami crossed the car park, pulled his wallet out of his pocket and
handed over the card. The man studied it over the edge of his sunglasses. Sami could see his own anxious face reflected in the lenses.

'Sami. Do you work here?'

'I work in the building, but not for the agency.'

The man turned his head to the side, seemingly to stare into space
but probably to talk into an earpiece.

'He's here now.'

The man gestured for Sami to enter the building. Some of the officers had stepped in behind him, others were keeping an eye on the
street. Sami noticed curious faces peeking out from behind curtains
in the block of flats opposite. Cars slowed and rolled down their windows. Whatever happens, if something happens, at least there are witnesses, he thought, and went inside.

The fluorescent light was harsher than usual. Rasheed and he rarely
turned on all the ceiling lights at once but today the office was bathed
in light. The decorative palm trees drooped and he made a mental
note to water them. Sami looked around and felt vaguely annoyed at
the mess, the way you notice a toothpaste stain on your shirt instead
of taking in that your girlfriend just told you she feels you should take
a break from one another.

'Are you listening to me?' she'd said, the night before. 'You're working too much.'

'We'll talk about it next week, when we're back from Latakia.'

'I'm not going, it's just going to be you and Rasheed.'

Sarah's words were rushing through his head, or maybe it was the sound of the ceiling fan. Ten more members of the secret police were moving about the office. They were packing papers and binders in black bin bags, carrying out boxes full of routers and cables, grabbing armfuls of computers and antennae.

'There you are,' said an older man, who introduced himself as the colonel.

His white hair matched the pinstripes of his suit. In his breast pocket was a pack of cigarettes with the red Alhamraa label. The colonel was shorter than him but Sami nevertheless had the feeling the colonel was looking down at him. He had clear, intense eyes behind round frames.

'I apologize for disturbing you in this manner,' the colonel said. 'Let's step into one of the offices so we can talk privately. Don't worry, my colleague will look after your bag.'

They sat down in Rasheed's room, which looked the same as before, except that Rasheed wasn't there. The pictures of his wife and daughters felt out of place with the colonel behind the desk.

'We've heard a lot of good things about your company. If it were up to me, we wouldn't be here today,' he said by way of starting the conversation. 'But, as I'm sure you know, what you are doing is illegal.'

The colonel folded his hands on the table to let this fact sink in. 'Where is Rasheed, by the way?'

Sami ran his hands up and down his jeans, fidgeting with a few loose threads where the fabric had worn thin by the knee. Rasheed: he was the one with all the important contacts who could get them out of this situation. He swallowed and asked to go out in the hallway to make a call, which the colonel allowed.

'Are they in the office, are we in trouble?' Rasheed said breathlessly on the other end of the line.

'They just want to know what we do, that's all.'

'Are you sure?'

Rasheed's voice was high-pitched and shrill like metal, and cars were honking in the background.

'Completely sure,' Sami said. 'We pay and answer a few questions and that's it. But if you try to go on the run, that'll obviously look suspicious.' Was it him Sami was trying to save, or himself, or both? He wasn't sure of anything.

Rasheed arrived at the office an hour later, with sweat beading on his forehead.

'Where were you going?'

'Lebanon,' Rasheed whispered.

The colonel bade him welcome and asked them both to take a seat. He seemed genuinely curious about their business, how they went about installing cables and finding new customers and the speed of their network. After thirty minutes of chitchat, he leaned back in the office chair – the only furniture aside from empty cabinets and the desk that remained in the room, now that the secret police had confiscated what they wanted – and lit a cigarette. The colonel took a long drag and apologized for having to borrow their equipment. They seemed to be serious entrepreneurs. Truly driven individuals, he had to say, and wasn't it strange that despite their obvious intelligence – he dragged the word out – they didn't understand that they needed permits to install cables and networks?

'Consider what this looks like. From our perspective. Given how quickly your network has grown, it's likely only a matter of time before you expand into Israeli territory. But you'd almost think you didn't want to be noticed. Almost as if you were trying to set up a secret communication system . . .'

He said it kindly and unassumingly. Rasheed jumped to his feet and objected, his face white as a sheet.

'That's not how it is at all, not at all. We've even been singled out for praise at the Palmyra festival.'

The colonel raised his hand and waved away a tendril of smoke.

'Yes, the minister,' he said. 'He's why I'm here, to make sure everything is above board. You have two options, the way I see it. Either you come with me now or you come in tomorrow to answer some questions. It's up to you.'

Once again, he made it sound like it was all a formality, a friendly visit. The colonel dropped his cigarette on the floor but didn't put it out – a chemical smell spread from the hole in the plastic rug. Sami thought about Latakia's beaches, about the sound of never-ending waves breaking, swirling up shells and pebbles, and he nodded.

'Rasheed?'

'Of course, absolutely. We'll come with you.'

People had gathered outside in the pale sunlight to see what was going on. Others continued watching from doorways, across the street and nearby offices. The colonel invited Sami and Rasheed into the back seat of his own car, a black Land Rover, driven by a private chauffeur. When the colonel noticed they were being patted down, he waved his hand to signal that there was no need for that. The Pink Panther looked sad and alone on the other side of the car park, and Sami found himself wondering whether the food would stay fresh in the cooler.

Two motorcycles led the convoy, clearing the way. They were followed by two cars with tinted windows, the Land Rover Sami and Rasheed were in, then two more cars. The drive to the secret police headquarters would normally have lasted around half an hour, but since the driver had his foot permanently on the accelerator and the other cars made way for them, it took less than fifteen minutes.

Sami and Rasheed sat quietly in the back. When they drove into a courtyard and the black steel gates shut behind them, their thoughts were swirling like seaweed in a current.

11

THEY WERE QUESTIONED together and Sami slowly grew frustrated with his friend. In the interrogation setting, the differences between their strategies and personalities became starker. Most of what Rasheed knew about his native country, where he had only spent a couple of years as a child, he had heard from horror stories told by Syrians in exile. But he believed the country could be changed, and that a change was best effected through cooperation and openness. That was why he had suggested using flyers to advertise and initiating collaboration with government employees. If they were open and honest and invited Baath sympathizers to join them, everyone would be a winner.

His friend's idealism had appealed to Sami, but he had advocated an alternative strategy: to work in secret and silence. Which was a kind of innocent idealism too, since in practice no one could work under the radar of the regime.

During their questioning, Rasheed's answers were long and exhaustive, even though Sami did his best to make him be brief. It was always better to keep it brief. Never lie or say more than you needed to; that was a recipe for tripping yourself up. Lies always led to more lies and, in the end, it was impossible to remember what had and hadn't been said. But Rasheed was stressed and nervous and embellished his replies with names and details. When the colonel leaned forward and gave him an interested smile, Rasheed took it as a sign that he was on the right track.

'Remind me, did you have a lot of customers?' the colonel said.

'Some,' Sami said vaguely.

'Three hundred,' Rasheed specified, not without a measure of pride in his voice. 'And one customer could be an internet café, so the users were many more. Probably thousands.'

'Is it true you smuggled in materials from Lebanon?' the colonel asked.

'Maybe,' Sami said.

'Sure,' Rasheed replied. 'We paid a guy in Beirut who did deliveries every other week when he went to visit his grandmother, who . . .'

The only time Sami volunteered information was when the colonel was joined by two new interrogators, who were mainly interested in the technology they used. The questions were impossible to answer since they were along the lines of: how do you set up a router in a shower? How would you get unlimited download speeds? How would you set up the signal to listen in on your wife's phone calls?

'You don't put routers in showers,' Sami said. 'And the maximum download speed depends on a number of factors, not least the provider.'

That evening yet another interrogator, who was more direct, took over. Were they Israeli spies? Or terrorists from the Muslim Brotherhood? Thus the questioning ebbed and flowed and they were accused of being everything from spies to terrorists to regime critics to idiots.

After night fell, Sami was allowed to leave. Rasheed was kept until midnight.

'One last thing,' the colonel said before they were released. 'You can't leave the country for a month.'

It turned out the Mukhabarat had raided at least two other companies in Damascus and Aleppo. One of them was run by a teenager who had hacked the internet provider – in other words, the regime – to make cheap international phone calls.

A week later the internet was back but with some adjustments. The regime had lowered the price of subscription by a tiny amount. Information was sent out to internet cafés that registration would be required to use wireless networks. Users were also reminded that it was illegal to hack the system to visit banned websites, such as Facebook and Twitter.

And now, were they supposed to carry on as though nothing had happened? Sami and Rasheed cancelled their trip to the beach. To anyone who asked, Sami said it had been a routine matter and that they had been treated well. He wouldn't have even mentioned it to his parents had not Ali, whose computer shop was near their office, already told them what he'd seen and heard.

'Are you really going back there?' asked Sarah, who had decided to give their relationship another chance.

'Anything else would seem suspicious, wouldn't it?' Sami replied.

So he went to the office and started cleaning up the mess, sorting through the papers and binders that were left. The rooms were empty, aside from a man in a black suit and sunglasses who took a seat by the palm trees in the lobby.

'Can I get you anything?' Sami asked him.

'Coffee, three sugars,' said the member of the secret police expressionlessly.

At the end of the day, Sami got up to leave, as did the man in the black suit.

'So, when are we getting our computers back?'

The man emptied his coffee cup into one of the planters.

'Computers? You never had any computers.'

The same procedure was repeated the next day, and from then on, every other or every third day. The secret police pulled cables from their office and tracked down every last one of their customers. The people of Homs were disappointed but not surprised. Give us our Israeli network back, they said, it was so much faster and cheaper than the old one. Sami found it increasingly difficult to laugh in response. He slept less, and was woken up by dreams he couldn't remember but that lingered like a dullness inside him. It was like moving through murky water. The sounds around him were distorted and the light didn't seem to reach him.

One night in March, the electrician's neighbour called to let him know the Mukhabarat had practically laid siege to their block. Around ten of their cars had driven up in the dark. Armed men had banged on doors and finally found their way to Younes' home, where they had blindfolded and handcuffed him and taken him away. The neighbour had seen it all through his window and recognized Younes' shaved head.

'Does it have something to do with your network?'

The next morning Sami went to see the electrician's family, who were beside themselves. But the arrest had nothing to do with the company, they said, it was personal. Younes' girlfriend in Tel Aviv had made the secret police suspicious.

'They called him an Israeli spy when they took him away,' Younes' father said and blew his nose in a napkin.

Sami tried to reassure them; he and Rasheed had been treated well by the secret police, no violence or open threats. But he could tell how empty his words sounded.

So they had been accused of running an Israeli network and now one of their co-workers stood accused of being an Israeli spy.

'Since when is it illegal to have a girlfriend in Israel?' Rasheed said.

'Sure, but that's not how they see it. Do you think the colonel would be lenient if he received orders from higher up to arrest us? I doubt it.'

A month had gone by since their arrest. Nothing seemed to happen, but since they could now leave the country they decided to head over to Lebanon and lie low for a while.

Muhammed said Sami could have the car indefinitely and so Sami enrolled in a programming course at a university in Beirut for the rest of the spring.

'I miss you,' he said to Sarah.

'I miss the Pink Panther,' she replied. 'And you. But mostly the Beetle.'

He pushed the phone closer to his ear and listened to her breath.

'When will you be back?' she asked.

'In the summer,' Sami promised. 'We can rent a bungalow in Latakia. Go for swims, make fires on the beach and rest on a blanket under the stars.'

'You can't even swim properly.'

'You can teach me.'

'I mean for good, Sami. When will you move back for good?'

He was picturing the future but somehow he didn't believe in it. After the secret police's raid, everyday life felt like a puppet show, in a shadowland, off to the side.

II

'Do you think it's a matter of luck?' I ask.

'I was careful,' you reply.

But after hearing the story of you boiling water for tea by connecting a cable to a power line, I no longer believe you. It's possible you were careful sometimes. Sometimes, though, I think it was precisely your way of throwing yourself into things that enabled you to escape the worst dangers.

If you hadn't hurled yourself forward and been so confident, I'm not sure I would have dared to believe in us.

I'm at the outer edge of this narrative, far out on the periphery. What right do I have to speak with your voice and bear witness for you? Only the right you grant me. What is told here has grown like an ongoing conversation, a plait we pull ever tighter with threads of four languages. We break off and start over, then we cry and carry on.

To be honest, I do most of the crying, since your tears have long since dried. Children wrapped in white sheets and body parts sticking out of the debris is too incomprehensible. A couple of dusty teacups, left behind in a hurry. I inherit your nightmares and memories without knowing how to put them down, if not on paper.

Your grief takes different expressions; you chain-smoke and go for long walks. To you, it's not incomprehensible or fiction, since it has already happened.

12

OUTSIDE THE POLICE station, the city had rubbed the sleep out of its eyes and roused itself. It was the beginning of autumn 2009 and Sami was finally back home, in Homs.

Sarah had invited him to stay over in her student room and they talked through the late hours in whispers. When the first morning light fell on her face, he kissed her and sneaked out. He could still feel her lips on his neck, and was grateful they were slowly finding their way back to one another.

'What are you going to do about your military service?' she had asked.

'It's fine as long as I'm studying.'

'But you're not studying here any more. Not since you left for Beirut.'

'I'm not officially missing from the service yet. I'm just a few months delayed.'

'So, what's your plan then?'

He had already weighed his options and found each worse than the next. Endure, like his older brother Ali and childhood friend Muhammed? It was unimaginable, to let the army steal a year and nine months of his life. Fleeing the country and living in exile was just as impossible. It entailed leaving Sarah, his family and his friends, in short, giving up his whole existence. The final option was to stay and go underground, waiting to be found out and sent to prison in Palmyra where people could be kept for years, or worse, be forgotten about and disappear.

At the same time, the country he lived in was a pragmatic one. There was almost always a spoken or unspoken way around things: money. You could stay abroad for a while and earn enough money to buy your way out of military service. That was why he was here, at the police station, to collect his passport, so he could head to Dubai to look for work. When he told Sarah about the plan, he thought she would argue or at least sigh. But she only stroked his hair and looked him in the eyes.

'I don't like it, but I understand,' she said.

While Sami went abroad and saved money, Sarah could graduate and start working as a teacher. They talked about getting married and living in Homs or Damascus. Anywhere they could have a library, Sarah said, with winding bookcases all the way to the ceiling.

'Be careful,' Sarah said before they parted that morning.

But going to the police station was not dangerous. It was a routine matter and besides, it was only the army that was interested in apprehending missing recruits. As an extra precaution, he had brought a fake certificate stating he had studied in Homs during his time in Beirut.

A waft of warm sweat and irritation greeted him when he opened the door to the waiting room. Sami entered just as a name was called out. If at that moment he had turned around, gone back out on to the street and then run until he ran out of air, maybe none of the things that awaited him would have happened. You never know which moments are pivotal ones. Maybe it wouldn't have made any difference at all.

His name was called. A police assistant studied Sami's ID and shook her head, as though she were dealing with an unusually troublesome student.

'You're a wanted man. Come with me.'

Sami was allowed to make one phone call. Not long after that, Ali turned up with a sports bag full of cash, but no bribe could help him. They had already passed his name on to other police stations. After a couple of hours his older brother returned, distraught, his eyes red.

'I promise, I did everything I could.'

He had called some people they knew, people with good connections, but with no result. Sami's heart stopped beating in his chest, or maybe it was beating so fast he couldn't distinguish the individual beats. After Ali left, two officers came to pick him up. His stomach was churning with hunger and thirst. Sami held his arms out and the handcuffs clicked shut.

'Where are we going?' he asked as stones crunched under the car tyres.

'To the cinema,' replied the officer in the driver's seat.

'Right,' said his colleague. 'Remind me, what's on tonight?'

'I don't remember, some kind of horror film.'

They laughed and the driver shot Sami a glance in the back seat.

'*Habibi*, you're the most ridiculous case I've come across in a long time. To show up here when you're wanted for military service.'

They turned the radio up. Fairuz was singing about Beirut, about a city that tasted like fire, smoke and ash. Sami sat quietly until they stopped outside a low concrete building on the outskirts of Homs. Inside, he was taken to an office, to a giant desk, behind which sat a man who introduced himself as the prison director. He had an unremarkable appearance – a wart on his nose, a thin strand of hair combed across his bald pate and chubby hands that rested on his stomach – but his voice was deep and melodic like an opera singer's. The prison director signalled to a guard to uncuff him and asked Sami to empty his pockets: keys, tissues, gum, wallet. The picture of Sarah slipped out and he tried to poke it back into his wallet before the prison director could see it.

'Who's this cutie?' he said, picking the picture up with both hands.

'My girlfriend.'

'Beautiful. Looks like my daughter. You do know it's against the law to keep pictures of your girlfriend in your wallet, don't you?' The prison director smiled at his own joke and proceeded to search the wallet, opening the currency compartment and shaking out a handful of change. 'We're done here,' he said, waving his hand dismissively.

The guard who had escorted Sami stepped back out of the shadows. His pointy nose, sharp chin and peering eyes made him look like a light-shy, subterranean creature whose habitat was drains and sewers.

'I don't understand. What happens now?'

'You will stay here,' said the guard, 'until it can be determined where you will do your military service.'

He was brought to a cell that was cramped, dark and dank like a cellar. Maybe it was a cellar. A small window with bars up by the ceiling let in a faint, hazy light.

At first he didn't notice the slender boy in the corner; he thought it was a bundle of clothes. The boy was sitting with his legs pulled up and his arms wrapped around himself, as though he were trying to hold all his limbs together. On closer inspection, he probably wasn't that young, maybe seventeen or eighteen.

'So, what are you in for?' Sami asked when the door slammed shut.

The boy didn't answer. He raised his head and it looked like his neck was going to snap under its weight. His eyes were sunken. Twice, the guard came in and said he needed help, placing his hand on the boy's lower back as he led him out. Each time they returned, the boy threw up in the sink in the corner.

The cell door opened and two more prisoners were let in. They were men in their thirties, well dressed and freshly shaven; one wore a Rolex and the other a light grey Hugo Boss shirt. Both had on navy chinos and patent leather shoes with low heels. They were quiet and mostly whispered between themselves, but they did tell Sami they, too, were wanted for avoiding military service.

A couple of hours after that a whole group of prisoners entered, seven men who reeked of alcohol and smoke, talking loudly and cracking jokes.

'Some afterparty,' said one of them, whose lanky hair fell to far below his ears.

He was wearing a turquoise shirt with palm trees and pineapples and big stains under the armpits. The guard opened the cell door once more, looked over at the boy in the corner, who avoided his eyes, and asked if any of them wanted cigarettes. The partygoers bought two packs, at three times the price charged in shops. They seized the opportunity to ask the guard if he had a deck of cards to sell. He did.

'Do you want one?' the man in the Hawaiian shirt asked after the guard shut the door.

'Thanks, but I don't smoke,' Sami said.

'You mean you don't smoke tobacco?'

He nodded to Sami's black T-shirt, which had a star-shaped leaf on the chest. He hoped the gloom hid the fact that he was blushing.

'But you play cards, I hope, Mr Che?'

They sat down in a tight circle and dealt the cards.

'What did you do to end up here?'

'I extended my leave a little,' said Hawaiian shirt. 'And when they came for me, they arrested everyone in the room.'

'They didn't even let us finish our beers,' another person in the circle said. 'Party poopers.'

Smoke quickly filled the cell and Sami tried not to cough.

Some time in the afternoon, the guard came and took him to a different room. In it was an older man in uniform, whose most remarkable facial feature was a bushy monobrow. The officer checked his ID, hemmed a few times and introduced himself with the same family name.

'We're related?' Sami asked, unable to conceal his surprise.

The man's jaw worked and he stroked his eyebrow but said there was nothing he could do.

Sami was taken back to the cell where they played cards for a few more hours until the thirst and cigarette smoke gave him a headache, at which point he tried to get to sleep, to no avail. Eventually he did drift off and awoke when the cell door banged open.

'Line up,' the guard shouted, even though the faintest whisper would have reverberated in the cramped space.

He was accompanied by three other guards, and Sami gasped when he saw their camouflage uniforms and red hats.

'Where are we going?' asked one of the partygoers as he packed up the deck of cards. He must have still been drunk to dare to question the military police, and he was promptly dragged outside.

'Now, silence!' the first guard shouted, also seemingly nervous next to the military police.

As they were ushered across the dirt yard, their heads lowered, Sami felt a warm breath against his cheek.

'Boloni,' the boy whispered to him. 'They're taking us to Boloni.'

'Look down! I said eyes on the ground!'

They were shoved into a minibus with a bulletproof rear window, through which they watched the streets of Homs and freedom rush past.

All the emotions Sami had gone through during the day, which had raged and clawed at the inside of his chest, turned into desolation. Despite all the rumours and stories, he hadn't believed it until that moment: that this was the truth of their country, that you could kiss your girlfriend goodbye in the morning, go for a walk and that same evening be sitting handcuffed in a military vehicle on your way to a prison, the second one of the day.

13

BOLONI WAS ONE of the military police's prisons outside Homs. Dusk was falling when they arrived but Sami caught a glimpse of the building from the outside: a square block with armed guards on the roof. Chained together in pairs, they shuffled inside.

They were received by new guards who told them to take off everything except their underwear. Then they were told to take that off too and squat down twice. Sami decided to be a model prisoner while he tried to think of a different strategy. He took off his jeans and the black shirt with the star-shaped leaf, folded everything and rolled up his socks. Pulled his underwear down to his ankles, squatted down twice and put his clothes back on. The partygoers did the same thing, serious now. The two well-dressed men followed suit, equally grave.

The boy, on the other hand, stood stock still in his red boxers. One of the guards shouted at him to obey orders but the boy didn't move. It didn't seem deliberate. More like his mental machinery had ground to a halt, locking him in position with his legs inches apart and his arms hanging limply like a marionette's. Then the guard punched him in the nose; it sounded like something cracked, and he landed two more blows. As the boy slowly collapsed on to the floor, he received two kicks in the stomach. The guards pulled him up and pulled down his underwear – blood was dripping from the boy's member – and shoved him along.

'Leave all belongings and loose items,' the guard said, and pointed to their belts and watches. 'Shoelaces too, so you don't get any ideas about hanging yourselves.'

The guard was still massaging his knuckles when it was Sami's turn to hand over his things. Only then did the guard look up and scrutinize him.

'My goodness, Sami, long time no see. How are you, my friend?'

Haydar spread his arms wide and looked like he was about to hug him but froze mid-movement. He still wore a silver wristwatch, like he did when they were little and went to school together. His hair was greying and he'd lost some of his confident posture, but other than that he looked the same.

'Here are my things,' Sami said, looking straight ahead.

'Whatever you need, you let me know,' Haydar said. Then he looked away, as though embarrassed, or maybe it was just his knuckles hurting.

When they had all been stripped of their personal belongings they were taken inside. The prison was built like a cube, as he had surmised from the outside, but with a traditional open courtyard. Inside, in the gloom, all he could make out were long rows of doors with narrow, barred windows.

One of the doors opened and they were ushered inside, tripping over legs and feet before the prisoners who were already in there had time to shuffle out of the way. The first thing to hit him was the smell: a mix of blood, urine, sweat and excrement, some emanating from a toilet in one corner partly concealed by a yellowed shower curtain.

During the first night, the skies opened and they watched the deluge through the barred window. They were so many that they couldn't stretch out on the floor – they lay pressed against each other with their legs pulled up. It was early autumn but Sami was so cold he was shaking.

The next morning, they were awoken by the sound of the cell door flying open and pieces of white cheese being passed in to them. Sami was unable to eat so much as a bite.

In the light of day, he could see more of the cell. It was about 250 feet square and held close to fifty men. The previously merry partygoers were quiet and hungover. They had smoked all their cigarettes and were unlikely to ask these guards for more.

Most of the prisoners had bruises and open wounds. Sami hoped they were the result of sharp elbows and feet during the night. He was soon disabused of that. Not long after breakfast, the cell door opened again.

'Against the wall, against the wall! Idiots, are you all deaf?'

Like sheep, they were herded to one end of the cell. Whoever was too slow got a beating from the guards. Sami kept his head bowed, but he noticed one of the guards had wrapped his rifle in a white scarf. Two of the prisoners were dragged out crying and screaming, then a long, agonizing wait followed. He counted to one hundred and then started over. Ninety-seven, ninety-eight, ninety-nine . . . The next time the door opened, the limp bodies of two prisoners were dragged back into the cell.

Sami caught a glimpse of the guard's rifle again. The scarf was now deep red.

A man on the far side of the cell took his shirt off and soaked it in water from the toilet sink, and the rag was passed from prisoner to prisoner. The wounds on the two men's swollen legs, which were like black and blue logs, were dabbed.

Every hour and every minute until dusk, the torture continued. Sami was not called out to the yard so maybe his relative's contacts had helped him. He didn't see Haydar again, which was a small relief.

The following night, the temperature plummeted and he started shaking long before midnight. This time he noticed the bedbugs; he had probably been too exhausted the previous night. As soon as darkness fell, his entire body, particularly his chest and stomach, began to itch violently. When the first light of day seeped through the window, he looked for the men with the battered legs. Their wounds were teeming with bugs.

Breakfast consisted of white cheese again. Lunch and supper the previous day had been lentil soup and bread, with either bulgur or three potatoes each. When everyone was done, the guard came back and asked if anyone was still hungry and wanted more. Hawaiian shirt immediately put his hand up. Sami, for his part, only managed half a potato. He wasn't attempting a hunger strike, it was just that his throat was so dry he couldn't swallow.

'You have to eat,' Hawaiian shirt told him. 'Rule number one in captivity: eat when you can, since you never know when you'll be fed next.'

Shortly after breakfast the guards started opening and closing cell doors. The prisoners were dragged into the courtyard in groups. Soon they could hear the dull thudding of boots and fists colliding with human flesh.

'Still, this place is better,' said Hawaiian shirt. 'We're still considered part of the army, even if we are traitors who need to be disciplined. In other prisons, like Saidnaya and Palmyra, prisoners die every day.'

He listed the methods used to correct inappropriate behaviour: beating the soles of a person's feet, electric shocks and waterboarding. Palestinian hangings, where the victim was strung up with his wrists behind his back until his shoulders dislocated. Some of the guards were on drugs but the primary reason for the torture was another one: tedium. They viewed the prisoners as animals they could experiment on.

'People aren't born cruel but they learn,' said Hawaiian shirt. 'And they learn surprisingly quickly.'

He told Sami they were most likely being kept a week or two in this prison, but he knew about a man who had spent many years behind bars.

'Next to the cell door was a tiny hole he managed to conceal,' Hawaiian shirt said with a low voice, 'and through which he peered out from time to time. When a new guard arrived, he had a hard time looking at the corpses in the hallway after the hangings. He threw up and left that job to the other guards. But after a few weeks, he stayed on his post. He helped carry the bodies, and one day, he was the one joking around with a new guard: what are you, a weakling, can't take the smell of a little bit of shit, eh? And as he said it, he'd be prodding one of the bodies with his foot.'

Hawaiian shirt paused and looked down at his feet.

'It's something I've thought a lot about,' he continued. 'If it's possible to learn evil, surely it also has to be possible to learn goodness. Don't you think?'

Sami didn't reply, but that seemed not to matter. Maybe he was talking more to himself than anyone else.

On the third day in Boloni, they were taken into the courtyard for inspection and a scolding from the prison director, a short, robust man in his forties with sun-bleached hair. He yelled as much at the guards as at the prisoners, and sometimes took part in the torture, which he seemed to relish. The prisoners were ordered to sit on the cold ground with their heads lowered.

'Us too?' said the man who used to wear a Rolex.

'That won't be necessary,' replied a younger guard, glancing nervously this way and that.

When the prison director noticed that the two formerly well-dressed men, now sporting rumpled shirts and stubble, were standing up next to the other prisoners, his face darkened. He walked up to them, grabbed one by the chin, then the other, and spat out the words:

'Who do you think you are? Just because you're judges doesn't mean I can't beat you to death. Sit down!'

The two men sat down immediately, right next to Sami. They pushed the palms of their hands to the ground to keep from shaking.

Sitting soon became the worst form of torture. The concrete floor was too cold to lie down on and the lack of space made it difficult to stretch out anyhow. No matter which way Sami turned, he felt like his legs were being worn down. His body was growing numb. Bruises appeared around his knees, calves and thighs where blood vessels had burst.

After one week in prison, the gate opened and two guards entered the cell.

'Which one of you is Sami?'

His tongue froze and his throat twisted. So it was his turn to be dragged out in the yard, to be turned into a piece of bruised meat. One of the guards chewed impatiently and looked around in the cell.

'Either show yourself now or you stay another week.'

Hawaiian shirt put a hand on Sami's shoulder, and the guards grabbed him under his arms. He felt like he was passing out but a sudden slap shook him back to life. Instead of being pulled into the yard, he was taken through the main doors, outside, where an armoured car was waiting for him.

'Your lucky day,' the uniformed driver said. 'You're going to the army's recruitment centre in Homs.'

It was like stepping into a parallel universe where people were neat, sweet-smelling and had beautiful skin with no lacerations or bruises. As he walked into the recruitment centre, Sami looked up to see his father, Grandpa Faris and Ali standing by the registration desk. It felt like it had been a year since they last saw each other.

'My son!'

Sami walked slowly forward and his dad met him halfway, embracing him and kissing his cheeks. Grandpa Faris stroked his hair and Ali put a warm hand on his back. Sami breathed in their scents: oud and soap and clean, perfectly clean, skin.

'Sarah wanted to come too,' his brother said, 'but her bus was late and we didn't dare to wait for her.'

They were smiling but it looked forced and Nabil's eyes were wetter than usual.

'Are they treating you well? Have you eaten?'

Sami nodded and thought to himself that it was almost true. During his detention he had managed to eat two potatoes, and there was no point worrying his family. The fact that he hadn't showered was harder to hide. But they held him for a long time, until the uniformed woman in charge of registration noticed them.

'Why is he not wearing handcuffs?' she said, pointing at the guard who had brought Sami in.

'I was told to take them off while he met with his family.'

'This is no family dinner. Come on, you, visiting hours are over.' The woman rapped her gold rings on the desk.

'We're doing everything in our power to get you out of there,' Ali said and gave him a final hug.

The meeting was over in minutes. Sami would be taken back to the military prison in Boloni and wait for the decision about his placement. In the car, the driver handed over his phone.

'A gift from your brother. You've got five minutes.'

Sami called Sarah first, then his mother. He could hear Samira swallowing several times but her voice was strikingly calm. He must do what the soldiers told him to do, she insisted.

'Don't get riled up over nothing, conserve your energy and eat when they feed you.'

She said what he needed to hear.

Back in Boloni, the persistent rain kept the temperature low and turned the nights into protracted battles. Time stood still or moved in circles, even the sounds of torture blended with exhaustion and hunger. Sometimes he didn't know if he was awake or asleep, if he was sitting or lying down, if he was a body or a human.

On the eleventh or twelfth day, he had lost count, there was a break in the tedium. Together with the two judges, whose shirts were now virtually transparent, he was handcuffed and taken to a new location.

Al-Nabek was on the road between Homs and Damascus, known for the nearby monastery Mar Musa. The city was in the valley and the monastery up in the mountains. A British archaeologist had recently found ten-thousand-year-old remains next to the monastery: stone circles, the foundations of walls and graves. Traces of people who had lived and died. The thought boggled his mind, that humans were so short-lived compared to the objects they surrounded themselves with.

Having left the crowded cell, Sami was now standing in an endless field. The autumn sun was high in the sky, warming his neck, and the air was dry with sand. The din of voices and feet intensified. Five thousand men surrounded him, ready to be assigned to their new divisions. Most had registered more or less willingly when called up. A small number of women had joined of their own free will. They often came from Alawite families and did not attend the usual military service but went to military school to be placed on administrative services later. Around a hundred men had, like Sami, come straight from prison.

The field was surrounded by numbered lorries and a soldier with a megaphone called out names and numbers. When Sami's name rang out, it felt like when he was younger and had to go and get the football from the old man's house. Mud and quicksand, like the world was losing its contours.

The lorry he was placed in was followed by two more vehicles. Similar convoys drove off in different directions. From above, it must have looked like a snake pit scattering; caravans of dark military vehicles slithering through the barren landscape.

Sami didn't speak during the drive. He wore the same clothes as when he was arrested, the jeans and black T-shirt now covered in white sweat streaks. The sports bag his father and older brother had managed to give him in prison sat by his feet. It contained a change of clothes, a first-aid kit with plasters, antiseptic and gauze. His mother had also put a miniature Quran in it, so small it fitted in the palm of his hand. He had held it since he took his seat on the lorry and now, as he opened it, a folded note fell out.

I love you, my son.

14

THEY HAD PASSED evergreen forest and little villages and turned on to a dirt road. Now, the military convoy slowed down. They were in the mountains, somewhere outside Damascus, that was all Sami knew. Up here, the air shredded his breath and he shivered in his short-sleeves. Everyone climbed out of the vehicles, hundreds of strangers eyeing one another. Some tried to find reasons to laugh, spotting an acquaintance or relative to talk to, but Sami kept quiet.

'Can anyone here write quickly?' the soldier who had driven them asked.

When no one raised their hand, Sami did, if hesitantly. Considering the soldiers he had encountered so far, he thought it safest to show a willingness to help from the start. He was told to make lists of the new recruits. First he was to tell them about himself.

'I'm twenty-two years old and from Homs.'

'Do you have any special skills?'

'Networks and computers.'

The soldier contented himself with that and Sami breathed a sigh of relief. The row of soldiers-to-be inched forward and Sami noted down their names and details, one after the other. They were from Damascus, Aleppo, Daraa, Idlib and other places all over the country. They had studied law, economics, art history, medicine or just graduated from secondary school. They were pimply, thin, muscular, long-haired, shaven, swarthy, ginger, freckled, with or without facial hair. What many of them had in common was that this was going to be the first time they had lived away from their parents.

'Name?'

'Hussein,' said a young slim man in an ankle-length shirt, whose long, dark eyelashes framed his serious eyes. He was from a village outside Raqqa in northern Syria, where white cotton fields spread out from the shores of the Euphrates. When asked about his education, he looked the soldier straight in the eye and answered calmly, in the accent typical of the northern countryside, 'I have never been to school.'

'Do you have any special skills?'

'Herding sheep,' Hussein said.

The other recruits smiled, someone laughed, but the soldier in charge of the registration nodded curtly.

'Next. What's your name?'

'Look, I don't speak Arabic,' a large man said in English. He had a bleached fringe that hung down over his eyes and wore a Nirvana T-shirt, apparently unaware of the regime's views on rock music. 'There must be some mistake,' he continued. 'I was at the airport. I have no idea why I'm here. I'm from Canada, I'm a Canadian citizen. I was just visiting my father's family. You have to call the embassy.'

'What's your name?'

'I don't understand Arabic. What's he saying?'

'He wants to know your name,' Sami translated.

'Bill. Or, well, Bilal, but everyone calls me Bill.'

The soldier flipped through his papers and said they would check his documentation again. But, he said slowly, according to the government's information, he was eighteen years old and a Syrian citizen and therefore obliged to do military service.

'What's he saying?' Bill asked.

'He's saying he will look into your case,' Sami replied. 'Don't worry.'

The Canadian swallowed several times.

'Next,' called the soldier.

When everyone's names were on the list and any mobile phones had been confiscated, they were shown around the camp. It sprawled out in every direction as far as the eye could see. The division consisted of almost twelve thousand soldiers.

The soldiers giving them their tour were patient and almost seemed sympathetic. Not too long ago, the soldiers had been in the new recruits' shoes. It'll be easier if you let go of the past, they said.

'Forget about free time, forget about sex, forget about girlfriends. From now on, you're going to have to get used to a different way of life.'

Their new way of life would entail basic training, then more advanced training over six months. Then they would be given their assignments and the work would start in earnest.

Sami and the others were shown to a bare barracks with rows of triple bunk beds. They each signed out blankets that were to be returned at the end of their service: in one year and nine months. The time could not be fathomed. Sami tried not to think about the hundreds of days and nights ahead of him.

Before bedtime they were allowed a couple of minutes in the showers, Sami's first since he was arrested two weeks before. He rubbed the hard piece of soap until it lathered. Afterwards, he noticed the others were no longer keeping their distance and he remembered something he had forgotten over the past two weeks: the smell of his clean body.

Sami claimed a bottom bunk and put down his coarse blankets – two as a sheet, two as a cover. He lay down on the solid mattress and looked up at the doodles drawn on the underside of the middle bunk by soldiers who had slept there before him: genitals and women's names, a countdown of days, a pig with initials Sami assumed portrayed an officer. The bed squeaked and moved under the weight of the Canadian, and Sami heard a short sob muffled in a pillow.

'Don't worry, it'll be all right,' Sami whispered.

The crying stopped and for a long time he heard nothing else;

maybe the Canadian had fallen asleep. But then, 'You really think so?' Bill said softly.

Sami couldn't remember what he answered as he sank into the much-needed oblivion of sleep. He fell deeper and deeper, and remembered none of his dreams the next morning when they were woken up by a persistent banging on the steel door.

Sami, Bill, Hussein and the other men shuffled out of bed, half dressed and with their blankets in a tangle. Curses rained down on them and moments later their beds were made and everyone was dressed.

Hussein, the Bedouin shepherd, was the only one who seemed happy and relaxed. He didn't talk much but had eaten his meagre meal as though it were a feast, praised the hot water in the shower and contemplated his bunk for a long moment before tying his arm to the frame with a scarf.

'What are you doing?' Sami had asked.

'Making sure I don't fall,' Hussein said as he made himself comfortable.

'From now on, no lie-ins,' said a soldier standing in front of them with his feet wide and his arms crossed.

He looked like a soldier from the movies. A caricature of a strict officer, with a neat moustache and rolled-up shirtsleeves that fitted snugly over bulging muscles. Everything felt cinematic and surreal. At any moment, someone would step through the backdrop and say, Cut, let's try again. They were given heavy boots, thermal underwear and green camouflage uniforms. Outside in the yard, barbers were waiting to shave their heads, cheeks and chins. Bill's bleached fringe fell to the ground, as well as Hussein's dark beard. They both looked younger and somewhat naked afterwards, even if the uniforms added some years.

Sami's own hair fell on to the dirt in soft tufts. There and then, the events of the past few days and weeks sank in, the open fields in al-

Nabek and the meandering journey to the camp. There was no going back. From now on, he was a soldier.

The second morning they were woken up at half past four by the same banging on the steel door. They put on their uniforms, tied their boots and assembled in the yard. The lower edge of the clouds showed a glowing fringe. The sky turned a rich red and pink, which was then watered down by the light of the rising sun. It was as though someone was taking a firm hold on the blanket of clouds and lifting it up, and underneath was the dawn, cold and clear like spring water.

The morning began with a workout: push-ups, lunges and squat jumps. The Canadian asked when was breakfast. Soon, was the answer, they just had to go for a run first. The run was two miles through forest and over hills and then the same way back. Hussein was the only one who managed with ease. Bill threw up in the bathroom and Sami saved some breakfast for him: two eggs, bread and bitter tea. He felt like he had barely eaten at all, his body not yet recovered from his weeks in prison. Hunger was like a wild animal, tearing at him from the inside.

Their first class was weapons training, then they duck-walked for four miles, which entailed moving at a squat with their hands raised behind their heads. Lactic acid started pumping through their legs after just a few steps. The morning was wrapped up with a double session of martial arts and military strategy.

'You are the pride and backbone of this country,' said their instructor.

He told them Hafez al-Assad had joined the Baath Party at sixteen and shortly thereafter become a fighter pilot. He quickly rose through the ranks.

'As we hope you will.'

Everyone knew that was a lie because in practice only Alawites were able to advance into the highest echelons. Their instructor continued by telling them how the Baath Party had saved the country from annihilation by assuming power in 1963. Hafez al-Assad had become head of the air force and later the country's defence minister. Then he seized control of Syria, through a corrective revolution, in order to get the politics and the country back on the right track.

'Finally, Christians, Sunnis, Alawites and Druze could live in peace and security together,' their instructor concluded, leaving out the Kurds, since they didn't exist in his eyes anyway.

Their instructor was called Bassel and was named after Hafez's eldest son, who had been expected to take over the rule of Syria one day. Bassel al-Assad had been famous for his love of fast cars and horse racing. But Bassel never got to take the reins as the leader of the regime. One foggy January morning in 1994 he was driving his Mercedes to Damascus' international airport. There was a car crash on a roundabout and Bassel, who was not wearing a seatbelt, died instantly.

There had been three national days of mourning. Schools, shops and offices had closed. Luxury hotels had abstained from serving alcohol. Bassel was declared a national martyr. Hospitals, sports arenas and an airport were named after him. When the confusion and grief had subsided, people started looking around. Who would now shoulder the burdens of governing if something were to happen to Hafez? It was Bassel's less well-known brother Bashar al-Assad, the British-educated ophthalmologist, who stepped up. Granted, he lacked charisma and gravitas, but one day he was going to follow in his father's footsteps.

When Hafez al-Assad died at the turn of the millennium, people didn't believe it at first. He, the eternal father of the nation, couldn't just die. Bashar was given the epithet 'Son of Hafez' in an attempt to have some of his father's radiance rub off on him. At first, Bashar banned the public posting of pictures of himself and ruled more as his late father's proxy. In time, however, he assumed his new role wholeheartedly and then some.

Naturally, their military instructor didn't tell them all that. He also didn't tell them that Assad, which meant lion, was an assumed name:

Bashar's grandfather had been a farmer who changed his surname from Wahesh, which meant savage or monster. Their instructor did, however, say that from now on, whenever they were asked where they were from, they should answer 'Assad's Syria'.

The afternoon and evening were conducted at the same tempo. Theory and training, a final lesson until eight o'clock, then dinner and rest until ten. Sami's feet were red and swollen and full of blisters from his shapeless boots. He sent his parents a loving thought for having packed plasters for him.

Darkness engulfed the barracks when they fell into their beds. Snores ebbed and flowed in the dormitory until the banging and shouting woke them at half past four, and everything started over again.

15

SAMI SOON REALIZED the officers were targeting the weak. Either the physically weak or the ones who didn't have the mental stamina to do the drills. And then there was Bilal, or Bill, who didn't know Arabic. He had been given language teaching back in Toronto but only knew a few phrases he had practised with his grandmother. One of the other recruits was always with him, translating the officers' commands, but sometimes it didn't help.

'Where are you from, soldier!'

'Canada,' said Bill.

The officer smiled and paused to draw the situation out.

'Where did you say you were from?'

'Assad's Syria,' Sami whispered, but Bill had already repeated: 'Toronto, Canada.'

'Wrong answer. Go to the shit pit.'

Bill went over to the shit pit, which was exactly that: a hole full of mud mixed with excrement from the latrines. The smell was putrid and sickening and a swarm of flies hovered above it. A fever had recently devastated their division and the officer had pointed out in their previous class how important personal hygiene was: wash your hands, don't share cutlery, keep your feet dry and clean.

'*In the shit pit, you piece of crap.*'

No translation was necessary because the officer was pointing with his whole hand. Bill hesitated for a second, then started unbuttoning his uniform with trembling hands. When he bent down to unlace his boots, the officer stepped in and gave him a kick in the behind. Bill fell head over heels and the mudhole swallowed him with a splash.

On the fourth night, they were woken up at two. From now on, a new element was added to their training: punishments. This usually started with them being forced into the yard in nothing but their underwear. Nine! Everyone did squat jumps. Seven! Everyone dropped to the ground and pushed their chests up and down. Buckets of ice water were poured over their backs if they didn't work hard enough.

Some were broken by the training. One morning during the first few weeks of training Sami was woken by loud cries from outside. He quickly put on his uniform and ran out, and saw that several other soldiers had gathered in a circle on the yard where they had their morning assemblies. In the middle stood one of the newcomers, dressed only in his underclothing, dark with sweat or some other fluid. Sami recognized him as one of the young men he had taken notes of on the first day. It was the first and last time they had talked. Now the young recruit stood shaking on the frosty ground. Beside him lay a big, empty can.

'Stay away. Don't get any closer.'

Despite his shaking, his face was strangely still. Wet hair stuck to his cheeks. The young man lifted his hands but Sami couldn't see what he was holding. A needle? A tiny box?

'I swear, I'll do it . . . Anything but this.'

It was then that Sami smelled the petrol. He took a step closer and released a sound that he didn't know came from himself. The young man struck the match and the flames rose up.

Sami found he couldn't move, couldn't comprehend how quickly the body became black, how fast the smell of burnt meat spread. From a distance, he saw how Hussein and two other recruits threw themselves over the burning soldier and tried to quench the fire with their own bodies. Paramedics were summoned but it was too late.

That night, Sami heard Bill sobbing from the bunk bed over his. Sami lay silently and listened, then sat up and walked over to Hussein's bed.

'How are you?' Sami whispered.

He could see that Hussein's eyes were open. He lay on his back with his arms crossed over his chest, white bandages covering the worst burn marks.

'You know,' Sami continued, 'I think everyone's in shock. It's OK to feel sad or angry or afraid, or whatever you feel . . .'

It was as if Hussein didn't hear him. Sami turned and took a few steps in the dark, then heard Hussein's muffled voice behind him.

'Fear is like poison. If you let it grow roots, you will be lost for ever.'

Not long after the fire incident another soldier died of a heart attack. In both cases their trainers explained it away as personal weaknesses, physical or mental. Sami no longer felt as if the pain penetrated into the depths of him. He woke up, he did what he was told and then he slept. But it was as though something happened to him at night, a slow transformation.

Gradually Sami started to consider it a challenge to break the rules. To drink a bottle of contraband wine, just to see the look on the sergeant's face when he didn't react to the ice water. Sami and Hussein also made a habit of stealing from the pantry, and Bill happily shared with them, even if he was afraid of punishment. They would take a carton of eggs or tinned beans. Once they got their hands on an entire chicken, which they roasted and ate in silence, an unadulterated joy.

During Sami's first night watch he started smoking cigarettes, and it soon became one of his few pleasures. The night watch was otherwise a psychological challenge. All sounds were amplified in the dark, from the barking of wild dogs to the hissing of hyenas in the distance. One time a soldier came running back to base camp, white as a sheet.

'What happened? You look like you've seen a ghost,' Sami said.

'Not far from it,' the soldier mumbled.

He couldn't speak until he had sat down and collected himself.

'Do you believe in jinn?' the soldier asked. 'I thought they were made up, myths. But after tonight . . .' He shook his head to cast off his unease. 'I was sitting by the fire, smoking, when I spotted a cat slinking along the tent wall. A cat in this cold, can you imagine? You won't believe me but it's true, *wallahi*. The cat crept closer and closer and in the end it was so close I could touch the tip of its tail. The fur was stiff with frost. And then . . . then it got up on its hind legs and opened its mouth so I could see its pink, coarse tongue. And it said, "Pardon me, but do you have the time?" Get it? The cat was talking to me!'

Sami laughed and asked what he'd been smoking. But there was no question the soldier was serious; he had a wild look in his eyes and his hands were shaking.

Nocturnal spirits or no, the soldier was sent to the clink for abandoning his post.

'My advice is simple,' their commanding officer said when the soldier was released. 'When a cat asks you for the time, just answer her. Tell her the time. But whatever you do, don't leave your post.'

Sami slept in double layers of clothing and thick woollen socks at night. In the morning, they blew smoke rings and pretended they were from cigars. The temperature was below freezing almost year-round up in the mountains, but on some spring days their bodies thawed in the pale sunlight. Like nocturnal insects, they would all turn to the sun and stare into the blindness.

During one drill, in a frosty field, Hussein rubbed his hands together and said, 'A cup of tea or coffee would really hit the spot right now.'

Sami looked around and said: Sure. He walked over to the flatbed truck and pulled out a handful of cables they used for the tents, which he twisted together with a few thinner cables to stabilize them.

Bill watched in shock. 'Have you lost your mind?'

'Put the kettle on the ground here, with the cable there. Then we'll lift the other end up with two sticks and touch it to the powerline.'

'Do you know how many volts are in something like that? You're going to fry like a piece of charcoal.'

'Fine, so don't then.'

An hour later, even more cold and hungry, Bill suggested they try again. Hussein and Sami balanced the stabilized cable against the powerline. It took them less than a second to get the kettle boiling.

Days and weeks passed, darkness fell and ice water was poured on their backs. From time to time soldiers had to be brought to the military hospital after passing out or not being able to feel their feet. *I choose this*, Sami thought. *I choose this and it won't kill me.*

After the initial training period, they got some time off. He counted down the days until each small break. He could endure the physical punishments tolerably but some things were harder to deal with than others. Like one particular sergeant. The sergeant had an arrogant way about him and enjoyed insulting them during training. They were weaklings. Vermin.

'I could put a bullet in the back of your heads and no one would care. I could fuck your sisters and little brothers.'

Sami was just getting up from doing push-ups when the world went black and he lost his balance. A foot between his shoulder blades and the sergeant's scornful voice: 'Eat shit.' White lightning shot through his body. Sami got up slowly and groggily, braced himself and kicked the sergeant so hard in the stomach that he fell headlong on to the stony ground.

In the barracks, several people patted Sami on the back and laughed at the whole thing. Except Hussein, who shook his head.

'They're going to punish all of us.'

The next night, they lined up as usual, dressed only in their underwear. It was cold, well below freezing. This time their instructor was present to personally oversee the evening's punishments. A few people bent down to start the push-ups.

The instructor held up his hand. 'No. Tonight, we have a different task for you.' He wrapped his scarf around his neck, pulled up his leather gloves. 'It's very simple. Tonight you are to stand still.'

A numb feeling spread through Sami's body. Stand still? He had expected some sort of consequence after the kick. For them to pull him out of bed in the middle of the night for extra punishment. For them to send him to the clink, even though soldiers weren't supposed to be sent there during their basic training.

At the same time, he figured the sergeant was ashamed. The instructors were supposed to demonstrate good morals and serve as an example for the new soldiers. In order to explain the kick, the sergeant would sooner or later have to admit that he had broken the honour code of the army by insulting the recruits' families.

Sami had almost started thinking of his kick as a nightmare, as something imagined, a cat standing on its hind legs asking the time. But now, with the instructor right in front of him, the event acquired a crisp clarity. After a few minutes, he began to understand the severity of the punishment. Because standing still was much worse than moving around. Doing exercises made the body warm and gave the mind something to focus on instead of the cold.

After a few minutes, his teeth started chattering uncontrollably. He clenched his jaw but the shaking spread through his body. After half an hour, he couldn't feel his legs. After an hour, he heard a thud, then another. Sami didn't dare to turn to look, but out of the corner of his eye he saw soldiers dropping around him. They fell and stayed down. Their hands were claws in various shades of purple. Only after some time did the instructor signal to the medics to take them to the military hospital. Bill managed to stay up, as did Sami. Hussein seemed unperturbed by the cold, but when they got back inside their barracks he wrapped himself in all the clothes and blankets he had.

The next morning, the ground was covered with glittering ice crystals, the tussocks of grass stuck up like spiky hedgehogs. Fourteen people were in the hospital with frostbite. The others were woken up to begin the day's drills as though nothing had happened.

16

WHENEVER SAMI HELD a new pen, he would assess its weight. See what kind of nib he was dealing with: wide or thin, straight or diagonal. It was the pen that inspired the writing, not the other way round. In the beginning was the word, his mum used to say. He pictured instead a golden pen, the original pen that wrote the world into existence, that drew light in the night of the universe.

Quite unlike the pen in front of him at this moment, which was barely usable. Sami moved the broken-off felt tip across the paper. A broken line of ants, a parade of grasshoppers. The sergeant held up the notepad and studied it in silence.

'What's your name, what's your number?'

After almost six months of basic training, Sami and the other re-cruits were about to be split up. They continued to perform the same drills but noticed they were watched less meticulously than before.

One day, a jeep had pulled up to where they were doing their morn-ing workout and a sergeant had climbed out. If anyone were to draw his face, lead pencil would have been the inevitable medium: grey eyes, placed close together, a thin moustache and a thin mouth. Outside of the army, he would have been someone you found in an office, in some unassuming bureaucratic post. But here everyone looked up when he cleared his throat. The sergeant had come from a military base outside Damascus and he was looking for someone with good handwriting. Since the military base in question was the core of their division, where the important decisions were made, it was a place most people wanted to be. Most of all because administrative work was a dream for the soldiers. Being there meant not being in active combat, not getting punishments. And certain perks could be negotiated, too.

'Who here has the best handwriting?' said the sergeant.

Sami was just about to raise his hand when the group thronged in front of him.

'Me, me!' one of them shouted and was given the notepad to write a sample.

The sergeant raised his eyebrows and sent the pad on to the next volunteer.

'Write in your neatest hand,' he urged them, and one after the other, they were dismissed.

'Please, try your best.'

One of them tried so hard he broke the blue felt tip. When it was Sami's turn, the pen was all but unusable. Did he have another? The sergeant shook his head. Sami wrote as best he could and tried to perfect all the fine lines, curlicues, dots and marks needed.

'Which script?' the sergeant asked, scrutinizing the paper.

'Al-diwani,' said Sami.

'Do you know others?'

He filled the page with sentences and words. For a moment, he was so engrossed in the familiar task – taken back to the writing competitions in school and writing signs for his siblings' doors – that he forgot the officer.

'OK, that's enough.'

During the following weeks, Sami and the other recruits waited to be given their assignments. If there was one silver lining, it was that their bodies slowly adapted to their trials. Sami suffered from constant sleep deprivation but was now able to do the drills without too much pain.

They had a day and a half off every other week. When they rejoined the camp, they would have a potluck with the food brought back from home: bulgur balls filled with lamb and pine nuts from Aleppo, rich red wine from Suwayda and grainy, matured cheese from Homs, dipped in silky smooth olive oil from Afrin.

Every morning, they ran out into the vast evergreen forest and back again. Whoever made it back first was given an extra day off. It was an almost unimaginable luxury. Yet even so, no one wanted to be the fastest, because that meant being added to *the list*.

No one had seen the list but they all knew about it. The soldiers in the combat battalion had the hardest physical job and the list contained the names of the recruits assigned to it for the final part of their service. So they jogged at a leisurely pace, careful to return to camp in a group.

Their drill instructor grew increasingly annoyed. Granted, they did follow orders and ran, but they seemed to have discovered a loophole in the regulations. An unspoken agreement. A collective resistance. Whenever someone felt impatient and wanted to sprint the last half mile, they reminded each other about the list.

One morning they were shivering in the yard, in long, sleepy lines. The sunlight broke through the haze and their commanding officer began to speak.

'Today, you will not be going for your regular run. It will be the same route but whoever finishes first will be given something extra.'

He looked around and straightened up.

'Nothing special, just a little bonus. Four days' leave.'

Waves now rippled through the formation. A confused din rose around Sami. Bill turned to Hussein, who for the first time raised his hand in the morning assembly.

'Do you mean in addition to the regular weekend, the one we get every other week?'

The officer nodded. Four days, an ocean of time. They would be able to go home, see friends and family. But they hadn't forgotten the threat of being selected for the combat battalion.

'I'd rather die,' Sami heard someone say.

'It's a trap,' whispered someone else.

'I'd rather run with my legs lashed together than end up on that list,' said a third.

The officer clapped his hands and the din subsided.

'Yes, and another thing. If I catch you coming back as a group, everyone will have their weekend leave cancelled.'

An angry clamour surged through the group. Being offered something you had never had was one thing, having your privileges rescinded was another.

They started to run in silence. A few people tried to talk but soon ran out of breath as the group cranked up the pace. Sami followed, still unsure if it was worth it.

'Aren't you already on the list?' Hussein asked.

'Yeah, I've been on the list since the first time we did target practice. But I see no need to push my name further up it,' Sami replied.

Or maybe it was worth it? He pictured driving the pink Beetle to the sea with Sarah, picnicking on the beach. Sitting in a café in Damascus, smoking the hookah, apple-and-mint flavour, maybe spending the night in a hotel. Without noticing it, Sami accelerated and left the group behind. The ground disappeared underneath his feet. Wet leaves, slippery. Two miles in, he considered stopping to wait for the group but he turned and set his sights on two runners up ahead. Only Hussein was keeping up with him.

'What are you thinking about?' Sami asked to flee his own thoughts.

Every breath pressed against his ribcage. The rushing in his ears. He didn't expect Hussein to answer.

'I'm thinking about the sea,' he said. 'I've always wanted to know what it sounds like when the waves break against the shore.'

They were approaching the densest part of the forest when they saw one of the runners trip over a root and fall. The guy behind him didn't have time to swerve and so tripped over him. Sami and Hussein lengthened their stride, caught up and passed them. They were coming up to the final stretch. One of them was going to sprint. Sami sensed Hussein would win; despite his sinewy body, he was used to roaming across vast distances. They had found another rhythm now. His throat was burning and his chest pounding but his legs were light. They could keep running for ever and beyond, past the horizon.

'What the fuck . . .'

Just then, three people dashed out of a shrubbery. They must have hidden there on the way out and were completely rested. Hussein stopped and bent over with his hands on his knees and spat on the ground. Sami stopped, too, and felt his lungs heaving. They walked the last hundred yards to the finish line. Their instructor patted the first three runners on the back and congratulated them.

The three winners laughed and Sami frowned at them, but Hussein put a hand on his shoulder.

'Let it go.'

The four days of leave had just been a fantasy anyway. Military service was built around creating vanishingly brief moments of hope that were then instantly dashed.

Living in the camp you had to hold on to the moments that kept your head above water, like the taste of fruity lip balm. On Saturdays, the soldiers in training were allowed visits. It was a two-hour window of brief happiness, which he could live on for a long time.

Sarah came to visit Sami a couple of times, and neither time did they talk about the future or the past. In fact, they didn't talk much at all, just sat on the bench behind the barracks, kissing.

'Have I changed?' he asked when they came up for air, but she was evasive.

'What does it feel like to shoot a gun?' she asked instead.

'The recoil hurts your shoulder, but you get used to it.'

'Tell me more.'

106

'I don't know, it feels strange . . . Like it's a game.'

'Well, you've always liked games. At least on the computer.'

'That's different. You know, sometimes we practise with the cold weapon, the bayonet, on dummies that look like humans.'

He swallowed and didn't continue but Sarah took his hand and smiled, like it wasn't that bad.

'Do you aim for the throat or the thigh?' she asked. 'I've heard a person's brain is drained of blood in less than a minute after a stab wound to the thigh. That is, if the person's standing up.'

They didn't have a minute, Sami told her. They weren't knives for slicing bread or cutting firewood with. They were straight, pointy blades, part of the rifle, and with the enemy that close, you only got one chance.

'So where?' she insisted.

'You stab at the heart, through the ribcage.'

He didn't tell her he had dreamt of the crunching sound of ribs. That he had woken up clammy with perspiration and looked at his hands,
relieved they weren't red, that it was still training and make-believe.

Soon enough, though, it became real. It started with the assignments being announced. Hussein's shoulders drooped when he found out he was going to the combat battalion, as were the three runners who had cheated in the foot race. Bill was going to work in communications, which was ironic since he didn't speak the language, but he was good with technical things.

Then Sami's name and assignment were called out. Several people in the assembly turned around and looked at him in surprise. Cartographer?

Sami would be going to the military base outside Damascus, the heart of their division, to work as one of three cartographers among twelve thousand soldiers.

17

WITH SAMI'S NEW posting came two new roommates, Ahmed and Rafat, who were also going to be trained as cartographers. They shared a windowless room with three steel beds and a stove in the corner.

Ahmed was from Aleppo and had two degrees, in philosophy and sociology, because he had tried to postpone serving by studying. In the evenings he read in bed, with thin frames at the tip of his nose.

'Do you know when I really started losing faith in our country?' Ahmed said and turned a page without looking up; his hands were long and fine for belonging to the tall body. 'In the summer of 2000. When all the TV channels showed Hafez's funeral instead of the European Championship.'

'You can't say that. Not here,' Rafat said and shook his head.

'Why? We're all alone. Are you going to snitch on me?'

'No. Not at all. I just think we should be careful.'

Rafat frowned and put his arms around his legs. He was younger than them, a quiet teenager who bit his nails when he got nervous. He hadn't been to university yet because he wanted to get his military service out of the way. His hands were narrow but scarred. His skin was tanned from working in his family's olive groves in Afrin, a small town in the north, surrounded by red soil and blue mountains.

'What are you reading anyway, the holy book?'

Sami meant it as a joke, but Ahmed snorted. 'If you consider Nietzsche holy.'

Ahmed was one of the first people Sami had met who openly identified as atheist.

'I'm
fine with religion,' he said. 'As long as it doesn't worship al-Assad.'

Overall Sami was happy to have them both as roommates, apart from the slight downside of Rafat's snoring at night.

'It's impressive, don't you think?' Ahmed said with a clear voice in the dark room. 'A mouse who sounds like an elephant.'

When certain recruits from basic training accused them of having bribed their way into jobs at the military base, Sami pointed to Rafat, who was a Kurd and would never have been able to get ahead through bribery. If bribes had been involved, they would have been placed elsewhere, where they weren't in charge of maps or invited to participate in strategy meetings.

In Homs, Sami had mostly spent time with Sunnis and Christians, but at the base everyone lived cheek by jowl. The army was a place where people from every corner of the country came together, irrespective of religion and ethnicity. Friendships were based on being there for each other, sharing your food and telling entertaining stories at night.

It was during such evenings that he found out details of other parts of the division, such as that there was a group of North Korean teachers who taught martial arts to the commanders, and a chemical battalion in the event that the country was hit by chemical attacks.

Sami also tried to ask about Younes, the electrician at his old IT company. But no one knew him or could say where he was. In the end, Sami gave up hope that his friend was still alive, even though he always kept up appearances when he talked to Younes' parents. Sami thought back to another time, when they worked under swirling blue skies, and how the world looked slightly different from up there, on the rooftops, and how the happiness could suddenly give way to a feeling of wanting to jump. He must take care not to fall for those kinds of thoughts.

Sami, Rafat and Ahmed worked in a dark room with grey concrete walls. The square glass drawing table was lit from underneath. Their pencils were the German brand Faber-Castell and similar to the ones he had used in school: sky blue, sand, light pink and grass green. One box was enough for about ten maps; the tips wore down and needed constant sharpening, the shavings scattering like confetti on the floor. After months of digging and shooting practice, Sami slowly got back into his old craft. War fronts and brigades materialized under his hands. Red dots denoted hidden armouries and tanks. Their task was to draw different scenarios. How would they counter, say, an Israeli airstrike against an important armoury? The maps showed five to eight strategic steps to follow, to show how the Syrian army would move its battalions and brigades.

The brigade general who was in charge of the maps trusted Sami. There were two keys to the room with the codex maps and he was given one of them. It was one of the base's most highly classified buildings. It was also the dustiest, with cobwebs in the corners, since no one was allowed in to clean.

Sami's new role came with certain privileges. All brigade generals were required to produce and submit a local map of their area every month. Since they were unused to drawing, they asked Sami, Rafat and Ahmed for help. In exchange they were given boots, fuel for the radiator and extra food. Whenever an officer of higher rank passed by, all the sergeants had to stand to attention. But Sami and Ahmed stayed in their seats during their breaks and smoked with their army-issue shirts unbuttoned. Rafat too, who started to relax in their company.

When they crossed the line, they were sent to the clink, but it was nothing compared to the prisons Sami had been in. Sami had his own corner; the guards allowed him to smoke; someone always brought a guitar and played it. They were fed and not beaten. In fact, it was one of the few times he could catch up on sleep. He had a special blanket and pillow for the clink. In time, he became friends with the guards and could sneak in a toothbrush, water bottle, gum, cigarettes and sometimes even mosquito repellent. Some of the guards played cards with him.

Sami was usually detained for minor infractions, like skipping morning assembly to get some extra sleep and have his coffee in peace. Or procrastinating on a time-sensitive map, handing it in a day and a half later than promised.

'Six days in the clink,' the general would declare.

But Sami was usually let out after a day or two when a map needed to be completed because he was considered the best colourist.

It was when he was under arrest that Sami got to know the shepherd Jemal, another regular in the clink. They were the same age but Sami had grown up in a major city and Jemal had lived all his life in the country. Every time Jemal was put in the clink, he declared himself innocent, saying it wasn't his fault one of his goats had slipped away and trespassed on the military base. At the same time, he readily admitted the grass was better at the base. After a few days, the general would let Jemal out, confiscate one of his goats and say, 'See you soon.'

Sami wondered what his life would have been like if he had grown up in a different family, in a different part of the country. Maybe all change starts that way: with a simple question. You suddenly discern a possibility in what used to seem preposterous, unimaginable. What if your life had been different? What if society were different? What if you could actually change it?

Everything would change that spring, 2011. Sami had almost completed his military service and was counting the days until he would be discharged when rumours started flying around the base. At first he didn't believe them because they were so improbable. There was whispering about a demonstration in Daraa, a city on the Jordanian border.

The police had caught some schoolboys writing on a wall, Ahmed told Sami when they were making a map together, something about the people wishing for the fall of the regime. Their families were forced to hand the boys over to the secret police, who tortured them. The whole city was in uproar.

The officers at the camp didn't say a word about the demonstrations. They did, however, cancel all leave and announce that everyone in the military would have their service extended.

'For how long?' asked Ahmed and polished his glasses on the uniform, like all of this was normal procedure.

'Indefinitely. Probably a couple of weeks, maybe months. This decision comes from higher up.'

Sami swallowed hard. The buzzing in his ears intensified as though there were a wasp in his head. *Indefinitely.* After that, the rumours spread like wildfire. More demonstrations had been organized, it was said, in Damascus and Homs and Hama. Not Hama? Yes, even in Hama. The state news showed a sea of people marching through the cities, waving the Syrian flag.

'They want to show their love and respect for the president,' the reporter said.

In later broadcasts, the demonstrators had switched to the revolutionary flag used to protest against French rule in the previous century. At that point, the reporter looked straight into the camera and said, matter-of-factly and without batting an eyelid, that the people taking to the streets were junkies and criminals. Only now did the officers start talking openly about the demonstrators. They were terrorists, armed terrorists.

One day at the end of March there was an order to confiscate all TVs, satellite receivers and mobile phones at the base. It was to be done within twenty-four hours. The next day, the military police went through each and every room to make sure no prohibited equipment had been overlooked. The military base was allowed to keep one TV set that showed state and Lebanese channels.

Sami didn't know what to think. Before he handed in his mobile phone, he had read news from Tunisia, Egypt and Libya that the people in those countries were demanding freedom and democracy. But the demonstrators were said to carry weapons, which made him feel torn. An armed struggle? Led by whom?

One of the generals showed Sami a video of a colonel supposedly shot dead by Syrian protestors. The film showed his bloody corpse and grieving family.

'This is what the terrorists' so-called fight for freedom looks like,' said the general.

Sami asked Ahmed about the murdered colonel. He told him there was a rumour that the colonel hadn't been shot by protestors at all. No, he had been stopped at a checkpoint and refused to show his ID card, which led to him being shot by a member of a regime-friendly militia.

Regardless of one's opinions, it was safest to keep them to oneself.

'Finally, the people are rising up,' one soldier said during breakfast.

Sami looked around to make sure he wasn't the only one who had heard it. Even Ahmed, who usually didn't hesitate to speak up, stayed quiet.

The next day, the soldier was gone.

Sami's doubts soon crystallized further. From time to time, he was asked to take notes or send deliveries to other battalions. He was also good friends with Issa, a soldier who received messages from other battalions in a bunker. Issa had managed to hide a TV that received international channels, partly to follow the news, partly to watch soap operas to help pass the time. Sami immediately won his affection by humming the theme music to *Kassandra*.

'I wish I was rich and could pay my way out of here,' Issa said dreamily. 'A bunker, seriously? If someone had told me that from the start, I would have been born a girl. No doubt. I would have stayed in my mother's womb until my dick turned into a vagina.' He quickly scrolled through the channels. 'Ah, look at her! Gorgeous. And don't get me started on the uniform. I need more colour in my life.'

It was on one occasion down in the bunker that Sami saw a report about a demonstration that had been organized recently. *Unarmed.* Sami read the sentence over and over. There it was, in writing, in a military report: the protestors were unarmed. And the army had responded with teargas and bullets.

Ahmed had handed over only one of his phones to the officer and hidden the other under his mattress.

'God, you're crazy,' Sami said.

'God is dead,' Ahmed shrugged.

'We can take turns to hide the phone if you sometimes let me use it.'

In the evenings, when Rafat was out and they were sure to be alone, they took it out and listened to the revolutionary song 'Ya Haif'. They listened to it over and over again, its lyrics and melody like a drug.

In the mornings, the military speaker car would stop in the yard and regime songs would fill the air. Then the president's voice came on, blaring out his message for the public. The demonstrators were a disease, he said. A virus to the body of their country. And the only cure was to cut off the sick parts.

In April, thousands of people in Homs filed into the square around the famous clocktower for a peaceful sit-in. Sami watched it on the TV in the bunker with Issa. The minarets urged everyone to come to the square. Young people cut up their ID cards to show that they were not going to leave the country until the dictator was gone. Sami glimpsed people in T-shirts whose logos he knew all too well – they were from Abu Karim's restaurant, his first place of work – handing out food to hungry protestors.

114

As they watched, three words echoed out across the crowd: freedom, dignity, democracy.

We are blossoming like an infatuation, Sarah wrote to him from Homs, texting Ahmed's secret number.

Sami read her messages and erased them, in case someone found the phone. Sarah seemed to have entered a state of bliss, as though she and the other protestors were in the process of writing their own future, their own history. Maybe it was the adventure she'd always been waiting for.

We're like a kaleidoscope, Sarah wrote. *Voices and hands are raised in the square, a cascade of mirrors. We are glass, shards and fragments, and no matter which way you turn, twist and shake us, we overflow with colour, improbable patterns. We fit inside a single broken ray of light that contains the echo of every spring.*

Sarah's next message came only an hour later. It was just one sentence:

They're shooting at us.

18

THE ARMY HAD opened fire in Clocktower Square in Homs and people had fled in panic. Sarah had sought refuge in an alley and heard the rifles' crackle in the square, like heavy rain against a tin roof.

The blood, she wrote to Sami. *I've never seen so much blood.*

When he called her, he wasn't sure it was actually Sarah who answered. Her voice sounded different and distant.

'Were there many injured?'

'I don't know, Sami. I didn't look. I just ran.'

He listened to her breath and felt stupid because he wasn't there and couldn't hold her, and because he couldn't even come up with anything comforting to say.

'It is difficult to describe how it has been,' she said. 'All the feelings at the demonstrations. I really thought we could change something. I know it sounds silly but I didn't realize what was at stake, but now—' She stopped. 'I should hang up, Sami. Talking to me must be dangerous.'

'Wait, what do you mean?'

'You're with them now. You're on their side.'

Sami went to breakfast with a dizzy head and a lump in his stomach, the world turning faster with every footstep. Eggs and tea, tea and eggs, every day the same meaningless food followed by the same meaningless chores. He was stuck here when he should have been with her. Had there been doubt in her voice? Was she blaming him for what had happened? He sat down in the circle of soldiers and thought he would pass out.

'Filthy dogs,' one soldier said and spat in the grass.

Sami assumed he was talking about the soldiers shooting at civilians and was about to agree, spill out some of the anger and confusion that was building up inside.

'They have no respect,' the soldier continued. 'Blockading the square like it's their living room. I'm surprised no one's put their foot down sooner.'

The soldier was holding an egg, breaking its shell with a spoon. White flakes fell on to his boots like big snowflakes. The egg yolk welled up, soft and creamy. Sami felt his gorge rising. He wasn't sure what Rafat thought but after breakfast he pulled Ahmed aside.

'What are we going to do? Can they order us to shoot at protestors?'

Ahmed glanced over his shoulder and lowered his voice.

'Not us, but other battalions.'

'So, what are we going to do?'

'Nothing. We're going to wait and see.'

Ahmed's response surprised him but he was probably right. They had completed their military service and should be discharged shortly, in one or two months, when the protests died down.

But summer was approaching and the demonstrations continued all over the country. It was getting increasingly difficult to follow events from the military base. Ahmed didn't dare lend Sami his phone more than necessary and Issa in the bunker, who had the TV with international channels, also pulled away. Sami understood. Reporting someone was easy and people had to protect themselves.

Besides, Sami had his hands full with cartography work. The need for maps never seemed to decrease. They were still focused on potential Israeli attacks and Sami continued to draw possible defensive plans. He marked out combat vehicles and thought about the ones he had been in during training. You climbed down through a hatch and landed in a claustrophobic cockpit with a tiny reinforced window. From inside, the people on the outside looked like paper dolls, fluttering in the breeze. If a soldier wanted to signal to the driver, he had to stand off to the side of the vehicle and wave his arms about. From close up, you were invisible. It wasn't real. Israel wasn't going to attack but if they ever did, his division would probably be annihilated.

At the start of the summer, the brigade general came to them in a hurry with a rolled-up map. Sami was standing in the half light by the drawing table next to Ahmed and Rafat, slightly unfocused on account of the itchy mosquito bites from a recent visit to the clink.

'What's this?' Ahmed said and ran his fingers over the paper.

'I have a different task for you today,' said the brigade general.

He was a sinewy man in his sixties who wore his badge with the three yellow stars and eagle with pride. Furthermore, he wore a badge on his chest that showed he had completed parachute training. In his eyes, they were nothing but schoolboys, but schoolboys who held his reputation in their hands. Their work reflected on him and he scrutinized every map before passing it on.

Now he rolled out the map, pointing and explaining. When he was done and had left the room, they stood in silence. This time, the task was not about practice scenarios, about defending weapons and vehicles. Instead, they were supposed to map out the quickest way for the army to enter a small city. From when the first troops reached the centre, no more than fifteen minutes could elapse before the last soldier was in place.

But this wasn't a strange city in a foreign country. It was a small city in northwestern Syria on the trade route between Latakia and Aleppo. The city had made a name for itself as a rebel stronghold ever since the 1980s, when resistance fighters torched a local Baath

Party office. The regime brought in helicopters and crushed the rebellion, and hundreds were arrested and executed.

Now, three months into the revolution, there was a rumour that armed gangs had killed over a hundred regime soldiers in the town. His friend in the bunker had made an exception and let Sami watch the news. Much was unclear about the deaths. Activists in the town claimed the soldiers had in fact been killed by the army, either for openly deserting or for refusing to shoot at civilians. Either way, the massacre was now being used as an excuse for the regime to attack the town.

'What do you think they want?' Rafat asked, even though they already knew the answer.

'A takeover,' Ahmed said quietly.

They studied the map. There were fields and high mountains, and a couple of bridges that stretched across the river into the town. When the brigade general returned, they had barely put pen to paper. He gave them some choice words of warning and an extension until the next day. That evening, a light rain fell and steam rose from the ground, but inside the map room the air was close. They were sitting on the floor, their backs against the wall. Rafat was sweating heavily and suddenly got up.

'We have to do something. If we don't draw the map, it's over.'

Ahmed stood up too, and reached for the pencils.

'You're right. We have to do something.'

'Are you serious?' Sami said. 'As soon as we draw the map the military will enter the city.'

Rafat turned and looked at him, his chin raised and the sweat visible on his forehead. 'It's not like we have a choice.'

'Calm down, I have an idea.' Ahmed put his hand over the bridges. 'We draw the map as you say. But with some adjustments.'

'Leave me out of it,' Rafat said. 'I just want to get out of here as soon as possible.'

It was risky, Rafat was right about that, but Sami sharpened his pencils and coloured in the fields with the greatest level of precision. It was going to be the best map he had ever made.

The next few hours felt like walking on hot embers, and when the brigade general finally summoned Sami, Ahmed and Rafat to his office, he wasn't alone. The major general, head of their entire division, was sitting behind the desk with his brow deeply furrowed, like a newly tilled field. He was staring straight ahead, making no attempt to meet their eyes.

'I have only one question. Are you retarded or just regular idiots?'

The air was thick with tobacco smoke and they could hear bangs from the shooting range.

'Well? I asked you a question. A simple one at that.'

Ahmed coughed and opened his mouth but the major general banged his fist on the table.

'Did I say you could speak?'

The major general lowered his voice and articulated as though he were speaking to imbeciles.

'We didn't ask for the long way to the city centre. If that's what I'd wanted, I'd have asked my niece to draw the map, or a donkey.'

The plan had been doomed from the start. Of course they would discover that they hadn't put in the most important entry points to the town, the bridges. That they had instead drawn up a longer route and ignored the possibility of using armoured vehicles.

'Have they caused trouble before?' the major general asked, addressing their general.

'Never,' he assured him. 'They're normally very well behaved.'

'We should send you all to Palmyra,' said the major general. 'Who's responsible for this map?'

For a moment, time seemed to stop and the world shrank to that one room, its walls and the two eyes watching them. Their fates depended on the caprice and ill-will of a single person.

'I am,' Sami said. 'I'm responsible for the map. Rafat was on leave and Ahmed was working on other assignments.'

The brigade general looked like he was about to object but then he closed his mouth. Perhaps it was better for his reputation if only one of his apprentices had screwed up. Maybe it could be passed off as a mistake and not a deliberate act of protest. The leather chair creaked when the major general leaned back.

'Take him to the clink and I'll think about it.'

Sami breathed a sigh of relief.

In the clink the mosquitoes were more numerous and eager than usual but now that the tension had been released, Sami fell asleep immediately. He woke up with his blanket pulled up over his face, his arms red and swollen with bites. He felt palpitations under his ribs, the feeling of harbouring something that was baring its teeth. He would have to be more careful. Another transgression would not be tolerated, especially now the major general had his eye on him.

Sami was let out four days later. He almost expected Ahmed and Rafat to congratulate him but they were absorbed and barely looked up when he entered the map room. The light from the drawing table spread a halo around the brigade general's back.

'Ah, there you are.'

The concrete walls seemed to warp and Sami's field of vision narrowed. The map they had made was laid out in front of him. The general cleared his throat and straightened up.

'We are behind because of you, and now time is growing short. You have until tomorrow morning to finish the job.'

There was no need for him to deliver veiled threats or mention their families; they knew what was at stake. Their pencils lay where they'd left them. New paper had been brought in. The map table shone dully, white, like the new moon above the treetops in a dark forest. Ahmed and Rafat had been sketching out a new scenario that included the bridges. Sami just had to colour it in. He told himself it wasn't hard, that it was like the drawings he painted as a child, but a string had begun to vibrate and left behind a dull reverberation inside him.

The day after they submitted the map, Sami descended the steps into the bunker, which soon turned into an illuminated tunnel. The lights flickered and cast long shadows across the walls. The corridor wound ever deeper underground.

Sami's friend was normally always in the same room, eyes glued to a fax machine that at any moment could spit out a pivotal message from another division. How Issa was able to keep a TV that received international channels wasn't clear to him. It likely had more to do with his commanding officer wanting to follow events than with an oversight. There was always a certain level of anxiety when they were down here, even though unknown footsteps would be heard from very far away. Hafez and Bashar's eyes watched them from the walls. The kettle was sitting on the black iron stove. They normally drank maté, a bitter green herbal tea, but this time Sami was unable to raise the glass to his lips. His hands were shaking too much.

Sami remembered conversations they had had. Why them? Couldn't they just refuse? The answer was always: if they didn't do it, someone else would. But if they all refused, who would do it then? A system can only be perpetuated if people perpetuate it. The memory of voices, his own concerns and doubt, all the threads tangling together. The din intensified, drowning out all thought. Stop! It was too late, it made no difference. Not now.

The blue light lit up the room and the newscast began. The reporter summarized the events of the past few days. Thousands of residents had fled to the Turkish border, where they were being housed in temporary refugee camps. The town was virtually deserted, an activist said. And yet the army claimed armed rebel groups were holed up in there.

'Yesterday we could see the army lining up armoured vehicles and

surrounding the town. Most of its residents have fled,' the activist told
the reporter.

But far from everyone had left. Later, Sami would describe it as the
moment a missile hits. When matter seems to lose its original form
and firmness and contours dissolve. The floor swayed, the portraits
stared at him, the kettle whistled, slicing through the sound of guns
firing on TV. He didn't notice his hands cramping until he felt the
glass cut into his skin. Red blood dripped on to the concrete.

Hundreds of people had been killed and arrested. With the help of
their map, which he had coloured in. Just like he always did. Filled it
with colour.

Now the colours became reality, in the images that flickered past
and blended together. The green fields and the shadows of the mountains, which surrounded the settlement in the heart of the valley. The
water – wild swirls, deep streams – flowing past under the bridges
lined with lampposts, where tanks and soldiers were pushing forward.
Soon, black smoke rose over the rooftops.

Sami sat dead still in the blue light. To his shock, Ahmed collapsed
on to the basement floor and wept.

Issa, who minded the fax machine, had his head in his hands. His
aunt wasn't answering her phone. She lived in the town with her two
sons, his cousins.

'Maybe they fled,' he mumbled. 'Or were arrested. If they were arrested, there's still a chance.'

Later on, a returning soldier told them the takeover had been smooth.
They had lists of people to arrest but were told to bring in more. The
names went on and on, page after page. On TV, they said about one
hundred and seventy people had been killed – it was probably more,
said the returning soldier. Because he had seen the army load dead
bodies on to trucks and remove them.

Sami closed his eyes and the sound of the TV turned into a distant
buzzing. He and Ahmed and Rafat had followed orders and in that

moment crossed a line. And it was just the beginning. There would be new orders. They would draw new maps. Every time he reached a line in the sand, there would be another one beyond it, and when that was crossed, another. It would never end. It would continue for ever, until nothing human and decent remained in him.

How much remained in him now? He had drawn the map. Beyond this line there was no turning back. The bunker walls closed around him, numbing in their colourlessness.

III

There is a picture of the little boy in the penguin jumper. In another, he's wearing a camouflage uniform and cradling a rifle in his arms, squinting at the sun, his boots resting in the tall grass. The pictures blend together and drift apart. I try to make them co-exist in my mind, understand how they can both be of you.

What would another person have done in your situation? What would I have done?

My writing is becoming an obsession. It breaks free of my computer and becomes part of everything I do, a snake skin I can't shed. We watch the hundreds of video clips you have filmed. We flip through nearly twenty thousand photographs you have taken, most of them from the siege. We cook your favourite dishes, stuffed vine leaves and lamb-filled zucchini in a saffron stew. We listen to your father's favourite singer, Umm Kulthum. We study maps and street addresses, read reports on mass executions in the prisons and the composition of sarin gas. The more I think and read and see, the less I understand.

When I see the ad for the Swedish army's survival course, I think that's a step closer. I regret my decision before I even get there, but am given a uniform and a green plastic tube of chapstick. Sleep in a steel bed, fire a Kalashnikov and bandage a gunshot wound. Have a hood put over my head and am interrogated with blinding lights in my eyes. I'm surprised at the ease with which I and my fellow prisoners get used to it, how willingly we adapt to the rules of the game before they're even presented. Forget that you have a body, keep control of your mind. But can a protest live only in the mind without being embodied? How quickly we fall silent when someone else has a gun pressed to their forehead.

An obsession, yes. To understand you and what you've been through. And a vague sense of unease which refuses to subside, telling me that no matter what I do, I will never understand.

19

SLEEP PULLED SAMI under. When he awoke for short
periods, it lingered like a cold in his throat, a heaviness in his arms
and legs, like an apathy towards the things going on around him.
Shadows moved back and forth in the doorway. Sound and light
blended together, there were unfamiliar voices and dirges, he imagined bridges hovering above his bed.

After three days, Rafat woke him up and said enough already. The
brigade general had not given them any new assignments but it
wouldn't be long before they had to go back to drawing maps. The
problem was his hands would no longer hold pencils. He kept crum-
pling up sheets of paper. Lines were erased and blurred. He carried the
maps inside him. He folded and unfolded lakes, forests and valleys.
Moved cities and villages around. Watched a flame take hold in the
paper and eat its way towards the edges, until he himself caught fire
and burnt. In his dream, his face and skin were seared until he had no
eyes to see with, hands to draw with or heart to feel with.

As day turned into dusk, the black dog appeared. A wild dog. The
soldiers loathed them. They roamed the hinterlands and didn't hesitate to attack if you stepped into their territory. The black dog was
mangy, its ribs visible and its breath acrid. Even other dogs disliked it:
its right ear had been torn off by a pack that had lain in wait and am-

bushed it. The soldiers shooed it away with kicks and curses but the black dog continued to visit the military base. It slunk by, panting with hunger.

Then, one evening, it didn't come. Sami went for a walk in the mild summer night without admitting to himself that he was looking for the dog. There was something about it that reminded him of the mutt his little brother Malik had dragged home when they were younger. The next night, the dog was back and he felt involuntary relief. Sami gave it the remains of his dinner: a bowl of chicken stew to lick clean and a crust of bread to chew. From that day on, the black dog followed him wherever he went.

'What's the name of your stinky dog?' the other soldiers asked.

'It's not mine,' Sami replied.

But he continued to put out bowls of leftovers and, after a while, the dog's ribs were no longer visible. The dog slept outside at night, except for when it managed to sneak in and lie down outside his room. At first, he scolded it, but then he got used to it, and eventually he looked forward to scratching it behind the ears. The black dog became a reason to wake up in the morning. To gather up his limbs and exist.

After weighing up different scenarios, Sami, Ahmed and Rafat agreed that they would desert if ordered to fire at people. At present, however, it was safer to stay where they were. The revolution had blossomed during the first tentative, passionate spring months, and matured and gained new force over the summer. Then the temperatures fell. An undertone of pine needles and wet soil infused the mountain air and the leaves changed colour. There was no sign of the revolt cooling off or dying down.

Sami was normally woken up by the dog's eager scratching at his door, but one early autumn morning he was instead awoken by Rafat sitting down on the edge of his bed.

'Ahmed's gone,' he said and held out a mobile phone.

'Where did you get that?'

'Never mind, just look.'

The black dog lumbered into the room and curled up next to the bed, its tail languidly beating the floor. Sami sat up and swung his legs over the edge of the bed, watched the grainy video. Judging from the date, it had been uploaded the day before. When he recognized the face, his legs started bouncing up and down and he pulled a flake of dry skin from his lip.

'Enough already,' Ahmed said, looking into the camera, fixedly and slightly wild-eyed. 'The regime is shooting us, they are killing our sisters and brothers. Peaceful demonstration isn't enough any more.'

Ahmed held up his military ID and Sami thought about how often he had seen those hands illuminated from below by the drawing table. Long, thin, sinewy fingers, which would not have looked out of place on a musical instrument. It was with those hands, piano hands, violin hands, that he tore up his military ID.

'I'm no longer fighting for Assad's army, I'm fighting for the Syrian people. Long live the Free Syrian Army!'

The name was not unknown to them. The armed rebel group, the FSA, had been founded over the summer. It disseminated pictures and videos of deserting soldiers while rumours spread about what had happened to the deserters. Deserting was far worse than being a conscientious objector and almost always led to a bullet in the head or a disappearance.

'Your lips are going to be a mess if you keep doing that,' Rafat said.

'Have you talked to his family?'

'I can't get hold of them. People say his parents have been arrested.'

The black dog raised its head from the floor and studied them before lowering it back down and putting a paw across its nose. If Sami had been in a sleep-like state during the past few months, he was wide awake now. Why had Ahmed not warned them? They had talked about everything. Hadn't they? But Ahmed had made a decision, planned his escape and left on his own. In addition to his disap-

131

pointment and mounting restlessness, Sami couldn't help but feel a tiny pang of jealousy. Ahmed had dared to leave.

Although they were not brothers, they had lived so closely together. It made him think of Homs and how much he missed his family. He hadn't been able to visit since the New Year and asking for leave was pointless. The more soldiers deserted, the more restrictions were introduced. After his infraction with the map, the general had decided Sami would not be given any opportunity to go home. Perhaps he sensed Sami would choose to stay and join the protests, or maybe it was just his way of demonstrating his power.

'What's it like in Homs?' the brigade general had said as he and Sami stood together in the gloom by the drawing table. 'I've heard they're planning to grow potatoes there.'

Because of the strong turnout over the past year, Homs was called 'the capital of the revolution'. 'Growing potatoes' was code for crushing the resistance and levelling the rebellion. A chill ran down Sami's spine. It meant complete destruction, and he knew that the same expression had been used before the massacre in Hama.

'I thought you were familiar with Homs,' Sami said as neutrally as he could.

'I am,' said the general and straightened up. 'Haven't I told you I did my training there?'

'Then you should know how cold the nights get. A pretty unsuitable place for growing potatoes.'

The general snorted and said Sami was never going to be granted leave anyhow.

So he would have to sort it out himself.

Sami went to bed with his uniform on. Instead of sleeping, he lay down and waited for the night to turn into greyish light. He finally sat up in the steel bed, carefully, but it still gave off a squeak. He stiffened, but Rafat's snoring rose safely from the other side of the room, where he slept on his back with a slightly open mouth. Sami tied his boots and took the backpack he used for leave and sneaked out of the room. Outside the door was the black dog, who drowsily lifted its nose when it saw Sami.

'Ssh,' he said and patted the rough fur. 'Want to join me on a little adventure?'

He handed out a piece of dried meat and the dog waved his tail happily. Not only had it put on some weight, it was even getting a bit round.

The sky was still grey when they began to walk through the base but soon the dusk began to dissolve.

'Come on, we have to hurry.'

The dog sometimes ran before him, sometimes after him, clearly excited about the excursion. After half an hour the trail began to de-scend and they were out of sight of the camp. Sami changed clothes in a shrubbery and put his uniform in the backpack. If anyone asked where he was going, he had faked a permit to leave. He would spend one night in the clink for wearing civilian clothing, but in the best-case scenario that would be the worst of it.

The black dog moved playfully up and down the path, then sud-denly became quiet. Sami stepped out of the bush in his new clothes, jeans and a woollen sweater over a washed-out T-shirt, and whistled low. No dog in sight. He continued down the path and froze at the sound of an angry growl. Two wild dogs blocked the trail, puffy and with yellow eyes fixed on him. They were smaller than the black dog but long-legged and sinewy, and above all they looked at him with starving eyes.

'Hey, careful . . .'

Sami patted his breast pocket for dried meat but realized that it was in the military jacket in the backpack. Instead, he held out his hands and spoke softly.

'Stay calm, I won't do you any harm. Good dogs . . .'

Sami took one step forward and one of the dogs began to bark, white froth foaming in its mouth, and soon the other dog followed.

133

Sami moved back and felt the thorns penetrate his sweater. The dogs barked breathlessly and approached, glaring at him, when he heard a sound beside him. The black dog rushed out of a bush and stood between him and the two wild animals. It took only a few lunges before the wild dogs turned and left, tails between their legs.

Sami breathed out and hugged his rescuer. The black dog panted back, its tongue lolling; if he hadn't known better, he would have thought it smiled.

'Now, we're almost there.'

The vegetation on the last stretch changed from jagged shrubs to trees with orange-brown leaves as if the crowns were in flames. Just before he reached the village, Sami said goodbye to the black dog, and it seemed to understand, turning back and going the same way they had come from.

The village was small and there was a shop that sold mobiles. He just had to wait an hour before it opened. The shop was similar to the ones he used to pass on the way to school, with a similarly short, grey-haired man behind the till and a box of fresh bread next to him. Sami bought two croissants in addition to a cheap phone and a SIM card.

'Are you from the military base?' said the man, peering at him.

Sami considered lying but realized it was obvious where he'd come from. Hopefully the man wouldn't call and tell on him.

'Yes, I'm on leave,' he said and handed the man an extra note.

He jumped on the first bus to Homs and called his older brother. The signals echoed and faded away. When Ali finally picked up, it felt like Sami was already there, that he was sitting in the kitchen with his family around him. And Sarah, he was going to call her too and ask her to come over. After the shooting at Clocktower Square, they had only kept brief contact. But seeing each other, face to face, they could talk things over. He would make sure she was well. Tell her that he would soon be out and they could make a fresh start. Finally, he dared to let longing swell in his chest and lungs, like rainwater filling the cracks in dry soil.

'Hello, are you there?'

But the reply wasn't what he expected. 'You can't just come here,' his older brother said. 'Things have changed since your last visit.'

Silence fell, only the low rumbling of the bus engine.

'I'm sorry,' Ali went on. 'Of course I'm happy that you're coming, but you'd better get off the bus before you reach the city centre.'

'Why?' Sami frowned, even though his brother couldn't see him.

Outside the bus window there was field after field of orchards, the fruit soon to be harvested.

'Temporary checkpoints are popping up everywhere. I'll tell you more later. It's not safe to talk on the phone.'

His older brother gave Sami an address where he would pick him up in what had once been an industrial part of Homs.

For the rest of the journey, Sami tried to collect his thoughts. What had Ali really meant? But when they slowed down and Sami disembarked, he started to understand.

It was like arriving in a foreign country. Dark clouds towered over the rooftops, as if even the sky had descended over the city. Several stores were barred and on their metal shutters were tags and graffiti he hadn't seen before. The street vendors had disappeared. Instead of the normal commuting traffic, the streets were full of funeral processions. Instead of car-honking, there was the sound of songs, cries and tears that rose and sank like waves. People in mourning clothes gathered in groups that dispersed at the rat-tat-tat of bullets on asphalt.

The fear drained out of Sami when he spotted his brother's face across the street. Ali ran up to him and gave him a long, hard hug.

'What's with the rubber bullets? Seems a bit over the top.'

'They're real bullets. Come with me.'

Ali pointed out the snipers and took Sami's hand, since he wouldn't have budged otherwise.

'Don't worry,' Ali tried to calm him. 'They're mostly to scare the people off gathering in big groups.'

Sami looked over his shoulder and hunched down, his pulse racing. During all his target practice in the army, he himself had never been the target. It was an eerie feeling of being watched, that every step could be your last.

It was afternoon by the time Sami was finally sitting in his parents' kitchen, with steam on the windows from all the people in the room. Samira kissed his cheeks and stroked his newly shorn neck. Hiba smiled and moved her youngest over to his lap, took off her slippers and stretched her legs out under the table. The child cooed and grabbed Sami's thumb. Ali was in a good mood but was moving about the room restlessly, topping up coffee cups and checking the time incessantly. Malik was the only one who seemed reluctant to hug Sami, and afterwards he sat silently on his chair with his arms crossed. He had turned thirteen but his plump cheeks and large puppy eyes made him look younger. Nabil looked across at Malik.

'Well, I for one am proud to have a soldier in the family.'

'Two soldiers,' Hiba said and glanced at Ali, but their older brother shook his head.

'Not any more. Not ever again.'

'Like you would have a choice if they called for you.'

'Please don't argue,' Samira said and turned to Sami, stroking his cheek. 'Now, tell us everything. Have you made any friends? Are they hard on you? What do they give you to eat? You look thinner than before . . .'

'Mum.'

They inundated him with questions and Sami tried to answer but it was as though their voices were echoing underneath the surface. He was still short-circuited from the snipers and funeral processions. Being home was like opening a door to the past. All the furniture stood as before, each item had its place. The black leather sofas, the crocheted cloth on the TV, the remote control in its plastic case. On the stairs to the front door stood a plate with leftovers in case one of the neighbourhood's stray cats passed by.

'Don't you drink coffee any more? Maybe you prefer it with sugar these days?' Samira said and pushed the sugar bowl towards him.

It fell to Hiba and Ali to tell him about what had happened since his last visit, while Nabil stroked his moustache and looked displeased. In July, a demonstration had been organized in Damascus and a number of famous actors, musicians and authors denounced the regime. One of the most powerful voices belonged to the actress Mai Skaf, who had subsequently been forced to flee the country. Ibrahim Qashoush, the man who wrote the popular revolutionary song 'Yalla irhal ya Bashar', was said to have been killed the same month. His body had supposedly been discovered in a river with its throat slit and vocal cords ripped out. In August, the well-known satirical cartoonist Ali Farzat had been pulled into a car by regime supporters by Umayyad Square in Damascus and had his hands and knuckles broken.

But the violence had crept in closer than that. Their cousin and a friend of the family had been killed at checkpoints controlled by regime-friendly militias. And regime soldiers had forced their way into their neighbour's house and raped the daughter in front of her parents.

'To dishonour the family,' Samira said.

'Isn't the daughter's pain worse than the family's shame?' Hiba said and stirred her cup violently. The child began to cry and Hiba took her back, rocking and shushing.

Samira told Sami about a newlywed couple further down the street. They had still been in their wedding clothes when they were stopped at a checkpoint and the man was told to leave his wife with the soldiers.

'So, what did he do?'

'What choice did he have?' His mother lowered her voice. 'They would have shot them both on the spot.'

Samira glanced at the baby. 'Sorry, I didn't mean to . . .'

'Don't worry, she's too young to understand.' Hiba kissed the child on the forehead, then turned to Sami. 'Why aren't you saying anything? Is this the kind of behaviour they teach you in the army? To act like animals?'

'I've never heard anything like it,' Sami said.

But he wasn't really surprised. Not once had their commanding officer talked about protecting the civilian population. Ethics and good behaviour extended only to fellow soldiers and the leaders of the land, as fighters in Assad's Syria. Every story intensified his shame at the army he was a part of.

'Sleepwalkers without any will of their own . . .'

Sami looked up and met his little brother's eyes. It was the first time Malik had opened his mouth since he'd come home. Sami was about to answer him but then Ali said he had to go.

'Where are you going?'

'There's a small demonstration down the street before dusk.'

Sami looked again at Malik, who was tilting his chair back and staring out of the window.

'I'm going with you,' Sami said.

Hiba shot him a crooked smile and put a hand on his shoulder; his little brother stopped tilting his chair. Nabil shook his head, leaned on the kitchen table and stood up slowly. Samira asked if anyone wanted more coffee.

'Me too,' Malik said. 'I'm coming too.'

20

IT WAS THE first time Sami moved in a group of his own volition. A group that was not ordered to line up in the schoolyard, in military formation or in mandatory manifestations of support for the president. A group that was not united behind a leader, but united nevertheless. Someone began to chant and someone else joined in. Then the shouts grew louder and the group found a collective rhythm.

'Freedom!' they shouted. 'Dignity! Democracy!'

There were about a hundred of them in a small square, surrounded by residential buildings with revolutionary flags hanging from their windows next to flower pots and washing lines stretching over balconies. He remembered jumping rope with his sister here when they were younger, and old women ordering him to help carry their food bags.

'Hey, boy, don't be lazy. Do you want me to break my back?'

He smiled at the memories and looked in amazement at the transformation of the square. A couple of armed rebel soldiers from the Free Syrian Army kept a lookout, ready in case the military tried to break them up, but none of the protestors seemed to be armed. It was an intoxicating feeling to stand up as a group. They were naive and at the same time strong. Their bodies were the body of the people and their voices were the voice of the people.

On the bus to Homs, Sami had called Sarah, who had promised to try to make it into the city centre. Now she called back and Sami pressed the phone to his ear.

'What did you say? I can't hear . . .'

The shouting escalated, a stereo was turned on and the protestors joined in the singing.

'. . . impossible to get past . . . completely surrounded . . .'

'Sarah, I'll call you in a bit, OK?'

He had never experienced anything like it. All the frustration that had built up inside him during his military service, all the punishments and days stolen from his life. All the stolen lives.

'*Yalla irhal ya Bashar*,' they sang. 'Get out of here, Bashar.'

The demonstration lasted about an hour. Then the sky crackled with lightning; at first the rain fell in big, gentle drops but it soon turned into sharp needles. People scattered and smaller groups splintered off until only Sami and his brothers remained. They were brothers in a different way now, overcome with adrenaline, participating in something bigger than themselves.

'What do we do now?' Malik said, his big eyes beaming.

Ali put his arms around their shoulders.

'Now, my brothers, we go home.'

They found their mother and father still in the kitchen, though they had swapped the coffee cups for tea glasses. The flame of the kerosene lamp made the shadows dance playfully on the walls but their parents' faces were grey and furrowed. They clutched the gold-rimmed tea glasses like they needed something to hold on to. How did you endure it for so long? he wanted to ask them. Why didn't you put your foot down ten, twenty, forty years ago? Were you really trying to protect us or were you simply clinging to your own comfort and security?

'Our neighbour just stopped by,' Nabil said. 'The army is planning to go in tomorrow morning and arrest all suspects.'

So that was what Sarah had been trying to tell him. New checkpoints had been erected around the city. She hadn't dared make her way to the centre, afraid somebody might recognize her from the protests. His father hid his face in his hands and Samira stroked his back.

'You have to leave, my son.'

'I have a travel permit. I'm OK.'

'You have a counterfeit permit and you're a soldier,' Ali said.

He was talking to him like an older sibling again, an older brother, not as though they had just walked side by side, sharing their first demonstration. But Ali was right. At best the army would think he had tried to sneak out for a few days of leave; at worst, that he had deserted.

'I'll stay the night and get out in the morning.'

As he said it, something was extinguished inside him. He had seen this as a chance to stay. Not to take up arms like Ahmed but at least to leave the army. He hadn't realized how much he missed his family until he had come back and felt the quiet everyday life in between the walls. The city was changing but his home remained. Now that the soldiers were poised to go in and search the houses, he wouldn't even have a chance to escape. He would be arrested the moment he deserted.

'You have to leave,' Ali announced.

'I'll call the general. He can talk to the guards at the checkpoint so they'll let me through.'

'You really want to take that risk?'

He was annoyed at Ali for making it sound like a choice. It was midnight and the soldiers would start going door to door at dawn. It was already going to be complicated, if not impossible, to get past the checkpoints.

'Call Muhammed,' his father said and walked over to stand next to Sami by the window.

Nabil put a hand on his shoulder. That he had to reach up reminded Sami how much his parents had aged over the past year, how they had deflated. The soft honey light of the streetlamps fell on young men with packed bags and cars. They were saying goodbye to family and friends. The people who were staying behind wiped their tears with handkerchiefs and went back inside.

His father was right. If anyone could get him out of this situation, it was his childhood friend who'd always been at his side, ever since the walks to school.

Muhammed's familiar, languid voice exuded calm on the phone.

'Pack your things, I'll be there in fifteen minutes,' he said.

It took almost an hour, but then there he was at the door, his hair as unkempt as ever. Muhammed ran a hand through his fringe, pushed his glasses up with his index finger and politely greeted Sami's parents.

Nabil took both of Muhammed's hands in his. 'Make sure he's safe.'

'Of course. I promise.'

Sami turned away, embarrassed, but Muhammed kept a straight face.

'How did you afford this?' he said when they had climbed into his car, a red BMW with the smell of pristine leather.

'Borrowed it,' Muhammed replied.

He scrolled through the radio channels until he found one playing classical oud music. The strings of the lute vibrated and darkness engulfed their vehicle, which was no longer a car but a javelin hurtling through the night. This was a different beast from the Pink Panther, which had long since drawn its last, rattling breath and stopped in the middle of a steep incline. They drove past their old school, the ice cream café they went to as children, all the well-known streets that had turned foreign. Muhammed explained that the regime still believed the rebels were mainly members of the lower classes; driving a car like this through the rich neighbourhoods minimized the risk of being pulled over.

'But where did you get it?'

'We have a couple of showroom cars at work. It just took me a while to deactivate the alarm.'

Once they had left Homs, Muhammed let Sami off at a bus stop. He rested his arm in the open window and gave him a wry smile.

'Good luck, my friend.'

'And you?'

'I always get by.'

Sami didn't doubt it. Moreover, Muhammed had completed his military service before the revolution began and was not in danger of being drafted. At least not right now. He had launched into a long monologue in the car, unusually long for Muhammed, the message of which was that their time had come. To make a difference, he meant. They were twenty-something and what had they really achieved in life? These were the years they were going to look back on. The tipping point people would say changed everything.

'For the better?' asked Sami.

'Of course for the better,' Muhammed said. 'Of course.'

And so, less than one day after secretly leaving his division, Sami was back. He had failed to desert, but he had heard stories of the revolution, taken part in his first protest and fled from his own hometown.

Back on the base, the other soldiers swarmed around him. Were the demonstrators outside FSA really unarmed? Then why did the regime want soldiers to shoot at them? Was it true what they said, that the only thing they were asking for was freedom? Other soldiers turned their backs on him. The less you knew, the better. One sergeant threatened Sami in front of the others.

'If you keep talking like that, this will be the last night you spend here.'

Sami realized he had to be more careful, that it was pivotal to learn how to tell friend from foe.

Sami let the black dog, who had found its way back to the base on its own, crawl into his bed and rest its heavy head on his stomach. Before, sleep had been an escape, but now he couldn't get so much as a wink of it. The voices of the protestors echoed inside him. He longed for Sarah, to feel her body close to his. He listened to the dog's sighing and counted the minutes until the first light of the new day broke through the window.

21

A NAME, WHAT was in a name? He remembered the signs he wrote with his siblings' names on, his yearning to name the sparrow on the roof terrace, the pet names Sarah had whispered to him in the night. In the army, a name wasn't worth much, only the stripes on your shoulders mattered.

'Sergeant!'

Sami let the shout echo behind him and ran his hand over the bark. A thin layer of splinters and woodchips covered the ground. The knife he had used wasn't sharp but it was still legible: his name and today's date. More than two years had passed since he signed out his uniform and blankets. It was finally over. This was the day he was leaving this hellhole for ever. No more nights when he collapsed into bed with aching feet and a pounding headache. No more early-morning runs over frosty moss with the air stabbing at his lungs.

The brigade general looked through Sami's papers and raised his eyebrows ever so slightly as though the documents amused or annoyed him.

'This must be some kind of record,' the general said. 'On average, you've spent one week of every four in the clink. We won't be sorry to see you go.'

'The feeling is mutual,' Sami said and saluted him.

The brigade general signed his name and handed back Sami's military ID.

'Get out of here.'

The same day, as he prepared to leave, Sami tried to find the black dog. He looked for it and had almost given up hope when he finally heard whimpering coming from a shrubbery behind the armoury. There it was, licking two newborn puppies. When she spotted Sami, she lit up; it was as though she wanted to apologize for disappearing. A third puppy had died and she had carried it away and covered it with a thin layer of sand: the wet tip of a nose and one paw were still visible. He contemplated bringing them home with him. But the dog was better off here, where she could roam the open fields with her puppies. The roof terrace at his parents' house, where he was going, was no place for semi-wild animals. He patted the dogs, fetched his bags and snuck out of a back door.

As arbitrarily and randomly as the soldiers had been brought together, their groups were now split up and scattered across the country. Bill was even leaving the country. He had booked a plane ticket to Canada for the same day he was discharged and was planning to become a language teacher. Whatever else you might say about his time in the army, his Arabic had improved, at least as far as insults were concerned.

Rafat would return to his family's olive groves in Afrin. He gave Sami a long hug in the windowless room they had shared, where the three steel beds would be filled by new recruits. They promised to be in touch if either of them heard from Ahmed.

Before Rafat left the room, he turned at the door and looked at Sami.

'He was right, you know. We've stayed silent for too long.' Rafat's face seemed older and paler than when they first met.

Hussein was the only one who asked to stay on in the army. The salary was meagre but it was still better than herding sheep.

'What about the ocean?' Sami asked, and Hussein smiled and patted him on the shoulder.

'It will still be there.'

On the bus home, a sense of freedom filled Sami's chest. His body was no longer owned by anyone, he was free to come and go as he pleased. Outside, the landscape rushed by, the air had a new edge of cold and the evening sun dipped the trees in gold. He rested his forehead against the window and drew his name, once more, on the foggy glass. A constant that was him, unchanged.

Sami's bus drove into Homs as night fell and the shooting intensified. His military ID got him through the checkpoints where Ali was supposed to pick him up, but his voice sounded distant on the phone and his sister took over.

'Dad's in the hospital,' Hiba said.

The rest of the words flowed past him as though he were standing under a waterfall, catching only random words and sentences: something about numbness in Nabil's face, dizziness and vertigo, collapsing in the kitchen.

'Are you still there?' Hiba asked. 'We can visit Dad together tomorrow but it would be safer for you to come home right now.'

He swallowed and asked if it was serious, and heard his sister take a deep breath.

'They are doing everything they can. Don't worry.'

That was answer enough. Sami asked in the bus car park and managed to find a taxi driver who, after inspecting his military ID, agreed to take him to the hospital.

The hospital hallways seemed endless. When he found the right door, he still wasn't sure it was the right room. The body under the starched sheets was a shadow of his father, sunken and fragile, with a tangle of tubes connected to his body. His moustache was unkempt and bushy. Sami pulled up a chair. From close up, his father was even more birdlike.

'My son,' Nabil said with both tenderness and reproach. 'It's after dusk.'

'How are you, Dad?'

'I'm just fine. It's your siblings I'm worried about.'

'Hiba said you had a stroke.'

'Just a little one. I'm fine now. My son, don't let them drag you into their folly.'

'You mean the demonstrations?'

'Only petty thieves and other criminals would . . . would . . .'

Nabil's lips continued to move but he couldn't find the words. Sami tried to see if the corners of his mouth were drooping or if there was any other sign of the tiny explosion that had occurred in his dad's brain. Weren't stroke victims usually semi-paralysed, amnesiac and changed beyond recognition? He must have been lucky. That did nothing to calm Sami, since his dad might just as easily be unlucky the next time.

'Can I get you anything from the cafeteria – juice or coffee?'

'My only wish is for you to stay away from them.'

His father took his hand and they held on to each other for a long time; he couldn't remember ever sitting like that before. He felt the warmth of his father's body rise towards his face, like the fog on the bus window. As long as a person is warm, he's alive, Sami thought. From the hospital window the streetlamps looked like waterlilies floating in the night.

His father was discharged a few days later as snow fell in big, airy drifts. Over the next few weeks Nabil quit smoking, or at least tried to wait to have his first cigarette until after lunch. He also tried to see to things he seemed to think had been neglected, like the fact that Sami and Ali were still not married and that Hiba didn't visit as much as she used to since having children.

147

And Nabil made one last attempt to persuade at least one of his sons to grow a moustache. Malik, who had entered puberty, surprised everyone by willingly agreeing, and it started auspiciously with a couple of downy hairs on his top lip.

'Dryer lint,' said Hiba.

'Bum fluff,' said Ali.

The only person who didn't mock Malik was their mother, but her words were the ones that hurt the most: 'You look so youthful with your moustache!'

Sami realized he had missed the family's breakfast-table discussions. He had moved back into his old room and while contemplating what to do next lived off the small amount of money he had earned during his military service. It no longer seemed as important to work from morning to night. It had partly to do with his father's stroke, and partly with him looking forward to a freer life.

In the end, it was Nabil who suggested his little brother shave after all.

'I'll lend you my razor,' he offered generously.

22

EVERYDAY LIFE WAS not much different from before, and yet so much was different. Some changes were obvious, like the army's building more checkpoints in Homs. Heavy armoured vehicles drove into the city, leaving sunken tracks in their wake as though the frosty asphalt were made of chocolate.

Other changes were subtler. Sarah had cut her hair short and there was a new fire in her eyes. If the shooting at demonstrators had scared her at first, it now seemed to have made her more convinced. She talked about the revolution the way she used to talk about novels and poetry. Aside from participating in the protests, she also collected testimonies and published them online. At first they had organized demonstrations at the university, but now the Shabiha or the Mukhabarat patrolled the hallways and almost only Alawite students dared to attend. Instead, they organized smaller protests across Homs on practically every street.

Sarah wanted to introduce him to a friend, who was a role model and leader among the protestors.

'You have no idea how brave she is,' Sarah said. 'One time, she walked right up to a checkpoint and handed one of the soldiers a flyer – just like that. You should have seen the look on his face. I thought he was either going to shoot her or propose.'

They gathered at dusk in a small square. People arrived in small groups, excited and nervous, pulling their scarves closer and rubbing their hands to keep warm. Sami remembered again the intoxication of his first protest and the feeling of an extended siblingship, of being brothers and sisters. Sarah checked her phone repeatedly.

'She said she was going to be here . . . Wait, there she is.'

Sami turned around and it was as though the world turned white, illuminated by a bright light. She pushed through the crowd and was stopped several times on the way because people wanted to say hello and pat her on the back. She didn't seem to make a big deal of it, just pulled up the hood on her baggy top – which only partially concealed the camera underneath – and pressed on towards them.

'Yasmin, is it really you?'

'Sami! What a great surprise.'

It was his childhood love, older and without braces and a hijab covering her hair under the hoodie, but unquestionably her.

Yasmin embraced him like when they were little, like before Haydar.

'You know each other?' Sarah asked. 'Why didn't you say something?'

'It was a long time ago,' Yasmin said and smiled. 'We took English together, didn't we?'

'You were top of the class.'

'Don't know about that . . .'

That was all the talking they had time for because the music was turned up and the flags raised. Yasmin handed Sarah and Sami a placard each, while she herself took out her camera from time to time to take pictures. He glanced at her and thought about how keen she'd once been to abide by the rules. How she'd kept reminding him that the walls have ears.

After the demonstration Sarah had to leave, but she suggested that Sami stay with Yasmin to catch up.

'That's so cool you know each other,' she said before she left.

They went to a nearby café and sat outside under the heaters. It was one of those places where men usually gathered to play cards and smoke but Yasmin didn't mind their looks.

'I'm so happy to see you again,' Sami said. 'What have you been doing all this time?'

'Studied law, mostly. After my dad died I realized how fragile things are. There's no time to lose.'

'Sorry, I didn't know about your father.'

'You don't need to be sorry. It was more of a relief, to be honest.'

She started on a new cigarette before the first one was finished – her voice was as hoarse from chain-smoking as it was from shouting – and spoke quietly but earnestly.

'My dad wasn't very kind to my mother. That is sort of the reason why I chose law. We were all witnesses to his abuse but didn't do anything.'

Sami thought of the military map and felt a strike of pain. He too had been a silent witness for far too long.

'You know, the revolution is the first step towards equality,' she said. 'I was a coward before but now I see clearly.'

It sounded simple and obvious when she put it that way. Sami envied her that clear vision. For his part, he felt things around him were growing murkier and murkier. He considered telling her about Haydar, their school friend who had become a prison guard, but decided against it. If he did, he would have to tell her about his time in jail and the army, and maybe she would think of him differently when she realized he hadn't deserted.

'Do you want another coffee?' Sami asked.

'Why not?' Yasmin answered and smiled. 'Two is better than one.'

The world had changed and they had changed with it. Or had he? There were more demonstrations, and Sami watched Yasmin and Sarah standing at the head of the protests, chanting on the barricades. What had he accomplished?

'Can't you hear I'm talking to you? What the fuck are you doing here?'

When the voice came closer Sami realized he was the one being addressed. Standing in front of him was an old acquaintance from university, dressed in leather jacket and high winter boots. The name escaped him – he used to be late to lectures and had copied Sami's notes.

'I thought we were nothing but shit to you.'

He spat on the ground and stepped in closer, lowering his chin and staring Sami in the face. Sarah backed away and he failed to find the words to defend himself.

'Come off it, he's here now, right?' Yasmin said.

'How do we know you're not an informer? That you're not here to gather information?'

'Good god, calm down,' Yasmin said.

'Shut up, I am calm. And you, you fucking traitor.'

'Take that back,' Sarah said and took a step forward.

'Traitor? Sure I take it back.'

He spread his hands, palms out. Then he leaned forward and Sami could smell the alcohol on his breath; he had never known a face could express so much contempt.

'Soldier swine fits better.'

It happened in a split second. Sami saw Sarah squeeze her eyes shut and raise her fist. It was like a switch flipped and he instantly knew what he had to do.

'Ow, let go of me! He was coming at you. Aren't you going to defend yourself?' Sarah twisted free of Sami's grasp and rubbed her wrist. The university acquaintance had already turned his back on them and was staggering off.

'But he was right, wasn't he?' Sami said.

Sarah turned abruptly and walked away. He took a few steps in her direction but a new group of protestors moved in between them.

'Don't worry.' Yasmin shrugged. 'All choices are political these days, even when you don't have a choice. I don't blame you,' she continued. 'My brother's doing his military service, and he says they'll come after me if he doesn't.'

He hesitated but in the end asked the question he had been thinking about.

'Do you know how to organize a local protest?'

Yasmin lit up. 'Do I know?' The revolution council of Homs provided organizers with a megaphone and video camera, and other than that it was simply a matter of handing out flyers with a time and a place. 'Supply bottles of water. Make sure you have a few people on lookout.'

The Free Syrian Army was ready to intervene if regime soldiers broke through. But they were more of a symbolic protection, since the rebels were loosely organized and would be unable to withstand a coordinated offensive.

It was easier than he had thought. During the first chilly weeks of the year, Sami spent all his waking hours organizing daily local demonstrations, with fifty to a hundred protestors at a time. He spent his days in the house, painting placards and arguing gently with his father. In the evenings they gathered, sang and filmed their meetings. Every gathering was a victory and a risk. The army was not the only danger. The regime covertly supported street gangs who attacked protestors on their behalf.

'We need to arm ourselves,' said Sarah one day, restlessly picking at her red nail polish. 'Look around. We've been protesting for almost a year and the graveyards are getting more crowded by the day.'

Yasmin disagreed. 'We have to be patient.'

Despite her unassuming air, she was one of the strongest voices in the group, precisely because of her thoughtfulness and ability to take a step back.

'Our strength is that we're sticking together,' she continued. 'The moment we fight violence with violence, they're going to call us terrorists, spies, traitors – God knows what – and deal with us as such.'

'Yeah, let's give it some time,' Sami agreed.

'That's easy for you to say.'

Sarah didn't say it straight out but Sami knew what she meant. He had only been protesting for a couple of months, hadn't seen and heard everything. He tried to ignore the accusatory tone in her voice since this was not the time to have a row. Either way, their friends had come to the same conclusion: when demonstrating for peace, peaceful methods were required. The Free Syrian Army was taking care of the armed struggle.

Sami and Sarah didn't talk about the future because this was their future. Freedom, and the new society they were trying to create. They met at each other's houses and planned activities, usually in the evenings when the military patrols were less frequent.

But it was dangerous work. One night, in the gentle glow of the streetlamps, Sami witnessed the security police breaking into their neighbour's house to seize the son, a well-known media activist. When they didn't find the one they were looking for, they took the father instead.

Sami watched from across the street as the elderly man was forced out in plaid slippers and a blue robe. He blinked in the streetlight and was reaching for something in his pocket when he got a hard push in his back and stumbled on the icy step. Sami saw a pair of glasses fall out of the old man's hand and land on the asphalt. One of the security officers stepped on them, almost unknowingly, while he lifted the man by his arm and shoved him into the black car.

By the morning someone had swept away the splinters and the broken frames. The glasses had vanished without a trace, just like the old man, who never returned to the house.

23

THE ARMOURED VEHICLES were not there just for show. Shops began to close and people began to hoard tinned goods. Some families sought refuge in the countryside. Yet even so, most remained calm. The regime would never dare, they said. As soon as the first missile is fired, the US, France and the international community will react. They said.

In the early spring of 2012, a year after the birth of the revolution, the first rockets were launched at Homs. Until that day, Sami had thought there was a limit, a red line of decency. Yes, he knew tanks had rolled into Daraa at the very start of the revolution. That demonstrators greeting the soldiers with flowers had been attacked with tear-gas and bullets. And yet he couldn't shake a seed of doubt that it was all really happening.

It wasn't just the situation he was unfamiliar with, it was himself, too – or more accurately, humanity. People were created equal and the same, which meant the light that existed in others, existed in him too. The darkness that existed in others, he could summon too. Inside the armoured vehicles were soldiers Sami had served with, soldiers who were now shooting at their friends' homes.

Rockets and missiles darkened the sky. Sami started taking pictures of the damaged houses. As evidence, he told Sarah. This kind of rocket was from the previous century and had a target radius of one hundred to two hundred yards; nothing you used if you had an exact military target.

Yasmin agreed that they needed to document things. They needed a media centre to coordinate and disseminate accurate information. They took turns meeting at each other's homes or finding other premises they could be in. Yasmin came to Sami's house sometimes, when she needed help editing photos or designing pamphlets.

'Hello,' she greeted Malik, who always seemed to show up in the hallway when she arrived. 'What are you up to, *ya albi?*'

Malik was too big to be called a sweetheart any more but still smiled and blushed. Yasmin leaned down to take off her shoes and Sami came just in time to see his little brother straighten his back.

'Oh, you know,' Malik said. 'I'm thinking of joining the rebels.'

'Don't listen to him, he talks nonsense,' Sami said.

'I don't. I want to do something, too.'

Yasmin nodded and said that the media group always needed volunteers. Maybe he liked to photograph or collect testimonies?

'I mean something real,' Malik said. 'Something that changes something. Between a man with a camera or a man with a gun, who would you listen to?' Malik twisted his hands when he realized what he had just said. 'Not that I mean that your work isn't . . .'

Yasmin shrugged like it wasn't a big deal but Sami felt the anger rise.

'First of all, you're not a man. You're thirteen.'

'Soon fourteen.'

'Second, go and do your homework.'

'We've got vacation from the school.'

'OK, brothers,' Yasmin interrupted and turned to Malik. 'Just tell us if you change your mind.'

Sami remembered the impression Yasmin had made on him when they were young. The feeling of being in the spotlight when she listened or talked to you, as if every word had meaning. As if you meant something yourself. Of course Malik was now feeling the same.

'Your little brother is cute,' Yasmin said and continued to Sami's room, where Sarah was waiting for them. 'He reminds me of my brother.'

The media activists printed newspapers and posters, shared images and texts on social media. Over time, structure emerged. Yasmin became the informal leader of the work and the forty or so activists engaged in it. Their work became more serious as circumstances became so. Sami's inner doubt grew stronger and stronger, but all outward doubt disappeared with the vibrations in the ground. When the missiles hit, he threw himself on the floor and covered his ears. Blood throbbed at his temples. The wall of a building further down the street collapsed, but not where he was. Time lost all meaning, at least in terms of how it had flowed before, divided into hours and minutes. Now he divided time into chaos and impending chaos.

For the first time he saw the bodies of young people, whose faces were covered in dust and whose skin steamed with heat. He had been wrong. Apparently, a body could continue to emit heat for a short while after death. The shock that rushed through his body, however, wasn't something he could talk about.

In the middle of March, late at night, he had a call from Muhammed. At first he didn't recognize his friend's voice. He was speaking in clipped, jerky sentences from the top part of his lungs.

'Come, you have to come.'

A massacre had taken place in Karm al-Zeitoun, one of the poorer parts of Homs. The army had gone in with armoured vehicles, broken into homes and handed the arrested families over to the Shabiha. The bodies needed to be moved before the army attacked again, and Sami and Muhammed's job was to make way for them.

Sami hurried to his friend's house and helped empty the rooms of furniture. Muhammed's glasses were smudged with grease and one of the lenses was cracked; his T-shirt was dripping with sweat. They moved like sleepwalkers, lifting up furniture as if for a weekly clean, sweeping and hosing off the floors. They let the water cool a little before pouring it down the drain to make sure they didn't disturb the jinn.

Later that night, a flatbed truck pulled up outside the house. The sight that greeted Sami etched itself permanently on his retinas. The bodies were stacked in the flatbed, legs and arms entangled. The smell was of smoke, burnt flesh and hair, sweet blood. The militia had shot or stabbed the people to death and set some of them on fire. Sami turned away and threw up.

'Hurry!'

Sami, Muhammed and the two men carried the bodies into the house and lined them up in the rooms. As he carried them he thought: *One day, someone is going to carry me.* One boy looked like he was resting when seen in profile, his eyelashes sticky with sleep. The other half of his head had been blown away, his brain seeping out. A woman was missing her jaw. They stared wide-eyed. Several of the children had knife wounds. What kind of person walked up to a child and stabbed it in the belly?

After midnight they had another call, another car was on its way. The street was dark and deserted. There wasn't enough room in the house and they had no choice but to leave the bodies in the street overnight. Sami counted thirty-nine dead, in the house and on the street. Nineteen children, thirteen women and seven men, of which three were old enough to be his grandfather. They were going to bury them at first light.

The video camera panned back and forth. When Sami watched the clip back he could hear himself sob, even though he didn't remember crying. He filmed it even though it felt pointless. But it had to be illegal, according to some international convention or higher law. He didn't think about revenge or justice, only this one simple thing: that there's a limit to what you can get away with. That life couldn't be allowed to continue as if nothing had happened.

A girl, no more than five years old, had been shot in the forehead. The flesh rose from the miniature crater like a flower, while the back of her head flowed out like a flaccid balloon.

As dawn broke, they began the work of burying the bodies. People joined them and cried with horror and shock. Sami regretted having been unable to take the bodies inside to spare them this sight. At the same time, they now had help carrying. Most of the bodies were buried next to a mosque, others in a nearby garden. Others still were collected by relatives.

Later that day, Sami undressed and rinsed the blood off his hands as rumour of the massacre spread and the mass exodus from Homs began.

24

THEIR CITY WAS being taken from them, imperceptibly at first, then more conspicuously. The army shot at the buildings where the Free Syrian Army were said to be hiding, but most of the victims were civilians. In one day, Sami counted forty rockets raining down on them. There were holes in streets and buildings where the metal points had driven themselves in and remained.

Sarah went back to her family outside Damascus. Sami encouraged her to go.

'You'll be safer there,' he told her, not knowing if it was true.

'I need to be with my family.'

'I understand, don't think about it.'

'I'll return to Homs soon.'

Soon, he thought, when was soon? They lived one day at a time.

One morning, Sami's dad put the radio under his arm and announced they were leaving. His mother packed a few changes of clothes. There was no talk of fleeing, no, they were simply going to leave town for a few days until the regime came to its senses. They would stay with a couple of relatives in the countryside. Hiba had already left with her husband and two children. Ali had hung up a handwritten sign on his computer shop: closed for vacation. He was wanted for military service again and had decided to stay hidden. Sami only knew he was staying somewhere in the al-Waer neighbourhood on the outskirts of Homs. Malik filled his back-

160

pack with comics instead of school books; the spring term exams had been cancelled anyway. As he helped his parents and little brother pack up the car, Sami said he would join them soon.

'They'll give up in a few days. Somebody has to look after Grandpa Faris.'

Because Grandpa Faris had decided to stay. Nabil and Samira had tried to persuade him to come but, in the end, they realized it was futile to ask Grandpa Faris to leave the city where he had lived and worked all his life, where he had met and buried the love of his life.

'Water the plants,' Samira said and kissed Sami's cheeks. 'And don't forget to feed the turtle on the roof.'

Sami didn't sleep at all the night after they left, only finally dozing off when morning had already broken. When he woke up, it was to a new kind of noise: the deep whistling of rockets being fired by the regime's artillery from the hill that was home to Homs' ancient citadel. This was different from the shoulder-mounted rocket launchers. Every strike vibrated for miles. Fire and black smoke billowed above the rooftops.

That first day on his own he called Muhammed, who had also elected to stay. Together they went out into the neighbourhood to see if there were any old people who had been unable or unwilling to leave.

Grandpa Faris stayed in his bedroom, where he complained about his aching legs and chain-smoked in bed. After three days, his costume was rumpled and his oil-combed hair dishevelled. The room was stuffy with sweat and pipe smoke. Sami noted the artillery fire seemed to be intensifying. In the silence between the launches he could hear the tapping of Grandpa Faris cleaning out his pipe. Then Edith Piaf's husky voice from the gramophone on the nightstand.

'The little sparrow from Paris,' Grandpa Faris said and drummed his fingers against his leg. 'That's one of the cities I've always dreamt of visiting. The elegant cafés, theatres, boulevards . . . Paris seems like a Damascus in the heart of Europe.'

'When this is over, we'll go there,' Sami said.

He sat down and stroked the brown, marbled cane that stood propped against the bed.

'Walnut,' Grandpa Faris said.

'From Aleppo, I remember.'

'Would you be a good boy and fetch my tobacco?'

The tendrils of smoke rose through the air, giving the room an air of normality, as did the floral bedspread and the gramophone. Sami was reluctant to tell his grandfather but he couldn't hold off any longer. He was going to call his cousins.

'They'll come and get you as soon as they can.'

Grandpa Faris didn't object, just nodded and said there is a season for everything.

'Don't forget your bottle of hair oil,' Sami said.

'You don't want to keep it? I remember you used to like it.'

'I don't have much use for it any more.'

He stroked the closely shorn hair at the back of his head, one of the habits he had picked up in the military. They listened to Piaf's raspy voice, *Non, rien de rien*, and the distant booms, *Non, je ne regrette rien*, blending together.

'I know you and your father don't always agree,' said Grandpa Faris. 'But you know, parents have a different job from children.'

Sami jutted his chin out and shook his head, mostly to himself. 'They could have protested when they were young.'

'Some did and paid a steep price. Others tried to protect themselves and their families by keeping quiet, but it didn't always help. There is something you need to know,' continued Grandpa Faris. 'Just after the massacre in Hama, before you were born . . . did you know that the secret police searched thousands of homes looking for people who might have ties to the Muslim Brotherhood? One night, they broke into your home.'

'Our home?'

'Yes, your older brother was still a baby.'

Grandpa Faris coughed and took a couple of deep breaths before he started smoking again.

'Your mother tried to push past the soldiers to get to Ali, who had just started sleeping in his own bed. She was stopped and pushed back on to the bed while your father was pulled out of the blankets. By streetlight, Nabil was dragged outside. He was taken behind a car, in nothing but his underwear, and surrounded by soldiers aiming their guns at him.'

Grandpa Faris held up his hand and looked in the palm as if it was a mirror.

'The general studied Nabil in the rear-view mirror. Then he waved his hand and your father was released.'

Sami blinked and tried to take that in. His dad, dragged into the street.

'I don't understand . . . did he have anything to do with the protests in Hama?'

'No, nothing at all. Your father was always eager to do right. He wouldn't hurt a fly.

'Sami,' Grandpa Faris continued, 'I could tell you that you will never be able to save yourself or anyone else by keeping on the right side of things. That the only thing that can save you is to fight for what's right. But it's more complicated than that. How do you know, at any given moment, what the right thing is? Even just talking about this and showing signs of hesitation would be seen as treachery by the regime.' He waved his hand through the air, scattering smoke. 'Yes, I know, the walls have ears and all that. But they're still our walls and our home. Right?'

Grandpa Faris smiled but it looked forced. He leaned back into his pillow, stretched his legs out on the bedspread and sucked on his pipe.

The next day, Sami's cousins came by and took Grandpa Faris out of the city.

It's going to be over soon, Sami thought, and every morning it continued unabated. But there was still water in the taps, still food in both fridge and pantry, and his photography gave him a reason to get out of bed. He shortened his walks and avoided the regime checkpoints. He spent most of his time at home. He watered the house plants. Played the gramophone and was soothed by the crackling tones. Grandpa Faris hadn't wanted to take the gramophone – that would be tantamount to admitting he wasn't coming back.

Sami flipped through the comic books Malik had left behind. He found a whole box of pictures of his brother as a young boy and surprised himself by feeling jealous. Malik would always be a child in their parents' eyes. The child who was conceived at the eleventh hour, possibly not planned, but deeply wanted. Maybe Sami had been wrong about his little brother. Maybe all his joking and talking wasn't a way to please and be loved, but a sign that he already was loved.

He tested out the chair in Nabil's study. On the desk a marble ashtray, a fountain pen engraved with his father's name, a portrait of Samira. He spun the ashtray around and discovered a small, flat key underneath. He held the key in his hand; it weighed almost nothing. It reminded him of the keys Hiba had used for her diaries when they were little, the diaries Sami was strictly banned from reading. He read them anyway, and realized with disappointment that she only wrote pointless nonsense about boys in the other class in school and who had the coolest trainers.

Sami looked around and pulled out the desk drawers at random. In one he found a silver flask with a couple of coffee beans next to it. He already knew Nabil drank on the weekends sometimes, that he preferred to do so alone out of respect for Samira.

None of the drawers contained anything the key might be used for. He opened the top drawer again and there, under a stack of papers, he could feel a sharp corner. He pulled out a box and put the key in the lock. It fitted. Inside was a collection of letters tied together with yellowed string. Sami touched the paper but snatched his fingers back as though they'd been burnt. These letters must be very important to his father, so much so that he kept the key to hand, yet hidden. Sami felt embarrassed for his father. Another woman, could it be that banal? Someone at his work, since he was always home early and never travelled. Whatever his secret was, Sami didn't want to know. Even so, he untied the string and picked up the first letter.

Dear Nabil, it started. Sami's cheeks flushed, but he forced himself to read on. *You have no idea how much I appreciated the book of poems by Qabbani. I know my parents don't want me to write to you any more, but I can't possibly stop myself . . .*

A young girl too! This was too much. Sami read on and his cheeks turned redder. She wrote about his hands and lips, even complimented his sticky-out ears. *Your moustache*, she wrote, *is the most handsome one I've ever seen on a man.* When he turned the page, he saw the name. It was signed *Your Samira, for ever.*

Sami smiled to himself, still embarrassed but for a different reason now – for catching a glimpse of his parents as young lovers. He tied the string around his mother's love letters and locked the box. He wondered what kind of person his father had been back then, when Nabil met Samira and tried to get her attention with poetry, the oldest trick in the book for the infatuated. He thought about who he had been a few years later, when they were married and his older brother was a baby and the secret police had forced their way into their home. When they pulled out books, opened drawers and toppled furniture. When his father was dragged into the street and his fate was decided by a glance.

Sami put the key back under the marble ashtray. You could get used to most things, even the whistling sound of incoming rockets and missiles. But maybe not the knowledge that everything can be taken from you.

The next morning, his cousins called again, this time with sad news. Grandpa Faris had passed away during the night. Not from a rocket or a bullet in the back of the head, but peacefully, in his sleep, of age or sorrow.

25

SAMI'S BLOCK WAS now right in the line of fire. He had tried to ignore the obvious but the black fire clouds kept coming closer. In a short time he had learnt to sleep despite the anxiety. It fired his dreams instead; he would wake up with a jolt and hit the wall.

On a warm spring night, Muhammed called and said Sami couldn't wait any longer. Sami reluctantly packed a bag and went, by the light of his phone, to his friend's house a few streets over. He hesitated at first, when he thought of the bodies they had carried there before burial. But it wasn't like Sami had many other places to choose from.

Muhammed's mother and three siblings had all gone now, to the al-Waer neighbourhood on the other side of the river. Their old house had now been transformed into a teenage lair with empty bags of crisps on the tables and pillows on the floor.

'I thought you'd cleaned the place,' Sami said.

'It's not my fault,' Muhammed said apologetically. 'I told Anwar to pick up his things.'

'The bookkeeper boy!' A large figure got up off the sofa and it took Sami a second to recognize him. As a chef he had always been impeccably dressed, rolled-up shirtsleeves, starched apron, but now Anwar looked like he had gone with whatever was at the top of the laundry hamper. His trousers were too short and his pale gut peeked out from under his shirt. But he still wore a black bandana, as a reminder of the smooth kitchen master he had once been.

'Anwar, I can't believe it's you.'

'And I, for one, didn't believe you would ever grow up.'

Sami embraced him and kissed his cheeks.

'How is Abu Karim? And the restaurant?'

'We had to close,' Anwar replied. 'Abu Karim said it was the rent but everyone knows it was because we handed out food to the protestors.'

Sami shook his head. 'I'm sorry to hear that.'

'You can take the other sofa,' Muhammed said and picked a few pillows up off the floor. 'If it drags on, we'll carry the beds down to the basement.'

Although Sami had known Muhammed since they were young, he had only been to his best friend's house a few times. In the beginning he had asked more often but Muhammed would say they had guests that day, or that his mother was cleaning, and another time would be better to visit. Sami assumed he was ashamed of the crowded space but he didn't mind. On the contrary, he felt at home immediately.

They had lived on one floor with a small kitchen, a living room and a bedroom for Muhammed's mum and one of the children. The basement consisted of another room, which Muhammed shared with two of his little siblings – the room lacked windows and had dark damp roses on the ceiling.

Muhammed's mum rented the apartment and basement from an elderly woman who lived on the top floors in the same building, who only asked for a low rent in exchange for helping her clean, shop, and care for the front yard. Sami had met the old woman once and remembered her friendly smile, a visible golden tooth, her wrists rattling with shiny bracelets. The old woman had left now but Muhammed occasionally went up to her apartment and cleaned, in case she came back. He watered the rose bushes until they had to save on water, and they saw the dark red petals fall to the ground.

A few days after Sami moved in, a pressure wave broke the windows. They taped black bin bags over where the glass had been. But that first night, Sami lay awake in the gentle darkness, watching the stars come out. If he listened carefully, he could almost hear the plough being pulled through space, the star-glazed wood cutting through the heavens. When he fell asleep he did it safe in the knowledge that he still had a home. But the next morning, his home lay in ruins.

Muhammed held up his laptop. A grainy mobile phone video was playing.

'There, see?' Muhammed said.

'Recognize that house?' Anwar said.

Sami sat up and frowned. Projectiles whistled over the rooftops and then plumes of smoke started rising. He watched the clip again, the dot speeding across the sky and the explosion that followed. Muhammed took off his glasses and polished them. The crack was still there. Anwar put a big, sweaty hand on his shoulder.

'Lucky you came here when you did.'

Sami couldn't help it; it bubbled up from some unknown cranny, like that time in the bank manager's office. He started laughing. Muhammed and Anwar exchanged a glance but he couldn't stop. It rose up from deep inside him, a convulsive sound that took over his body.

'You need to eat. I'll cook something,' Anwar said. 'Wait, where are you going?'

Sami had already got off the sofa and was tying his shoes.

'Let him go,' Muhammed said quietly.

Outside, the air was dry with dust and the smell of smoke. It was just a house. The main thing was that he and his family were alive. That was the most important thing, right? Yes, it was. Being alive was the most important thing. Just a house. He said it out loud, even though there was no one else around.

At first Sami had a hard time identifying his house among the others. The missiles had hit the façade on the street side. It was like looking into a dolls' house. The rooms were exposed, except on the top floor, which had folded flat like a cardboard box.

Sami had to climb over debris to get in. Twice he got stuck and had to wrench his foot free. The staircase was intact apart from a large hole halfway up. The unharmed and unbroken was as strange as the demolished. It was as though two photographs had blended together, underscoring the contrasts between before and after: on the one hand, bricks and debris littered the kitchen floor, the backs of the chairs were broken and the table snapped in two. On the other hand, the fridge was untouched, though without power. On the one hand, dust and shattered glass covered the floral bedspread and the black Singer sewing machine lay on the floor with a broken needle. On the other hand, the gramophone had come through virtually unscathed.

For every step he took, it felt as though someone else took a step behind him, another Sami. The one who had moved through these rooms before and was unaware that his childhood home lay in ruins. He had an urge to clean up and set things right in case his parents came back. He picked up things that lay in his path: the silver sugar bowl, the remote that had slid out of its plastic cover.

When he reached his parents' bedroom, his arms were full of objects that had lost their former significance. How was he to judge what was worth saving, which memories were significant to them? He let all of it fall to the floor and stopped moving.

He studied the pile he had collected, found the box with his parents' secret correspondence and put that in his backpack, even though the key was gone. He filled the rest of the bag with tins and dry goods.

Once again, he felt as though someone was right behind him. Not a shadow. There really was something watching him. He froze. A faint rustling, followed by a faint squeaking. He turned around and squatted down. There they were, underneath the sofa. Four newborn kittens the colour of mustard. They meowed and showed their pink tongues, climbing over his hands. There was no sign of the mother. Sami opened the unharmed refrigerator and put out a bowl of yoghurt. The kittens immediately lost interest in him and hungrily lapped up the tart whiteness.

Just a house. Sarah was always telling him he closed up instead of expressing his feelings. Maybe it was a way of protecting himself, or of protecting the people around him. He didn't want to put his troubles and worries on others. But just now, some form of venting would have been good, like crying uncontrollably or running himself ragged. Instead he walked around what had been his childhood home and felt the heat rise in his eyes and had no way to express his pain. Laughing didn't work any more, nor did crying or running.

The kittens meowed and blinked, and he wondered if they could see or were still blind. He picked one up; it squirmed around his hand, resisting, until it resigned itself and started purring. This innocent tenderness, this trust towards a living creature who had fed them, was enough for now. There, there, tiny kittens. Your mum will be back soon. He decided to return the next day or when the bombing had slowed.

There was still lettuce in the fridge. Sami took a green leaf and climbed up on the roof terrace, what was left of it, but hard as he looked he couldn't find the turtle. Maybe it had been crushed by a brick. Maybe it had seen a chance to live free and escaped. From the roof, he saw the utility pole next to the house and once again thought of his dad. One of the few transgressions Nabil had allowed himself, possibly the only one, was that he tapped the powerline out on the street to lower the family's electricity costs. Now the pole had snapped in two, the top half dangling limply.

Sami's eyes stung again. Just a house. What gave him the right to grieve when others had lost their entire families? It was just concrete, bricks, thresholds, wallpaper, door jambs, moulding. It was just a place he had lived for most of his life, his first and only home. He walked away without turning back.

26

IN MAY, WHEN the sun was warming the broken roofs and the Arab League monitors were allowed to visit Homs to inspect the damage, the blockade was temporarily lifted. People who had fled returned, but only to pack up things they had left behind.

Sarah wasn't among the ones coming back. Sami called her and her voice sounded distant, as though something had shifted during the past few days.

'I heard people are leaving,' she said.

'Not everyone. Some choose to stay.'

'And you, are you staying?'

He closed his eyes and saw her face in front of him, remembering how she used to raise her voice during the meetings and speak for arms.

'We're fighting for our future, remember? You always said that. You said we'd never give up.'

'But we can't fight if we're dead,' Sarah sighed.

'I know the army inside and out. I know what kind of people they are. When the rest of the world realize they're shooting at civilians, they'll be forced to withdraw.' He continued, though he wasn't sure she was listening. 'The whole thing will be over by the end of the week. By the end of the week.'

'Is this it?' she asked quietly.

'What do you mean, is this it?'

'Well, this, us.'

'I told you I'll be there in a few days.'

'Yes, so you said.'

Her voice sounded remote. He preferred it when she hurled arguments and opinions at him, when she spoke loudly and intensely, rather than these unspoken undercurrents of disappointment, or maybe anger, or grief. She had returned to her city; surely she had to understand he didn't want to abandon his.

'What are you reading?' Sami asked.

He wanted to talk about something that reminded him of everyday life, of what life used to be like when she would read her favourite passages out loud to him. If she could be made to remember that, she would remember the rest.

'Nothing,' Sarah replied. 'I don't read any more.'

The silence swelled and surged as though they were standing on opposite beaches, trying to persuade the other to cross the sound in between. They listened to each other's breathing: his slow and light, hers heavy and rapid.

'We'll stay in touch. We'll write every day,' he told her.

'Sure.'

'Every day that there's not a power cut.'

'Look, I think I have to go now.'

The call ended before he could say the most important thing. Normally he had no difficulty expressing his affection and love, but now it was as though words of that kind would have underlined the sense of an ending. And maybe this was the beginning of the end. He had a gnawing feeling one of them was right and the other wrong. He just didn't know who.

Sami's parents came back to their ruined house for a few hours. Nabil kept blowing his nose into a handkerchief, while Samira mechanically moved bricks and swept the broken staircase. Sami helped, even though the wind soon covered it with dust and dirt once more. His mother packed carrier bags full of photographs and clothes. Nabil walked around aimlessly, searching for his razor and putting the gramophone under his arm.

'This time you're coming with us,' Samira said. 'Come and see Malik and Hiba.'

'I promise I'll join you in a few days.'

'My son,' his dad said and shook his head.

Samira had to call out three times to Nabil before he left the house, or what was left of it, and walked slowly to the car. His father got in the passenger seat and looked straight ahead, one hand on the glove compartment. Sami watched as the car left. How could he make them understand? Homs was his home. No matter what happened, he wanted to see it with his own eyes, to bear witness. Especially since he had missed the start of the revolution. He had so many lost months to make up for.

A few days later Sami heard a familiar knock on Muhammed's door and, when he opened it, his ears filled with sound, like water seeping into a sinking ship, imperceptibly at first, then rushing in from all directions.

'What are you doing here?'

Standing on the front steps was a lanky fourteen-year-old boy. His little brother, who had grown up without him noticing.

It must have happened overnight, no, over many nights, years even. Malik, who followed his every step and listened to every word he spoke. Malik, who was disappointed with Sami for not deserting, for not joining the rebels, when he was trained to handle weapons and all. But then Sami had chosen to stay behind and that had made that possible for Malik too. Why hadn't Sami noticed that his little brother took after him, even when they disagreed? Now moments like this made it painfully clear.

'I'm staying,' Malik said and pushed his way into the room.

'You are not, you're too young.'

He understood all too well his little brother's frustration. How infuriating to see through the contradictory behaviour of the adults and still not be considered an adult yourself.

'Really, you're too young.'

'Everyone's needed in the revolution.'

Malik glared at Sami. The words sounded too big for his mouth.

'How did you get past the checkpoints?' Sami sighed.

His little brother jutted his chin out and pulled himself up straighter.

'It doesn't matter, that route is closed now.'

'I'm serious,' Sami said.

'So am I,' replied Malik.

He didn't want to think about what his parents would say when they discovered their youngest child had left them. Sami and Malik were of the same build and people said their eyes were identical. *Do you see what I see?* he wondered. *Do you see yourself with your arms crossed and your chin in the air, ready to be as old as the situation requires?* What did the situation require? Neither one of them knew yet.

'There's another thing,' Malik said, his eyes darting this way and that, as though he had just remembered something he had been trying to forget. 'It's about Yasmin.'

Sami hadn't heard from Yasmin in a week, which had worried him, but at the same time sometimes it was necessary to lie low, or there could be practical obstacles to communication. The last time they talked it was about the next issue of their newspaper. Now Yasmin's brother had asked Malik to relay what had happened.

'Come in,' Sami said. 'Tell me everything.'

Malik followed him but was too restless to sit down. Yasmin had been arrested but granted bail, he told Sami. When her brother arrived at the military detention centre, the officer had asked if he would like a cup of tea. Yasmin's brother realized he had no choice.

'Sure,' he said. 'I'd love some tea.'

They sat down in the office and soon after, there was a knock on the door. She entered the room, naked, carrying a tea tray.

'Serve your brother first,' the officer had told her.

Sami didn't want to hear the rest, and Malik was stuttering and didn't seem to want to keep on speaking, but he did.

'They let her go,' Malik said. 'After she had served them tea. The money was on the table and everything.'

'Yes?'

'But then Yasmin asked if she could have her camera back. And that was when . . . well, her brother tried to stop them . . .'

Malik sat down on the sofa now, exhausted, and looked at the floor.

'The officer gave Yasmin's brother her clothes back, after he shot her.'

Sami stood in the middle of the room and felt the walls disappear. The wind swept in and carried with it the smell of Yasmin's cigarettes, the pens they had used to make the placards, the sweet scent of low-hanging oranges from their school years. Once upon a time she had been his first love. Later on, along with Sarah, Yasmin had been the one to help him find a place and a role in the revolution. Now she didn't exist. Sami had an urge to tell Yasmin herself what had happened, to plead with her to go into hiding. The numbness started in his fingers and spread through his body but it was too soon to call it grief.

Malik took off his backpack and dropped it to the floor. The same backpack he had once used to carry his school books in. Sami remembered the stray dog Malik had dragged home and the olives he had thrown while he sat at the breakfast table, all the times he had reprimanded his younger brother.

'I know what you're thinking,' Malik said, 'but this is the way it is. I'm staying.'

And Sami knew it was Malik's decision to make, just like he had made his.

IV

In the beginning, while we are still learning to sleep together and share a duvet, you sometimes wake up in the middle of a scream and hurl yourself out of bed.

'Was it the checkpoints?'

Sometimes, it's prison corridors with hunting dogs. Sometimes, your nightmares are about the lack of tobacco. It's almost never what I imagine would be the worst of the worst. We drink tea with honey, interlace our fingers and decide you should sleep on the outside of the bed, away from the wall.

You tell your story and simultaneously translate it. Partly by using another language than your own, partly by dressing your bodily experiences in words. What happens in the translation and interpretation and description, to us and to the story? What disappears and what is gained? I would like to think something is gained.

Describing trauma is always overwhelming – powerfully emotional memories that don't slot into our constructed narratives. Events and fragments we can't fit into the rest of our experiences, and which therefore break through like uncontrollable flashbacks. It's only when we can deal with the trauma and intertwine it with our memories that the story can become whole, and we can become whole as humans.

But does telling the story always help? When you return to certain events your throat goes dry. You clear it and drink more tea. Your eyes look different. Your irises grow big, dark and shiny, as though you can see what's happening. I put a hand on your arm to remind you you're not alone. Afterwards, we talk about something lighter and return to the present. That is my promise to you: after following you into the dark, I also have to follow you back and show you the light.

27

THE MASS EXODUS entailed new concerns, like what to do with family pets. Some took cats and dogs with them; some left aquariums with neighbours. Others set their animals free, hoping they would survive over the summer.

The pigeon owners had the hardest time letting go. They handled their domesticated birds as tenderly as if they were relatives, stroking them and feeding them sunflower seeds and giving them names, but their cages were too much of an encumbrance. Before the war, you would see the doves flying above the rooftops of Homs in well-orchestrated formations. The birds had been a natural part of the city. That the sky was now devoid of the fluttering of wings was a clear sign life had changed.

May usually smelled of jasmine flowers, now it smelled of dust and fires. A couple of thousand civilians remained in the city centre. Many were elderly people who had been unable or unwilling to flee; others were families with young children who had not managed to get out while the roads were open.

Sami and his little brother stayed at Muhammed's house, as did Anwar. After a lot of persuasion, they managed to buy a pigeon coop from a reluctant seller. Of the twelve birds, they ate four, which Anwar turned into stew by cooking them with herbs and stock cubes. A couple escaped or were stolen. The rest were killed by alley cats or giant rats – the rats were the worst since they didn't even bother to eat what they killed.

Sami and his friends went around the other houses, scavenging for food. At first they only took food that wouldn't go bad, like rice and flour and tinned goods. They returned for the food they had passed over the first time, then a third and fourth time, until not a trace of rice or shrivelled chickpeas remained. When Sami remembered that some families saved chocolate Christmas decorations, he collected them and gorged himself until he had a stomach cramp.

From time to time, they'd spot a dead turtle with its shell covered in ash. They had once lived in fountains or ponds in people's courtyards. Muhammed, who was as solution-oriented and patient as always, showed them how to use a rock to crush the shell. Sami cringed, thinking of the turtle that had once lived on their roof terrace. Then Anwar took over and cut out the green cartilage and connective tissue on the inside, as carefully as he once rolled a sandwich. After boiling it for a long time, slimy lumps formed, which they ate in silence.

'Doesn't taste that bad, does it?' Muhammed said, trying to cheer them up. 'This would be a delicacy in the old times.'

'I'd prefer a burger and fries,' Malik muttered.

'I'll have your share then,' Sami said and raised his chin.

'No, never mind.'

When Sami was too dejected to take pictures of the destruction, he turned his camera on everyday life. The young children filling water cans on the street. A middle-aged woman breaking wooden chairs into smaller pieces for her fire. The dog man in his wide-brimmed felt hat and white beard, sitting on a wooden chair in the sun, talking to the passers-by. Before the siege, he ran a kennel and would only agree to sell a puppy if the new owners promised to visit occasionally so he could see how the animal was doing.

'Mind if I take a photo?' Sami asked.

'Only from the right.' The dog man turned his head. 'It's my photogenic side.'

Sometimes the camera lens was helpful. It became a shield against reality, something to hide behind. Sami stepped into private rooms he was both part and not part of. One time he saw a missile strike a building and an elderly couple burst out of it at a run. They were covered in grey dust from head to toe. But when they saw Sami and his camera, the woman stopped in the middle of the street and pointed. She wiped her forehead and beamed, because she was about to be photographed and tell the world her home had just been destroyed.

It was the shock, of course. But also a sign of the camera's power. He remembered when, at the start of the revolution, a Japanese photojournalist was lifted up and carried aloft by the protesting masses. Someone from Japan in Syria – it was taken as proof of the world's interest in their plight. Now the images would spread and the world would support the Syrian people.

He had a nebulous feeling the images might not have had the effect they imagined. Or rather that the world chose to see some images but not others. Among the most widely distributed and commented on were the ones showing injured animals. Two horses with flared nostrils and their legs in the air. A cat undergoing surgery for a bullet wound in a field hospital, getting a bandage around its tummy.

A woman wrote to Sami and asked him to follow up what had happened to the poor cat.

Yes, he replied. *I will try to shoot some more.*

No! the woman had replied. *We must save the cats, not shoot them.*

I meant shoot more pictures, Sami wrote.

Before the roads were closed, the activists had managed to smuggle in satellite equipment. Through it, Sami maintained contact with the rest of the world, where life seemed to carry on unchanged. He was primarily interested in news that could affect Syria. In the same spring that Homs became under siege, 2012, Vladimir Putin was re-elected president of Russia and François Hollande became president of

France. Every day, new deaths and massacres in every corner of Syria were reported. The outside world talked about a red line that was supposed never to be crossed, but somehow that line was always moving. A little further away, a little more blurred with time.

During the summer, new battalions were formed within the Free Syrian Army in Homs, each with a couple of hundred rebel soldiers. Some were deserters from the army, others were civilians who wanted to take part in the armed struggle, and each battalion and each leader had their own opinions on how to conduct the struggle.

In order to achieve more cohesive action, a military council was established for the rebel groups in Homs. The Free Syrian Army also ran social charities for distributing food to families with children. In that way, a city within the city was created and people adapted to their new life under siege. No one could leave the fourteen city blocks the regime had surrounded, but within those blocks, everyone was free. They could speak freely, assemble and organize. Sami for his part continued working with the media centre for journalists and activists. They got their electricity from diesel generators, which were still available – most buildings had a back-up diesel tank on the roof, used for heating in the winter.

'Why don't you pick up a gun and join us?' asked Muhammed, who had joined the rebel soldiers.

With a scarf around his head, the crack in his glasses and a nascent beard, his childhood friend now looked like a pirate. It was as though their roles had been reversed. While Muhammed was able to find a calm at the eye of the storm, Sami could feel stress gnawing its way out of his insides. He told Muhammed he was done with weapons and the military.

Instead, he, Anwar and a couple of other media activists started a photo blog on Facebook and Instagram.

'I've never held a camera before,' Anwar said, 'but I need something to focus on.'

In a way, cooking and photographing had something in common, Anwar argued. Both were about capturing the moment. To create the perfect food or perfect picture, soon to be gone, was to live in the present.

'As long as you don't lose the battery charger,' Sami said.

The everyday pictures seemed to fulfil an insatiable need. They had a hundred followers after one day, five hundred by the end of the week – then thousands. Before long, they reached one hundred thousand followers.

Activists in other cities copied them and started similar blogs under a shared name. The photographs spread and drew comments; international newspapers called for interviews or to license the images. Syrians in exile wanted to see what was happening on their streets and the world wanted to know what everyday life was like in the war zone. The only one who didn't share or comment on his pictures was Sarah, who had also stopped mentioning the revolution in her messages to him. Her texts got shorter and maybe his did too.

Hayati, he wrote. *Khalina nehki?*

Can't talk, Sarah answered. *We're moving again. More tension here now.*

OK, be safe. Miss u.

He knew she was still in Eastern Ghouta, the area outside Damascus where they had lived until now. But all the other details that they used to share, from what they had eaten for breakfast to conversations with friends, fell like sand between their fingers.

While Sami and his Nikon lived under constant threat, he was still much safer than the activists who lived in the regime-controlled neighbourhoods, where they could be monitored and arrested at any moment. Sami thought about Yasmin and felt like a bit of the revolution had died with her – but then the media group declared it was safest to choose a new leader from among the besieged activists, and their choice was Sami.

He delegated but sought to make decisions collectively, often via online chats or video conferences. Sometimes this slowed down the work, but it was important to conduct their business that way, to create democratic micro-structures. If they were making a poster, what should its message be? And which campaign would be more effective, one that called for hunger strikes or one urging people to send letters of protest to their governments? A lot of it was satirical, partly because they themselves felt a need to laugh, partly because it was an effective weapon against power and powerlessness.

Sami had sporadic contact with his parents and older siblings but he was cautious on the phone. Ali was still hiding in al-Waer to avoid conscription, while Hiba lived with their parents at a relative's house in the countryside. On occasion he felt a pang of guilt, but his mum assured him she felt calmer with him and Malik on the inside, protected by the rebels.

'You're the big one now, Sami. You have to look after your little brother.'

'I will. Don't worry about us.'

'And how are Muhammed and his friends doing? I hope they are safe.'

There was a warm undertone to her voice when she talked about the Free Syrian Army, even if she never mentioned their name. Samira would never admit to supporting the revolution, especially not in front of Nabil, but she seemed to dream of a different future. To understand what they were fighting for.

'I heard it's been raining,' she said, which meant the falling rockets.

'I keep myself dry, don't worry. Say hi to Dad.'

Sami didn't tell his parents about the other dangers. You had to pay attention to details, say, the beginnings of chafing on your feet. Sami's trainers were worn out and the sole was flapping loose, so Muhammed had lent him a pair of his shoes. Sami was so busy digging around the debris that he didn't give the fact that the shoes were half a size too small a second thought. The chafing was nothing at first. It started with the skin being worn smooth and slightly wrinkled, like when you've been too vigorous with an eraser on a piece of paper, then it started to swell. The blisters grew and merged, blueish-purple and boil-like. Eventually they burst, oozing with bloody pus.

Sami paid no attention to that either. He was constantly on the move and simply slapped on regular plasters. But the plasters fell off because the wounds were wet, and only then did he notice his feet. The skin on top of them was stippled with holes that wouldn't stop bleeding. He tore up strips of fabric and wrapped them around his feet, swapped his shoes for bigger ones, but they kept bleeding. The chafing didn't heal for weeks. He asked at the field hospital why that was, and the doctor replied: vitamins. Or rather, a vitamin deficiency. That was the first sign of starvation.

Another sign was how challenging it was to think about anything other than food. It would have made sense for his body to forget about the hunger since there was nothing to eat. But his body refused to be reasonable, and he swallowed and thought about food to get the saliva flowing. He heard about a friend who tied rocks around his stomach to trick his body in thinking he had eaten, as though one weight could stand in for another. There were things the camera couldn't capture; there were wounds that didn't show on the outside.

28

AS THE MONTHS went by and the leaves started falling from the trees, the children learnt where the red line was – the invisible zone where the rebel streets turned into regime-controlled neighbourhoods – and played soccer and other games among the ruins. Sami saw one little girl who wore a necklace made of empty cartridges. He saw a little boy standing by the bare foundations of a building, red cheeks under his knitted cap, holding a plastic camera, the kind you might have bought at a carnival for nothing and change.

'What are you doing?'

'Documenting,' the boy said without looking up.

'That can be dangerous, you know. They might think you're working for us activists.'

'I don't care, he's a duck. Bashar *al-batta*. He destroyed our house and the whole world's going to see it.'

Sami bent down to hug the boy but he kicked him in the shins and ran off. Sami stayed where he was, studying what was left of the house, when he spotted something bright red among the debris. He carefully moved closer and picked up a toy tractor, polished it with his sleeve and put it down on the wet ground, in case the little boy came back.

It was Leyla's idea to start a school in the besieged area. Like Sami, Leyla was working at the media centre and was one of the activists who never seemed to sleep. There was always something more to do, someone to help. Leyla was a couple of years older than Sami and reminded him of his sister, not least because she was so stubborn. And Leyla seemed to see a sibling in him, too.

'I might adopt you as my little brother. Would you mind?'

Her face was serious and her eyes sad, and there was a scar on her left eyebrow that she never explained. Before the war started, Leyla had been studying philosophy and literature at the university, but her idea for a school didn't come from a moral and ethical angle. She said it was for the children, that they were bored and had nothing to do. They needed something more constructive than playing among the ruins, where they were targets.

'I don't even like children,' Sami said.

'But you don't dislike them?'

Underneath Leyla's mild voice and gentle gestures was a core of pure steel. She put her hands in the pockets of her lined coat and fixed her gaze intently on him.

'I don't have the patience to teach,' Sami said.

'You could at least try, it's only temporary.'

She wrapped her scarf around her neck and it was settled.

He didn't learn much about Leyla or her family except that they were Druze and came from the Golan Heights in southwestern Syria, the area annexed by Israel in the 1980s. The Heights sloped steeply down towards the Sea of Galilee, which was one of the specific flashpoints between the two countries, in addition to the area's general strategic importance. Syria wanted Israel to pull back from the shores of the lake, but it was one of Israel's most important sources of fresh water.

Sami knew the Druze didn't believe in predetermination. God had given humans the intelligence to choose and act freely, and it was their responsibility to shape their society and living conditions to suit the divine purpose. Maybe this was her way of doing it.

Sami would have loved to ask Leyla more questions but she disliked talking about herself and her background. Moving to a big city had been a way for her to have more freedom and room to act. Once she had told him all the choices we make are based on either love or fear. Sami pondered that for a long time. The Druze were not supposed to marry outside their religion. Maybe she had met someone her family considered inappropriate? He didn't know her well enough to ask.

Instead, Sami told Leyla about Sarah, expecting a certain level of interest or curiosity on her part. He thought the two of them would have got on well, felt they had a number of things in common, what with their passion for poetry and pedagogy. But Leyla asked no questions.

'So she left,' was all she said.

Sami wanted to defend Sarah – it was the ones who had stayed who were being selfish. People like him, who didn't think of how the separation would affect his family. Without taking into account that being apart from each other might be worse than any risk outside the siege. But Leyla didn't see it that way. She was going to stay with the children until the last bomb had fallen.

'First of all, we need to find a place to have the school.'

'I'll ask around,' Sami said.

So far Leyla had been tutoring in people's homes but she wanted to find a place where more children could participate. They found the solution with a man who distributed food rations to families. He offered to let them use his house in the mornings, as long as they kept it neat and tidy. Sami and Leyla printed up a couple of flyers and handed them out, and the man helped spread the news while he handed out rations.

The school was small but would do for now. It consisted of a big living room with a wood-fired stove that would keep the children warm. Sami and Leyla arranged the sofas in a semi-circle and put a big notepad up on the wall. Books, pens and notepads were collected from a bombed-out school nearby.

The day before the first day of school, Sami felt noticeably restless. He swept the thick carpets, even though this had already been done. Put books out on the sofas, gathered them back up and put them back out again. He opened the windows to air the room; a thin layer of powder snow had fallen in the courtyard, settling on the remaining leaves on the lemon tree. Leyla was sitting cross-legged, mapping out the week's lessons. She was planning to review the alphabet and assess the level of the students. He had no plan other than the task Leyla had given him: to teach the children mathematics and English.

'Would you calm down, please.'

Sami had reorganized his papers for the fourth time and accidentally knocked over a jar of colouring pencils. Much as he tried to suppress certain memories, the smallest detail was enough to bring them back. His breathing was shallow as he stood staring at the rainbow of pencils in his hand. The engraved letters: Faber-Castell.

'What if no one shows up?'

'They'll be here,' Leyla said calmly.

The next morning he shaved for the first time in weeks, and washed and combed his hair. The frosty streets were teeming with people. He was in a hurry and tapped a woman on the shoulder. She was holding a child in each hand, a girl with a side plait and a boy with an unruly fringe.

'What happened?'

'Something happened?' The woman stopped dead in the middle of the road while the girl tugged her sleeve.

'Mummy, hurry, we're going to be late.'

'I didn't mean to scare you, it's just so busy today.'

'Oh, it's the children, you know. They've opened a school in the area. Can you imagine? It's been almost a year since my daughter last went to school. She had only just learnt to read and my son never even started.'

Sami thanked her and continued at a brisk pace to the school house. Leyla was already standing at the gate, greeting people. She held her hand out to the children first, then their parents.

191

'Amin,' said the little boy he had just met.

'Mona,' said his older sister with the plait.

In the end the courtyard was so crowded they had to ask the parents to leave. *Come back at two, we'll look after them until then. See you soon, sweetheart, be a good boy and make your parents proud. Just leave, Dad, I'm fine by myself. There, there, I'll help you with your homework tonight. You are going to give them homework, aren't you, sir?*

Sami was taken aback but Leyla came to his aid.

'There might be homework,' she said. 'But the most important thing right now is to build routines and encourage the children's desire to learn. Don't you think?'

When the parents had left, twenty-four children remained in the courtyard. Leyla started things off with a game where the children had to line up in order of age. Mona raised her hand.

'But, miss, how are we supposed to know who's oldest?'

'I guess you'll have to ask each other.'

So the children turned to each other and asked about birthdays and soon the ice was broken. After much laughter and giggling, they had formed a line, with the little boy called Amin first.

'And how old are you?' Leyla asked.

'Five and three-quarters, miss,' Amin said, with his arms pressed stiffly to his sides.

Leyla divided the children into two groups, with the youngest students, from five to eight, in one. The younger group went into the classroom with Leyla while the older students, from nine to twelve, stayed with Sami in the courtyard for physical exercise. In the afternoon, it was Sami's turn to teach inside, first the older group, then the younger, by the heat of the stove.

We've started a school, he wrote to Sarah. *The kids call me Mister Teacher, can u believe it?*

For the first time in a long while, she texted a heart.

Mister Sami, it suits u. Bahebak kteer.
I love u too, he answered.

The next winter morning, there were thirty children in the courtyard. At the end of the week, closer to fifty. At first, Sami yelled at them when they fought or talked during class. But then he realized they were bored and viewed school as a break when they could see their friends. War was not constant battles, there were periods of tedium. At the end of the day, the children growing restless and playing was a good sign – better that than the apathetic look he had noticed in some children's eyes.

Sami changed tactics and practised patience, giving them space to both play and learn new things. Mona and Amin were among the hardest-working students, shy but always helpful.

However, external circumstances made teaching more challenging. The regime's airstrikes began with a couple of reconnaissance planes. Then the planes returned, circled above them and released their bombs. While the shells from mortars could weigh up to five pounds, the airdropped bombs were ten times bigger. The ground rumbled for miles. Smoke rose in mushroom-like clouds. During the airstrikes, hiding in a basement wasn't an option; the bombs obliterated everything in their path.

If it was the Free Syrian Army the regime was targeting, the aerial assaults were not particularly helpful. The rebels cleaved to the red line, while the bombs were dropped over the city centre, where the civilians lived. Bombs aimed at the red line would have risked hitting the regime's headquarters, since their strike radius was at least three-quarters of a mile.

Sami and Leyla continued to document events when they weren't teaching. Leyla filmed and painted murals, believing art to be a way of reclaiming the city. *Our hearts belong here,* she wrote. *We're going to return.* Sometimes she painted flowers and animals so the children would have something comforting to look at.

In an interview, much later, he heard Leyla describe her work. Body parts were the hardest things to film, she said. The man looking for a hand among the debris. The boy staring straight into the camera, in shock, not realizing he had lost a foot. The suffering of the animals was difficult, too. Limping pigeons and dogs without hind legs. The cats that gave in to hunger and ate human corpses. A porcelain cup could be devastating. Sitting on a table, waiting to be drunk from, no one coming to pick it up.

Sami agreed that the remnants of everyday life were unbearable. The children's coats on the hooks, covered in dust, in the empty houses where they were looking for food. School backpacks, workbooks and felt-tip pens. Death was ever-present, breathing in their stead, an endless wait. When it stepped in and snatched away a life, it left a black hole that was soon filled with more waiting.

Even so, the airstrikes, too, became a sort of routine, predictable: twice or three times a week the aeroplanes approached. You had to do your errands at the right time of day, in the right place, and keep an eye out for scouting drones.

They tried to continue teaching as usual despite the airstrikes, to distract their students from the world around them. To let the classroom be a reminder of what everyday life used to be. But it was only possible up to a point. Even if the school remained a haven, they couldn't protect the children for ever.

In the last days of January 2013, after taking pictures in the area, Sami ran into two of the children from school, Mona and Amin. The snow had melted and they were playing next to a blocked-off intersection near their house.

'Look at my bike,' Amin said proudly and climbed on the saddle.

'What do you mean, your bike? It's our bike,' said his big sister.

'That's great. Where did you find it?'

They pointed in unison at a house whose façade had collapsed.

'OK, but it's dangerous in there. Bricks can come loose and fall down.'

'How much does a brick hurt?' Amin asked.

'It depends on how big it is, obviously,' Mona told him.

While they argued about the brick and who should have first go on the bike, Sami got out his camera. It was the hour before sunset and everything was golden. The evening light was filtered through the spokes, drawing lines of shadow on the asphalt.

'Take our picture,' Amin said and leaned one arm on the handlebar.

Mona picked up a white kitten with a black tail, which had come to them in hope for food. Sami snapped a few pictures and said it was getting late; their parents were probably waiting for them.

'We're just going to play for a bit longer, sir.'

The mortar shell hit half an hour later.

The shockwave had broken the windows in the adjacent buildings and no people could be seen in the concrete cloud that rose after the explosion. Searching the debris, they found the bike, whose red lacquer finish was blanketed by grey dust. Then they found Mona's shoes, next to her braid with the pink hair tie. Amin's body was warm when they dug it out, his jeans soaked with urine.

Their father cried when he saw the picture Sami had taken of the children, the moment when everything was still possible. When the black and white cat was trying to wriggle out of Mona's arms. When Amin was balancing on the tall saddle with his tiptoes on the ground.

'Is there anything I can do?'

The children's father shook his head.

'Post the picture. Let the world see.'

Sami thought about Nizar Qabbani, who had written about his wife's death and expressed his grief and rage in poetry, in a poem that had outlived its author. But to what avail? It was still just words, as meaningless as the verses his grandmother had sung to him when he fell off his bike and broke his finger a long time ago. A life was a life. It could never be recreated in words or pictures.

Leyla told the other students about Mona and Amin's death. She said there was a fixed number of souls on this Earth and when someone dies a metamorphosis takes place, through which the soul from the deceased passes to a newborn baby.

'Where did you get that from?' Sami asked her afterwards.

'It was something my parents used to tell me,' Leyla said.

'Do you really think that's how it works?'

'What does it matter what I think? What matters is what the children think.'

29

'WHERE DID IT hit? Around yours?'

'No. And you, is everyone on your street OK?'

Sami let out a sigh of relief when he heard Leyla's voice but then they fell silent. Someone else had been hit instead, in one of the myriad airstrikes that had finally forced them to close the school, in the beginning of summer. Someone else was lying in the dark, staring up at a ray of light and a corner of blue sky, a window in the debris.

He ran outside and forgot for a moment where he was going. There, the silvery cypress trees. There, the sun shimmering over the rooftops, over the houses that still had rooftops. There, the wooden fence and, behind the fence, the park with its swings and patch of greenery. Sami had played there as a child, swinging higher and higher until he almost reached the sky. One time Sami had challenged his little brother to jump from the top, after he himself had made a perfect landing in the dust. Malik tried and scraped both knees, and Sami made him promise not to tell their mum. But even though Malik was hurt, he was the one who joked about it, so Sami wouldn't feel bad.

'Better practise,' Malik said and dusted off his wobbly knees.

'Practise for what?'

'For when God throws us out of heaven.'

'Don't worry,' Sami laughed. 'You'll go to paradise, I'm going to hell.'

'Yeah, I know. But someone should keep you company, right?'

Other times, Sami and Muhammed used to go to the playground in the evenings, sharing a cigarette, his friend's pale face and curly hair illuminated by the soft glow. All this seemed so long ago.

Sami took a step forward and felt a pain rise when his foot hit a brick. That was when he remembered – the missile.

After helping to dig out the dead, they buried the bodies in the former playground. Sami recognized one of the women he had seen as recently as the week before. She had been hiding in a stairwell, kissing a rebel soldier she had met at a checkpoint. She wore the same red headscarf now as they put her in the ground.

That night, Sami and Malik made a fire to cook soup, and the next day Sami went out and chopped down the fence by the playground. He didn't know why he hadn't thought of it before; the fence was dry and old and would burn well.

Sami chopped wood once or twice a day, usually at dawn before the airstrikes began. It might be old chairs, kitchen tables or thick limbs from damaged trees. Every other or every third day he scavenged for food, usually after a bomb raid when there was reason to expect a moment's peace.

The mortar shells, on the other hand, rained down on them both day and night. Sami brought his camera and took pictures, then returned before nightfall and hung out with friends until late.

He felt both relief and sorrow when the room began to grow lighter. It was all going to start over again. The future was narrowing until it was no wider than the barrel of a rifle.

I dunno if u were brave or crazy to stay, Sarah wrote.

Neither, he answered. *I was feeling guilty.*

But guilty over what, exactly? That he hadn't done enough or that he'd done too much? Or guilty to have survived so far, when so many others hadn't?

◆

After a while, Sami forgot his own smell. He reeked in the heat but there was no way of differentiating his own body odour from the smell of dirty and unwashed clothes. Sami washed when he could, but the choice between drinking water and clean clothes was a no-brainer. He boiled the water to kill the worst of the bacteria but his bowels were chronically unsettled.

It might have been the food they ate. Rice that had lain on the floor of bombed-out shops for over a year was collected and rinsed. Unripe fruit was eaten, peel and all. 'Bread' consisted of wheat husks they did their best to separate from rat droppings, glass and stones, kneaded together and baked over embers.

'One day, we'll be eating rats,' Muhammed said.

That was the line in the sand; the day they had to eat rats, it was over. Sami couldn't bring himself to eat cat either. At the start of the siege, when there was still food to be found, he had given the stray cats expired tins of tuna. They still gathered outside his door and meowed when they saw him, long after he had stopped feeding them.

One time, he saw a man aiming into the foliage of a tree.

'Shh,' the man said and looked up at two almond-shaped pupils.

'Shame on you, you can't shoot a defenceless cat.'

'My stomach's not ashamed. Would you prefer I shoot you? Great, now it got away.'

During another one of his careful walks, Sami heard his name being called from across the street. He looked up and couldn't believe his eyes. It was Younes, the electrician who had been arrested shortly after the raid on their IT company.

Four years had passed since they last saw each other. Sami looked around and dashed across the street, and Younes embraced him. It really was him. And he looked the same, if skinnier and with his hair grown out and a scar across his forehead. There had been no trial, Younes said. They asked questions about Esther, his half-French girlfriend in Tel Aviv, and his work for the IT company, and then they read out the sentence: terrorist and spy for Israel. He was taken to a prison outside Aleppo and subjected to torture. The scar on his fore-head was from a cable. His back looked even worse, he said. He thought he would die in his cell, as so many prisoners had done before him. But then, one day, he heard the sounds of gunfire and explosions and unfamiliar footsteps in the hallway. The Free Syrian Army had taken over the prison. They spent a week going through the prisoners' files, then Younes and other people they considered innocent were released.

'And now you're here,' Sami said.

'This is freer than I've been in four years.'

Younes carried a belt of cartridges over his chest and said he had joined the Free Syrian Army. He didn't have to pretend his street style any more, Sami thought.

'And Esther?'

The same moment he asked, he regretted it. What were the chances of them staying in contact over the years? But Younes smiled.

'She's good. We keep in touch. She was the first one I contacted when I came out of prison.'

A couple of days later, on Muhammed's birthday, Sami invited Younes for dinner. On the menu was, incredibly enough, pancake. Muhammed had managed to buy a batch of flour from a regime soldier – on a few occasions during the siege, a temporary smuggle path would open across the red line. Buying food from the enemy didn't make sense but he was a good contact and Muhammed trusted him.

They gathered on the sagging sofas. There was Sami and his little brother, who had turned fifteen and didn't seem so little any more. Younes was half lying on the couch, texting someone and smiling. Leyla, with her scarf tied round her head, talked with Anwar about opening a new school in the besieged area.

And there was Muhammed, who was the chef for this special occa-sion. He wrapped his scarf like an apron around his thin waist and borrowed Anwar's bandana to keep the curls from his face, and started cooking. Flour, water and oil. The smell was heavenly, bordering on magical. Their lips turned greasy and their cheeks rosy. They laughed and talked about what Muhammed should make with the rest of the flour. Round, fluffy *khobz* to fill with hummus. A sponge cake stuffed with nuts or fruit. Such wild wishes.

They ate until their stomachs ached, everyone except Malik, who was running a fever and had lost his appetite. They played poker for the last piece of pancake. Anwar won and devoured the last few bites while they enviously looked on. Sami licked his plate and felt a touch of vertigo.

Then they all went silent and watched Muhammed's hand move towards his breast pocket. He pulled out a packet of Winston Blue and shook out the miracle: a cigarette. Not a cigarette rolled out of newspaper or a torn-out book page, filled with tobacco extracted from butts picked out of bins or hoover bags. Not dried grass, leaves or whatever else you could smoke to pass the time and quell your hunger. No, a real, American cigarette.

Muhammed took the first drag, which was only right. They watched the blue flame of the match, watched the fire take hold in the paper and reach the tobacco. His lips closed around the filter, he breathed in and exhaled the first of the smoke. Then it was Sami's turn. He pulled smoke into his lungs until his eyes watered – the room suddenly seemed to be moving, as though they were on a ship – and exhaled. They all monitored each other as they took their turns. Millimetre by millimetre, the glow moved up towards the filter, until it fizzled out.

That night, the nightmare began. The cramps came in waves, pulsing like electric shocks through his body. Sami put a plastic bucket next to the sofa and threw up into it until his dizziness had abated. By morning, his blanket was wet and he hadn't slept a wink. Eventually, sheer exhaustion pulled him into a deep sleep.

When he woke up, night had fallen. The cramps had subsided but his body was stiff and empty. His little brother was sitting on the edge of his bed, dabbing his forehead.

'The others have been at the field hospital all night,' Malik told him. 'The doctors say Anwar almost died.'

Sami leaned over the bucket but nothing more came up.

'How are you doing yourself?' he asked his little brother.

'It was lucky that I wasn't so hungry.'

Malik's eyes seemed larger than ever, sunken in their holes, in the yellowish skin. Sami had a sudden feeling of wanting to embrace his little brother, but didn't. Instead he cursed himself for taking such an unnecessary risk. Food from the regime, what were they thinking? What would happen to Malik if Sami wasn't there?

'Come on now,' Malik said, helping him to stand up. 'Let's take you to the hospital.'

'Where have you been?' a doctor asked when he finally made it to the field hospital. 'You're lucky you all shared your friend's food, otherwise you wouldn't have made it.'

'What was in the flour?' Malik asked, since Sami could barely speak.

'Probably arsenic,' the doctor replied.

On the way out, they passed a room with eight more people, all with stomach pains. It turned out Muhammed had been kind enough to make a pancake for their next-door neighbours. He himself was lying on one of the gurneys, writhing in pain, his curly hair flat with sweat.

To get their friends' strength back, Sami sent his brother out to buy a kilo of honey on the black market, even though he loathed the men who made money off the war. They were people who avoided taking sides, who only cultivated contacts to further their business interests. Who hoarded food until people's hunger peaked and then sold tinned goods to the highest bidder. The honey went for the equivalent of three hundred pounds, while a kilo of tobacco was two thousand and rarely available at all.

But the honey did them good. It lasted two weeks, and gave Sami enough energy to move further than a hundred yards without stopping for a rest.

Sami had barely recovered from the poisoning when he was asked by a healthcare worker to come back into hospital.

'Hurry, come over.'

There had been one large field hospital and two smaller ones, until one of them was bombed. After that, one big hospital and one small hospital remained. The smaller field hospital was housed on the ground floor of a private residence and had five beds. It was always chaotic; people smoked and shouted at each other, and the staff worked in wellies because there was so much blood. As soon as a patient's most acute injuries had been seen to, he or she had to leave to make room for incoming ones.

The larger field hospital had twenty beds and a couple of trained doctors, a few medical students and a veterinarian. There was also a self-taught mechanic who had learnt how to extract bullets and suture wounds – sometimes people jokingly referred to him as the doctor. The hospital was located in al-Hamidiyah and under constant attack. But as it was housed in the basement of a former office building, it was as safe a place as any other.

A thick smell of blood and disinfectant greeted him. At the start of the siege, there had been morphine and drugs of all kinds, but now the stores were empty and most surgeries were performed without anaesthetic. A young woman on a gurney propped herself up on her elbow and asked Sami to hold her newborn child while she got to her feet. He held the infant girl in his arms; she couldn't have been more than an hour old and was no bigger than a kitten. The woman took her baby and thanked him, and Sami took her place in the hospital bed.

He was pricked in the arm and studied the bar fridge they stored the blood in. After a while, the medic patted the half-filled bag and said that was enough for today.

'You probably need to recover for a bit longer.'

Sami continued to take pictures and chop wood. It saddened him to see people chopping down the healthy trees. The trees had spent so many years growing and now they were cut down with a few well-aimed strokes of an axe, even though they were much too fresh and damp to even make good fuel. Some of the trunks bore traces of hand-carved hearts and names of long-forgotten lovers. Maybe there was a tree trunk that said *Sarah and Sami*, which was just now being thrown on the embers and turned into sparks and heat.

30

THE SKY HAD taken on new meanings. Clear blue meant good visibility for the pilots, overcast meant impending rain and a chance to gather water in tubs.

The siege of Homs had lasted more than a year. As time wore on, the conflicts between different leaders became more conspicuous. Sami and the other media activists formed a union to strengthen their voice relative to the military council.

In the autumn of 2013, Muhammed asked Sami and Anwar if they wanted to follow the rebels on a raid. The soldiers usually filmed themselves with their mobiles, but those images were used for propaganda and to strengthen morale among the rebel troops. Sami and Anwar, on the other hand, would be able to document the battle as it was, without embellishing.

Several of the rebels were hesitant, but thanks to Muhammed's powers of persuasion they were given the green light. It was going to be a night raid, an attempt at taking over one of the regime's most important outposts in the Qarabis neighbourhood: a clutch of high-rises that before the war was home to families but was now occupied by two hundred regime soldiers.

Malik asked Sami if he could join but Sami had to draw the line somewhere.

'Don't even think about it. You'll stay here.'

The attack was launched before dawn. It was the hour between night and day, the hour during which Sami often woke up with his heart in his mouth, unable to go back to sleep. Now he was wide awake and hard on the heels of the winding line of rebel soldiers. Nearly two hundred young men were going in and a similar number were waiting as backup above ground. Muhammed and another soldier lifted the heavy manhole cover. A black hole opened up, darker than the night around them. The soldiers climbed down first; Anwar and Sami followed.

Sami was grateful he had nothing but his video camera to carry. The smooth iron railings soon grew slippery and slick with mud and the tunnel went on and on.

'Halfway now,' Anwar whispered, almost out of breath.

If it hadn't been for the last months' lack of food, Anwar would have had difficulty getting through the tunnel. He still had some trouble, however, due to his extra luggage: a Kalashnikov on his back and two hand grenades in his pockets, in addition to the camera. Anwar was a media activist but his attitude to guns differed from Sami's. Neither one of them had a helmet or bulletproof vest.

They had to lower themselves down the last few yards. Jumping would have made too much noise, risking their covert operation. Sami landed in water. The damp climbed up his jeans and the cold spread through his body but he had no time to focus on it because the FSA soldiers were already continuing down the tunnel. One group had turned left, while most seemed to be turning right. Anwar nodded to the left and he followed.

They had a flashlight but wanted to preserve the batteries so they only turned it on when they had to. The first time Anwar lit up the tunnel, Sami saw the backs of the soldiers in front of him. The second time, he squatted down to tie his laces. The third time they turned the light on, the soldiers were gone. The flashlight flickered across the walls without revealing a single clue.

Sami and Anwar waded on, their backs tense from crouching, then the tunnel split, the ceiling rose and they could straighten up. Anwar sighed with relief. A faint light was trickling in from somewhere.

'Where did they go?' Sami said. 'Should we stop and . . .'

He was interrupted by the rat-tat-tat of a few rapid rifle rounds that hit the tunnel wall right next to them. Anwar backed into Sami, who tripped in the water but managed to regain his footing. More bullets whistled past, closer this time. Anwar was breathing heavily in his ear.

'Are you hit?'

'Shh!'

A new volley of shots, a few inches from their bodies. They pressed in closer to each other. Sami groped at the damp walls to find a way further into the tunnel when he realized – there was no way in. They hadn't backed into an adjoining tunnel but an alcove in the same one. They were in a dead end.

'Come on out, rats! We know you're in there.'

Judging from their voices, it was two or three regime soldiers in an access shaft about fifty feet down the tunnel. Sami and Anwar didn't dare use the flashlight so it was impossible to pinpoint their location. The two of them barely fitted in the alcove but there was just enough room for them to hide.

'Do you have your rifle?' Sami whispered.

Anwar nodded, sweating under his bandana.

'But there are only four bullets in it . . .'

Just then new rounds were fired from the opposite direction. It seemed there was an access shaft there too, about 150 feet away. After a while, Sami could make out another two voices. They were under attack from both directions and had nowhere to go. Anwar pulled a chain from under his shirt and kissed a ring.

'You're engaged. I didn't know,' Sami breathed.

'Was,' Anwar replied. 'She lived in Karm al-Zeitoun.'

Sami pictured Sarah's face in the dark. What was he doing here? Why hadn't he listened and left while he still could? The tunnel was dark, silent and damp; the only sound was from the soldiers climbing up and down. The soldiers seemed nervous about what was happening above ground, and at the same time scared of going into the tunnel. Their fear was Sami and Anwar's only hope.

Should they lean out and take aim? But in which direction, and what chance would they have of hitting anyone? Even if they managed to catch a glimpse of a soldier in one of the passages, they would also be abandoning their cover. The same was true of the two hand grenades; the chance of hitting anyone was minimal and the person throwing it would be exposed, if only for a second. No, they were going to hold on to the grenades as a final resort if the soldiers stepped out of the access shaft and into the tunnel.

Sami messaged Muhammed, trying to describe where they were. At the same time, they were straining to listen to the above-ground battle, if it was coming closer or moving away from them. If the rebels were advancing, that could be bad, too, since the regime soldiers would have nowhere to go but down the tunnels, towards Sami and Anwar. That would be the end.

Anwar turned on the video camera. It was recording when they heard one of the regime soldiers shout, 'So it's freedom you want? I'll show you freedom!'

A sharp white light lit up the tunnel. Sami was thrown into the wall as though he had received a blow to the head. Grenade shrapnel landed a few metres from them but not a fragment reached their hideout. Sami's ears rang and howled, his face was cold and wet. There was mud in his mouth but the only thing he could think about was where he had put his phone. He looked around and trod the water, until he realized he was still clutching the phone tightly in his hand.

Further down the tunnel, another grenade exploded. His head pounded, there was a rushing in his ears. He felt exhausted, as though he wanted to lie down and sleep. Anwar's lips moved but he couldn't understand him. He looked distractedly at his arms and hands as though it was the first time he had seen arms and hands. Anwar grabbed him and pointed at the water and he understood what was

208

going on. The water was up to his knees. It was rising slowly but steadily. When the regime soldiers had realized how the rebels were getting in, they must have turned on the water to force them out of the tunnel.

Sami was sweating and shaking and trying hard not to vomit. The only reason the regime soldiers were not climbing down into the tunnel had to be that they were afraid to get caught in a trap. Time passed differently in the alcove, where a second was an hour and an hour was a lifetime.

His phone lit up. Muhammed.

Soon in position. Pick u up when mission completed.

They had probably reached the regime stronghold. The rebels' tactic was to return to the same tunnel entrance they had set out from, which meant Sami and Anwar had to wait. His phone lit up again.

Hold on.

Like they had a choice. The regime soldiers climbed up and down in the two access shafts but they never stepped into the tunnel proper. They fired at the alcove from time to time and threw four hand grenades, all of which missed them.

Above ground, the battle was drawing closer. Sami, deafened by the explosions, could none the less hear the sound of gunfire. But when he saw Anwar's lips moving, it was as though the sounds were echoing up from the bottom of the ocean.

It was some time in the middle of the day that the guns fell silent and Muhammed wrote to say it was safe for them to climb up. Trembling, Sami waded down the tunnel behind Anwar to the access shaft from which the regime soldiers had been shooting at them for hours. He heaved himself up and started the long climb back into the sunshine.

The light hurt his eyes when he stepped out in a daze on to the battlefield. A white haze of smoke and dust surrounded him. He took a step and caught his foot on something, a bloody corpse in his path. A squatting rebel soldier was taking aim in the fog and signalling for him to get out of there. But Sami stayed where he was, frozen. He took out the camera and polished the lens and looked at the buttons, unable to remember how it worked. What was he holding? From the smoky mist, he saw Muhammed come running towards him; he grabbed Sami and Anwar by the arms and pulled them to safety.

As evening fell, the fighting died down. A grey dusk swept in between the buildings and for a moment Sami was unsure if it had all really happened. But when the bodies were lined up, it became impossible to deny. Around fifty regime soldiers had been killed, fifteen or so rebels. And thirty of the regime's men had been taken prisoner.

It took several days for Sami's hearing to return, and a monotonous beeping lingered. He started writing to Sarah, apologizing for staying, for not leaving with her. But when he was about to hit *Send*, he changed his mind and deleted the message. It made no difference now.

The action led to a gruesome aftermath that tarnished the Free Syrian Army in his eyes, even though far from all the rebels were involved. The rebels' military council had been sceptical about the al-Qarabis mission from the start. It was considered too dangerous. Afterwards, the rebels edited together a propaganda film with religious overtones that the military council considered inappropriate, and banned. But someone shared it on social media anyway, which exacerbated the internal conflicts.

Before the siege, prisoners taken by the rebels had always been detained and then set free in due course. This time it was impossible. They would be a danger to the civilians in the besieged area. It was decided that some of the prisoners would help build a barricade by the red line. Coincidentally, those prisoners managed to escape back to the regime-controlled neighbourhoods, and coincidentally, they all happened to be Alawites, while the remaining twelve prisoners were Sunnis and Christians.

The civilian population was in uproar. Rumours spread in the besieged area that someone on the rebel side had negotiated the release of the Alawite prisoners – that the rebels had colluded with the regime.

One of the Free Syrian Army's battalions in Homs proposed doing something drastic to calm the angry populace: the execution of the remaining twelve prisoners. A clear signal to the regime, which would also serve to regain the trust of the civilians in the area.

The proposal was unanimously rejected by the rebels' military council. But after days of negotiations, opinions shifted. One night in late September, even though the decision was not sanctioned by the military council, the executions were to be performed.

Sami found out an hour before they were to take place. When he reached the square in al-Hamidiyah, he was soaked from the rain. Around twenty soldiers were present; Sami and Anwar were the only media activists.

'You can't take pictures,' ordered the general of the battalion in charge.

Sami's body seized up and he found it hard to think clearly. It didn't need to happen, he was sure of that. There must be other ways to deal with this.

The twelve prisoners were tied up on the ground, face down. The rain was pooling around their bodies. Sami's field of vision narrowed to a tunnel without light.

'I don't want to do this,' said the FSA general. 'They're poor and were forced to fight for the regime against their will. I've talked to them. Several of them are really decent.'

Then he ordered the rebel soldiers to fire.

Two of the soldiers refused and stepped aside. For a few seconds, there was nothing but the sound of automatic fire. Then the general raised his hand, walked over to the mangled bodies and finished off the executions by putting a bullet in each head.

31

EVERYONE FOUND THEIR own way of surviving. Activists outside the siege zone supported them as best they could, by trying to smuggle in medical supplies and paying for satellite phone contracts. Others chose to stay and work for the regime while secretly supporting the resistance, using their connections to warn people about suspected airstrikes or help prisoners out. It required inventiveness and risk-taking, and it could be the difference between life and death.

One elderly man used to buy carp at a market in Homs. When the city centre was surrounded, this market remained open because it was in a regime-controlled neighbourhood. So the man continued to buy his fish, two or three at a time, until one day when he ordered a hundred carp.

'My niece is getting married,' he told the fishmonger, and took a photograph out of his wallet, leaning on his walking stick.

'Mabrouk, ya hajji. May God smile on them and give them many children.'

'Thank you, that's very kind. Do you have children?'

The fishmonger didn't but he hoped he would one day – God willing. Meanwhile, he would sell his fish and save his money to buy a house for his future family to live in.

'So, how many fish did you say?'

'A hundred of the biggest and fattiest you have. And if it's possible . . .' said the elderly man. 'No, never mind, it can't be done.'

'No, do say.'

'I really think it's impossible.'

That made the fishmonger insist, since problems were there to be solved and he was proud of his reputation as one of the city's best fishmongers.

'Since you insist,' the elderly man said at length. 'Fish is best served fresh, as you know, and if I take all the fish now, they're going to go off before the wedding. The best thing would be if they could be delivered fresh, straight to the grill. Then the guests would have the pleasure of seeing them wriggle on the hot coals!'

The fishmonger smiled and asked the elderly man to come back in two days.

Two days later, the fishmonger showed him twenty buckets with five carp in each. The elderly man was happy, overwhelmed. He thanked the fishmonger, paid and wished him all the best in life, both with his house and his future children.

Then the elderly man put the buckets in his car, waited until nightfall, and emptied the fish out in a stream which ran in the direction of the besieged neighbourhoods.

For the starving people on the other side, it really was like being invited to a wedding. Women and men gathered by the stream and fished in the moonlight.

Sami arrived too late, standing with cold water up to his knees for hours without catching a single fish. He pulled his net through the water and from time to time thought he glimpsed a silvery shard of glinting fish scales, but it always turned out to be one of the white stones on the riverbed.

Another idea to help alleviate the starvation, which was never carried out, was to round up a flock of sheep by the red line and shove chillies up their behinds, so the animals would bolt into the besieged area in desperation.

As food stores ran ever lower, the civilian population's patience began to run out and the siege seemed to enter a new phase. The regime was holding them hostage and the rebels had not been able to push them back as promised.

During the year, a group of battle-hardened rebels from the Free Syrian Army left and joined a branch of the terrorist organization al-Qaida, the al-Nusra Front. In Homs, the group was small at first, and unorganized, founded partly out of religious fervour, partly as a result of personal conflicts among the rebel leaders.

One of the members of the al-Nusra Front was called Tareq. He was a former university friend of Sami's, a twenty-four-year-old from one of Homs' more well-to-do families. He had neither lost a loved one nor suffered more from the war than anyone else, but he was prone to taking on the grief of others and considering it his own. It was not uncommon for him to end up in heated discussions with one of the imams who lived in the besieged area. The imam would urge Tareq not to mix politics and religion. The most important thing was to ease people's suffering, not to stoke hatred.

'You're a *kafir*, no better than any other infidel,' Tareq told the imam. 'God is the highest and his will must be reflected in every part of our society.'

Sami continued to meet up with Tareq on occasion, to have tea and talk to him, even though his friend had become an extremist. Socializing was limited under the siege and at least it was a breath of fresh air to have someone to argue with.

'How can you justify violence in the name of religion?' Sami asked.

'What do you mean? People do that all the time,' Tareq countered. 'The American president says "God bless America" and drops bombs on the Middle East. And the rebels are shooting at the regime every day . . .'

'You can't compare the Free Syrian Army's self-defence with a desire to take over the Western world and introduce sharia law.'

'Why not? Muslims are being killed and oppressed. We have to defend ourselves.'

Sami was having tea at Tareq's hideout, a miserable basement with no electricity or water, when Tareq informed him that one of the al-Nusra soldiers was spreading rumours about him. They were saying Sami was an atheist and an infidel, and that he should be taken care of. That usually meant death.

'But I've never even met him,' Sami exclaimed in surprise.

'He's seen your pictures and what you've written about us. You're shaming our leaders.'

'I write about anyone who commits crimes and transgressions, irrespective of their allegiances.'

'Either way, he says you're a bad Muslim.'

Before they could finish the conversation and without pausing to think it over, Sami got up and walked straight to the nearby house of the leader of the al-Nusra. He knocked, was patted down and shown into the living room. The group had about fifteen members in Homs at that point and most of them were gathered there, on sofas around a glowing cast-iron stove.

'What can we do for you, brother?' said their leader, a man in a black kaftan with prayer beads in his hand, who introduced himself as Abu Omar.

'I'm not your brother,' Sami said. 'And that doesn't make me a bad Muslim.'

'There, there, calm down.'

But Sami wouldn't calm down. Things were boiling over inside him. People who claimed to know the Quran should know better than to talk ill of others, especially if you didn't know them. And to create a so-called caliphate, were they out of their minds? How was that supposed to work, when they hadn't even been able to leave their own neighbourhood for over a year? When the regime kept shooting at them and dropping bombs? Non-Muslim lifestyles were hardly the enemy here and not worth starting a war over. Wasn't there enough war to go around anyway?

Sami left the house of the al-Nusra leader without waiting to see their reaction. Later, back at the basement, Tareq laughed and said Abu Omar had taken to task the person who had been spreading the rumours.

'Abu Omar thought you seemed well read. Maybe we should recruit you.'

'Over my dead body,' said Sami.

That would happen sooner or later, death, that is. But for the moment, he and Malik and Muhammed and Anwar were alive.

They had moved the sofas into the basement of Muhammed's house, even though it offered only limited protection against a barrel bomb. Barrel bombs were old oil drums filled with explosives and scrap metal, which scattered in the air like confetti.

The regime had also released sarin gas over Eastern Ghouta, the Damascus suburb where Sarah had grown up. Sarin was heavier than air and sought out low points in the terrain, like basements. Because of that, the nerve gas was especially effective in areas where people had already moved underground to escape the airstrikes.

We're safe, Sarah wrote. *But no word from my cousins yet.*

The longer time went on, the less Sami found the words to express what he felt. Maybe because he hardly felt anything any more.

I wish I was there with you, he finally wrote.

Sami, Malik and Muhammed had consulted the internet and made their own gas masks, even though they would make almost no difference in case of a chemical attack: sarin penetrates the body through the skin as well as the airways. Firebombs filled with napalm and other chemicals were also impossible to protect yourself from. They broke up like a rain of fire, like fireworks, in the pitch-black night.

Sami studied Malik's silent face as he built the gas mask. He tried to remember his little brother from before, sparkling with life, and realized he had adjusted to the situation all too fast, all too well.

There was no room in their lives for the suggestive or ambiguous any more. That was one of the biggest casualties of the war: the grey area. There was warmth and cold, being full and being hungry, friends and enemies – but in between, nothing of any real importance.

And then there was life and death. One day, his little brother was alive. The next, he was dead.

32

THAT OCTOBER MORNING Sami heard birds tweeting. He couldn't remember when he had last heard the sound of birds and thought he
was imagining it. But there, perched on a chair, was a sparrow. Sami
tried to beckon it but the sparrow twitched its head and refused to
budge. Then it spread its wings and flew out of the window.

He didn't know if it was because of the bird but he had a bad feeling
that morning. He didn't normally worry about his little brother, but
when it happened, he knew. He knew it when the doorbell rang and an
acquaintance was standing outside. He knew it when the acquaintance
said Malik was injured and had been taken to the field hospital. And he
knew it when he jogged towards the hospital in fits and starts, as though
he both wanted and didn't want to get there.

A couple of volunteers had put up bunting in the street, the kind
that had been used for parties and weddings before, to help people
find their way to the field hospital. The green and yellow ribbons ran
down ditches, into basements, through private residences where missiles had opened up holes in the walls, up staircases and over boulders.
The acquaintance tried to keep up with Sami. Outside the field hospital, he apologized to Sami for not having told him the whole truth,
then he leaned his hands on his knees and looked down at the ground.

'I'm sorry.'

Sami pushed past him, feeling no desire to be held up by this man when he could simply talk to his brother himself and find out what happened.

Malik was lying on one of the hospital beds, next to Anwar and two other boys. His little brother's body was less bloody than the others, but just as rigid. Anwar's tall body barely fitted the stretcher. He had grown lean in the siege and no longer resembled the healthy chef he once knew.

The heat drained out of the room and a white chill spread from Sami's chest to the rest of his body. He fell to his knees wanting to scream but no scream came out. It was Malik and at the same time it couldn't be him. Sami pulled himself upright again and stroked his brother's cheeks. Flies were buzzing around his eyes, which were white as though his irises had vanished into his body in terror. Maybe this was death's way: to freeze the features that had once made a body into a person.

'What happened to you?' he whispered.

A medic came up to him and told him in a soft voice. Malik, Anwar and the two other boys had gone to a street in al-Hamidiyah to put up cloth screens to block the snipers' view.

'That was when the missile hit. They were crushed under debris.'

Sami thought about his parents. They had thought he and Malik were safe here. At least here, the regime couldn't get to them. Here they couldn't be arrested, tortured or pressed into military service.

But there were missiles, every day.

A medic and two rebel soldiers helped him move the bodies. Sami carried his little brother and put him on a flatbed truck. He sat down next to him and held his hand, stroking his forehead. The truck drove a few blocks and then came to a stop. Sami looked over his shoulders, scanning the roofs for snipers, but all he could see in the sky was a pointlessly shining sun. The ashes and concrete only reflected its light.

It was not easy to find an open patch of ground by the mosque. They had no shovels so they dug with whatever they could find, scraps of metal and bin lids. Sami took his brother's ID card and searched Anwar's pockets, but there was nothing in them to give to his family. Then he remembered the necklace with the gold ring, gently removed it from around Anwar's neck, and carried on digging.

'Do you mind if I take his shoes?'

A skinny boy with streaks of dirt on his face was pointing at Malik's feet.

Sami stood still. Sweat was streaming down his face, or maybe it was tears, and the salt reached his lips. Then he bent down and pulled the shoes off himself.

'Here, they might need to be polished.'

When Sami's grandmother died, Grandpa Faris said, 'When there is nothing left, only rituals remain.' But now, not even rituals remained, at least not in their ancient form. Before the war, an imam would have read verses or said a few words at the funeral. Before the war, a procession of cars would have driven through the city and out to the countryside, either the same day death claimed its victim or the next. The body would have been swathed in white cloth tied at the head and the feet. The family would have hosted a three-day reception, in their home or at a mosque, where friends and relatives could come to offer condolences.

Now they had neither the time nor the ability to organize a procession or reception. The four martyrs – Malik, Anwar and the two boys whose names they didn't know – were lowered into the ground and covered with sand and stones. Dusk fell quietly.

Back at the basement Sami had half a can of water left but didn't want to wash. There was blood on his arms and hands but it was his little brother's blood. He sat on the basement floor, rocking back and forth. He was alone. Muhammed was out doing battle and didn't know what had happened.

When there was a faint but clear knock at the door, Sami was sure it was his brother coming home. He hurried upstairs and took a step back when he saw the three men in black trousers and kaftans. The man at their head was Abu Omar, the leader of the al-Nusra Front, who raised a calming hand.

'We're here to offer our condolences.'

They greeted him with bowed heads, kissing his cheeks, without seeking eye contact.

'I think it would be best if you . . .' Sami was unable to finish the sentence.

'Tea, my brother?'

Abu Omar stepped inside and unpacked a basket on the coffee table. What persuaded Sami to let them stay wasn't the thermos of tea, it was the glass jar full of honey.

After a while, he almost forgot who they were, and that they had threatened to kill him after he published their names and pictures on social media. Abu Omar said that was water under the bridge. And when it came down to it, wasn't a certain level of attention a good thing? It lent them credibility and made it easier for them to spread the word.

'Let's not dwell on the past,' said Abu Omar and put a teaspoon of honey in Sami's teacup.

'Martyrs,' he continued. 'God's sons and daughters who give their lives in the struggle for justice. Innocent teenagers who die for a higher purpose. Is it God's will? Of course not. But things are the way they are.'

The words blurred together. Abu Omar's voice was almost as soothing as the honey.

'Our country is at war and God has his hands full and we have to have faith, and to trust our faith to guide and support us in our darkest hour. Isn't it better to fall in the struggle than to lie down without resisting?'

Abu Omar stroked his beard and counted his prayer beads. His nails were strangely clean, neatly cut and manicured. Abu Omar and the others talked for hours, or so it felt, while Sami listened in silence. At midnight he almost dozed off, sitting on a cushion on the floor, but then he twitched and was suddenly wide awake.

'So,' Abu Omar repeated, 'will you come tomorrow? We have plenty of beds and our house is safe.'

'Yes, or I mean, let me sleep on it.'

When the three men had left, Sami gathered up his things and sent Muhammed a message.

I have to leave. Call u later.

He packed only his laptop, camera and water can, and decided to come back for clothes and cooking utensils later, or find new ones.

When he started to move through the city ruins, his heart eventually stopped racing and he was able to think back over the day before. His little brother hadn't died, it was just a misunderstanding and a mistake. Malik would appear before him any moment.

Had the three jihadists been a bad dream too? Sitting in his flat, talking about martyrdom? Rage surged inside him, caused in equal parts by them forcing themselves on him when he was in the throes of grief, and by it almost succeeding. After hours of talking and ingratiating voices, their words had got under his skin.

Sami tried to conjure a parallel reality in which his little brother was still alive. He heard Malik's voice, and went over the fights they had had and invented new endings, in which instead of standing his ground, he yielded and compromised. What had they even argued about? Silly things, like which movies to watch and who got the most attention from their parents. The stray dog that Malik had brought home to cheer up their mum. When he told Sami that he wanted to work in IT, just like his older brothers, and Sami had said it wouldn't suit him, when what he had meant was that his little brother was too social, too loving, to be stuck in an office. When Malik had chosen to stay at the beginning of the siege, as if he wasn't old enough to make a choice of his own.

He embellished old scenes to make himself less of a big brother scolding and looking for faults, and more of a sibling his little brother could have turned to with questions and problems.

He wished so desperately that he had been better at offering a warm embrace and a shoulder to lean on. But there was nothing in between, no space between the lines to rest in.

33

THE STREET IN Bab Tudmor was deserted. Even the cats had left. That was why he went there: no one would suspect the house to be inhabited. No sane person would ever consider settling there. There was no water or electricity, but the living room and parts of the kitchen and bathroom were intact, and that was where Sami set up camp after Malik's death.

Sami ran his hand over the cracked bathroom mirror and saw his brother. He stroked his brother's cheeks and beard and saw his eyes well up with tears. The reflection trembled but he was still, completely still. He saw his brother lean on the sink and only then did he become aware of his lightheadedness and collapsed on the cool stone floor.

When he woke, he saw the blood. He made a fire, boiled half of the water in his can, undressed and washed his clothes in a bucket. Scooped some of the water over his body and dried himself on a shirt he used as a towel.

His new accommodation had only one major drawback and it was a fundamental one: the house, or what was left of it, virtually touched the red line. Which was to say it was right on the frontline between the regime's army and the rebels. A six-lane motorway separated them; snipers shot at each other round the clock. He didn't have to worry about airstrikes but the Free Syrian Army's presence was weak. The regime's soldiers could at any time sneak across the road to conduct a night raid.

Sami decided to break his promise and buy a gun. Once upon a time Sarah would have been proud of him for daring to join the armed struggle; now it seemed not to matter. Her messages grew ever shorter and more sporadic. She apologized but claimed the power cuts were becoming more frequent, even in the countryside. In the end, Sami couldn't get his hands on a gun anyway. The prices on the black market had soared and he couldn't afford one. The irony was that food on the black market was even more expensive and hard to find.

During the day he lived with the constant sound of gunfire. At night he woke up thinking someone was in the house. He crept round and checked the adjacent rooms and peered out at the nearby houses, but it was just the wind. He lay down on one of the sofas and saw the contours of the room slowly take shape in the dark. He pictured the six-lane motorway and the bodies on it, on the red line, where no one could retrieve them for burial. He didn't believe in jinn, not really, but then there was the soldier who had met a talking cat. What if the spirits were feeling restless and looking for new homes? Maybe one had already taken up residence inside him; maybe he was one of the living dead.

From now on, he was alone. It was too arduous and dangerous to make his way over to Muhammed's or Leyla's. He almost hadn't been able to tell them about Malik's and Anwar's deaths because he knew that as soon as he said the words, it would be real. They would be gone. And when he did finally tell them, Muhammed cried, and it felt like he cried for them both.

Sami spent most of his time inside his newfound house aside from short outings every other or every third day to fill up his water can and look for food and clothes. One time he found a fungus growing on a wooden door. He broke it off and put it in his backpack, pondering whether he dared to eat it. He did. He left it to his stomach to work out whether or not it was edible.

Before, street names and addresses, maps and GPS had been used to navigate. But now the city had changed shape; it had turned into a maze and people had to find other signposts. He could go hours without seeing another person. The concrete had risen up like an iceberg and the city was shrouded in a blanket of ash and dust. Sometimes he had an urge to lick the wall of a building or grab a fistful of the reddish-brown, iron-rich ash and put it in his mouth. The whitish-grey ash, on the other hand, he associated only with death. He had heard it could be used as a natural disinfectant in lieu of soap but he couldn't bring himself to try it.

The dust got in everywhere. Even though he tried to brush down the sofa cushions and keep the rug clean of rat droppings, it was just as dusty again the next morning. The dust crunched under his feet and for a few hours that would be the only sound, aside from distant gunfire.

Sami spent several days setting up a parabola, a satellite receiver and a generator, so he could use his laptop and phone. That autumn he read about a former systems administrator working for the American intelligence service, Edward Snowden, who had revealed the extent of the United States' mass surveillance of its own citizens. Why all the fuss, he had thought at first. Of course the state spied on its citizens. How could it be otherwise? And then he understood. He had internalized surveillance. It had become part of being a citizen. That was the true extent of his government's abuse of power: you monitored yourself even before the state did.

In November 2013, the first snow fell, recalling a different time. The flakes swaddled the wounds of the city like cotton, filling its tears and cracks. It snowed outside the room and the snow fell inside Sami. He was cut off from the world. The streets were empty. One morning he feared his hideout had been discovered when he spotted unknown tracks by the front steps. But then he realized it was just the rats smearing the sludgy ash of his own footsteps.

He might have been the last person in the world. Civilization had been destroyed and the radio stations shut down in a larger war happening outside the one he was in. The Earth had been invaded by aliens or an epidemic had killed large parts of humanity, like in the time of the plague. A volcano had erupted and covered the planet in ash. Except right here, in Homs, where the ash was already so thick humans had learnt to live in the murky air.

He moved through the ruins like someone shipwrecked. Even if he were the last person in the world, he would never know. He would live and die and, with him, humanity would perish, but the Earth would continue its journey around the sun for a little while longer, before it was sucked up by the masses that constituted the universe, leaving behind an everlasting black hole.

The snow kept falling and he needed to find new, warmer clothes. He groped his way in the dark, pulled out dresser drawers and opened wardrobes. He had found two jumpers and a pair of jeans. He was reluctant to enter houses, even though they were abandoned and their owners would hardly mind their clothes and food being put to good use. But it was as though the houses themselves were people, empty and broken by grief. Would they ever be able to return to a time when you could have tea with your neighbour and exchange gossip while the sweet voice of Fairuz filled the background?

Sami's thoughts were interrupted by a familiar and ominous silence. The calm before the strike. He only just had time to throw himself to the floor before the missile struck the house next door. The roaring escalated and the tremors intensified. The walls shook, a heavy object thudded to the floor and then he heard a girl's high-pitched voice from the other side of the room. He looked up in the dark. The girl's monotonous voice made his blood curdle.

'You're a beautiful girl, you're a beautiful girl . . .'

He lay still and listened until the battery in the doll died before daring to get to his feet and gather up his scattered items of clothing. He had to leave; there was no guarantee the next missile wouldn't hit the house he was in – and yet, it was as though he couldn't bring himself to do it. Sami moved towards the window he had first climbed in through, but with each step he felt as though something was trying to hold him back. As though the house wanted to hold on to him, yes, devour him.

A new silence fell. In his head, he could hear the doll's voice ring out after him, hollow like a house without human life. That was when he decided to seek out Muhammed and Leyla after all, before the isolation drove him mad.

34

CHRISTMAS WAS APPROACHING and although Sami didn't celebrate it, he missed the sense of festivity that used to spread through the city, especially in his old neighbourhood, al-Hamidiyah, where many Christian families lived. The streets would be transformed in December, with holly wreaths and tinsel garlands and luxury gifts in the shops.

Sami had celebrated Christmas with Sarah one year. They had dinner with her family and then went to the midnight mass, where they sat close on the wooden bench and held hands, hidden under her Bible.

Both the church bells and minarets had been silent for a long time now, the muezzin no longer calling out for prayer five times a day.

The muezzin was usually chosen for his talent in reciting prayers melodiously or at least – as in Sami's old neighbourhood – loudly. The recitation was a special kind of art that touched everyone who heard it. Not least the *salat*, the dawn prayer just before sunrise, which many woke up to, or half slept through with the words finding their way into their dreams. But the muezzin in al-Hamidiyah had made people put pillows over their heads or turn up the radio. Finally, the priest in the neighbouring church had taken the matter into his own hands and walked over to the mosque to talk to the imam.

'Church bells sound the same regardless of the day,' the priest had said. 'A human voice is another matter . . .'

He didn't want to hurt the imam's feelings, especially since they were colleagues in the matter of religion, but the imam didn't seem to understand.

'You know how people talk,' the priest continued. 'Religion is also a matter of aesthetics.'

The imam fully agreed. 'Content and form can't be distinguished from each other and when they interact at best, the message is . . . elevated.'

'I'm sorry,' the priest finally said, 'but I have to tell you the truth: your muezzin is completely tone-deaf. You'd better change to someone with a better voice to keep your believers.'

Sami smiled at the memory and picked up his phone.

Hey Sarah. What do u want for Christmas?

It took some time before the small screen lit up.

Ask Santa for peace on earth. And chocolate.

His belly rumbled at the thought of food. Right now, between peace and chocolate, the choice would have been easy.

It was both the hunger and the thought of company that drove him out now, on to the dangerous road to Muhammed's house. Muhammed had stayed in his old home and promised he was going to make Sami and Leyla a feast. A phenomenal recipe, he claimed.

The passageways Sami used through houses and cellars were constantly changing whenever new ruins blocked the road. Several of the fabric screens set up to obscure the view of snipers had blown down. In addition, the ground had frozen during the night and he had to take extra care when moving in open spaces.

He arrived at Muhammed's house but barely recognized the building. The rose bushes had been cut down, probably for firewood, and black plastic now covered all the windows.

'My friend.' Muhammed embraced him on the doorstep as if it had been a lifetime since they last saw each other.

'It felt like I lost you at the same time as your little brother and Anwar. How are you?'

'You know.' Sami shrugged, then suddenly noticed the grey wool sweater Muhammed was wearing. 'Is that Malik's?'

'Do you mind that I'm wearing it? It's been difficult to find warm clothes.'

'No, not at all. It was just . . .'

His voice broke and the grief came over him without him being prepared for it. They walked inside and Leyla rose from the couch. She took his hands and kissed his cheeks, her lips cold and her fingers blue. Both she and Muhammed had become thinner since he last saw them. And although Sami was happy that they were all together again, he felt discouraged, because in their empty eyes he saw himself.

'How about your plans to start a new school?' Sami asked.

Leyla sat down heavily. 'It's not possible any more.'

She held out an arm and Sami sat down beside her on the sofa. Muhammed fiddled with a stereo until they could hear quiet music, then took a few steps into the room and declared that they were not under any circumstances to talk about sad things, for this evening was a feast.

'Did Abu Omar ask for me?' Sami interrupted and felt his legs shaking.

Muhammed nodded. 'But don't worry, I said you were dead.'

'Which is almost true. You look like a ghost,' Leyla said.

'You too. Both of you. Which makes this a ghost party, I guess.'

Muhammed raised the volume and Sami recognized the mixed rock classics they had played during the car trips as teenagers.

'Can you remember when you last had a decent meal?' Muhammed asked and waved a wooden spoon in the air.

'I remember the arsenic pancake,' Sami said.

'This is different, I promise. Smell that meat?'

Sami remembered the smell of roast chicken in Karim's restaurant and his mother's lamb stew; he remembered juicy steaks, kebabs and steaming beef *kibbeh*. And this, which Muhammed insisted was meat stew, smelled nothing like meat.

'Are you sure? Have you tried it?' Leyla asked and pulled her scarf tighter around her shoulders.

'It's one hundred per cent animal. You won't be disappointed,' Muhammed reassured her. 'When the revolution is victorious and we're living in a villa by the sea, I'm going to write *A Survivor's Cookbook*. It's going to be a bestseller.'

Their expectations rose dizzyingly. Something akin to saliva moistened their mouths. Sami and Leyla nestled into the sofas; Muhammed handed out bowls. A charred cooking pot sat on a moth-eaten jumper on the coffee table. Muhammed waited for silence, like a magician waiting to pull a rabbit out of his black hat. He lifted the lid. The pot contained a watery, brownish soup with flat rectangles floating in it. Their excitement was dampened somewhat, but they held out their bowls while Muhammed served. Leyla put a spoonful of broth in her mouth.

'You should probably come up with a plan B in case the cookbook thing doesn't work out,' she said.

'It's not that bad, is it? Sami, what do you think?'

He stuck his spoon in the soup and fished out a piece of meat. Sami chewed and thought to himself that it was like chewing a rug. A sheepskin rug, that had spent years on a dirty floor, collecting dust and grime, and then been picked up, rinsed tolerably, cut into squares and boiled for hours.

'Isn't it amazing?' Muhammed said. 'You just cut off the wool and boil the skin for a few hours.'

Sami was surprised to find it was possible to fall short of his expectations. But the so-called meat was in fact inedible. Afterwards they had tea with shaving gel, which gave the beverage a hint of sweetness.

Moments like this cut through the meaninglessness with a metallic white light and almost made him smile. What if anyone could see them there, in the basement, chewing boiled sheepskin? Wasn't it comical, this human existence? How your life contained many lives, layer upon layer, like a nesting doll or an onion? How you never knew what to expect?

Before, he would never have been able to imagine this. The way the rest of the world would never have been able to imagine this, because most people only know about their own lives and one or two generations back. If the world knew this, it wouldn't let it continue, naturally. And so Sami laughed, at the ignorance of other people and at himself, who only now realized that everything he had ever learnt was meaningless. He should have been learning how to make fire and to dress in layers. How to determine whether a plant is poisonous or not. How to find and purify water.

In the before times, he had worried about unfinished homework or a spilled drink. In the before times, he had been able to obsess about a rash word or a rash action. All of that was nothing. Insignificant. It was about finding warmth, shelter and water, in that order.

35

THAT WINTER, THE last one in the siege, brought a white storm in over Homs. The snow rose in plumes of smoke and whipped across the rooftops. The wind howled and whistled through cracks as though the house were an organ. Sami kept the small wood-burning stove lit around the clock. His fingernails were purple and his cuticles black with soot and oil. The sofa was too short to stretch out on; he spent his nights with his legs pulled into his chest, counting the seconds between the rumblings. His hair, which had grown long once more, started to fall out. He slept with two hats on and in the mornings they were full of tufts. He cut it himself with nail scissors but kept part of his beard for warmth.

It was during the protracted blizzard that Sami stopped praying. He had never performed the daily prayers with much dedication; he preferred to pray when he felt a need for it. But now, after burying his little brother, in their hometown, which was no longer theirs, what was there to hope or pray for? Sometimes he felt guilty about the shoes, that he hadn't let his brother keep his shoes.

A gun battle broke out in a nearby house; one half of the building was dominated by the rebel army and the other by regime soldiers. They were so close they could see each other's faces, so close they would be able to recognize an old classmate or neighbour or barber among the enemy, through the bullet holes in the wall.

But it was as though the fighting no longer concerned Sami. He slept and watched reruns of the cooking show *Fatafeat*, a kind of elaborate self-inflicted pain that still gave him some pleasure. Despite his hunger, he knew it wasn't hunger that was going to kill him. It was more likely he would die from dehydration or exposure on a night with sub-zero temperatures, or that a blood infection would eat him up from the inside. And yet, all those thoughts of food. It would be a long time before he could pick the first spring grass and the delicate green leaves of the bushes, and another few weeks after that before the first unripe fruits would appear on the few remaining trees.

The mice were another problem, even though he sometimes appreciated their company. At night, they climbed over his legs and back as though he were part of the sofa, an immobile piece of furniture, already dead. He slept with an arm over his face so he could swat away the most intrusive little tails.

Sometimes Sami wondered what the end of the siege would be like, if there ever was an end. The Free Syrian Army was too weak and fragmented now to resist the regime forces and liberate the city. They could possibly withdraw to one city block and regroup, maintain at least one stronghold. Otherwise, it was likely the army would go in and clear out the city centre.

In the spring of 2014, after drawn-out negotiations between the regime and the UN, there was an opening. The green city buses that people had used before the war now entered the besieged zone to evacuate civilians, but not without restrictions. Any young men were likely to be pressed into service. It was unclear whether there would be an amnesty for people who were wanted by the secret police. As a consequence, the people leaving on the green buses monitored by the UN were mainly women, children and the elderly.

'See you on the other side, little brother?' said Leyla.

They hadn't seen each other since the sheepskin meal with Mu-hammed. Leyla stroked his cheek. It was an unusually tender gesture, but then it might be their last time together. She had stuffed her back-pack full of textbooks, some of whose thick bindings had been hollowed out to hide memory cards.

'Remember what we agreed,' she said.

If he hadn't heard from her in twenty-four hours, she had probably been arrested, and he was supposed to get in touch with his contact at Facebook and ask them to close her account. If she was brought in for questioning by the secret police, she would be forced to tell them her password and thereby put others at risk. By closing the account, they could at least protect other media activists Leyla had been in contact with.

Sami asked her to send his love to his family and to Sarah, if she managed to see them. Leyla climbed on to the bus and waved through the window, but she didn't smile.

The green buses left, as did the UN, and the checkpoints closed behind them. He felt both sadness and relief. Several of the children from their school had also been given a seat on the buses. But not Mona and Amin, whose faces he involuntarily scanned the crowd for.

There was another way out but it could hardly be considered an opening. It consisted of relying on people outside the siege, people who had good connections and could negotiate the passage of their friends. But there were no guarantees. Some managed to get out that way but it was mostly a matter of luck. It only took one sniper not knowing about the negotiation or disapproving of people being let out, or one stray bullet, and it would all be over. There was also the risk of disappearing in the labyrinths of underground jails. To Sami, the odds seemed too long to take the risk.

'I'm doing it,' said Muhammed, who despite his placid nature was growing impatient. He was speaking faster than usual; his nails were chewed to the quick and he had lost more hair than Sami. There must be another way, Sami said to his friend. Wait a few days.

'I've waited long enough.'

When they hugged goodbye, he could feel his friend's ribs.

'Do you know the first thing I'm going to do once I'm free?' Muhammed said. 'Drink a Coca-Cola.'

'Are you serious? Pepsi is so much better.'

Muhammed shook his head and smiled.

'You don't know what you're talking about.'

Sami thought of everything they had been through together. From when they were young, trying to get each other to laugh during the military class at the schoolyard, to the excursions with the Pink Panther, and all the times that Muhammed had got Sami out of danger. Without him, the siege's difficult years would have been even more challenging.

'So, where are you planning to go?' Sami asked.

'Beirut, probably. My cousin has invited me to stay in his flat. You're welcome too, when you get out of this hell-hole.'

'If I get out.'

'Don't talk like that. We are both getting out.'

They stood in silence, neither of them wanting to leave.

'Hey, by the way,' Sami said. 'My parents are going to try to persuade you to testify.'

Muhammed bowed his head. 'You know I can't.'

'I know, and it's fine. That's all I wanted to say.'

It was about his little brother. In order to produce a death certificate for Malik, the regime required two witnesses to testify as to the cause of his death, which was tantamount to admitting you had been in the besieged area and were a rebel sympathizer.

'I'll explain to my parents, they'll understand.'

The two friends said goodbye again, then a fourth time and a fifth.

It was the last time they saw each other.

No one was able to explain to Sami what happened next. Maybe it was a sniper who didn't know Muhammed had negotiated free passage in exchange for leaving the Free Syrian Army and handing over his gun. Maybe it was a bored regime soldier doing target practice. Maybe Muhammed had a change of heart halfway and tried to turn back. Maybe he paused one second too long, a moment of hesitation. Whatever happened, his body now lay on the red line, in no-man's-land, only starving cats daring to approach him, sniffing interestedly.

Sami's deepest grief was not being able to grieve. One by one, they had disappeared from his side. His little brother, Yasmin, Anwar and now Muhammed – soon he would have no one left. He wasn't even there himself. He was a shadow, wandering through ruins.

In April, a third and last route out was offered. This time, the agreement to bus people out of the besieged zone to a town north of Homs had been brokered by the Russians and Iranians, both allies of al-Assad. But Sami would not be safe in that town; he had written negatively about FSA soldiers there. Once again, the green buses arrived and left.

April wore on and the situation became increasingly dire. It was only a matter of time before the regime forced its way in, reclaimed the city centre and purged whoever was left. Sami was still staying in the house near the red line and considered moving to a different street, but then what? It was like being back in that tunnel watching the water rising. Should he have tried to get out on the buses, even though he would have been arrested on the other side? He thought about Younes, the electrician, and how little it took for the regime to brand you as a threat. The cable mark on his forehead, the smallest of visible scars.

He needed someone to talk to about all of this. On occasion, he caught himself saying words or full sentences out loud to his little brother or his childhood friend. The mice squeaked in response and darted about the floor. There was nothing to look forward to; loneliness enveloped him like a blanket. He rarely left his room.

But he had a small quantity of ground coffee beans left, which Muhammed had given him before he attempted the leap across the red line. A good day was a day when Sami could make coffee, had enough tobacco to roll a cigarette and it was warm enough to sit on the roof. He took up a couple of sofa cushions. Turned his face to the sun and studied his garden: a six-by-six-foot patch of sand, rat shit and soil. He had found the radish seeds in an abandoned house. There wasn't time to let the roots grow; he picked the tender leaves and ate them like lettuce.

It was there on the roof that Sami pondered his future and finally concluded that there was only one way out. The way he had already rejected. The way that had claimed Muhammed's life: crossing the red line.

36

IT WAS THE biggest decision of his life. It was not only about escaping the siege. If he succeeded, he would also have to leave the country. To stay in the regime-controlled area would be too dangerous.

Having made his decision, Sami got in touch with a few people who might be able to help him: a distant relative, a childhood acquaintance and a woman he had got to know online through his work as a photographer. They in turn negotiated with people on the regime side.

While he waited, he found lentils. Sami ran his hand over the dusty kitchen counter and gathered them up: twelve pale red lentils. They were tiny, round discs, like miniature versions of doughballs before the baker rolls them flat. He put the lentils in his jacket pocket, scraping the last one from his greasy fingers and pulling the zipper closed. Not today, maybe tomorrow. It was easier to endure the hunger when it was voluntary, when he knew he could make a soup of water and twelve lentils whenever he wanted.

The question was whether he could have eaten if he had decided to make soup. As so often, his worries had lodged themselves in his stomach.

Then he was given the go-ahead, and told a time and a place. After midnight, at a certain corner of Bab Tudmor. The only thing Sami had to do was cross the six-lane motorway; a regime soldier would be waiting for him on the other side. It sounded easy but required high-level strings to be pulled both politically and militarily. Could he really trust that every last soldier watching from rooftops and through cracks in walls was aware he had permission to leave? And what was waiting for him on the other side?

After weighing up all possible scenarios, there was only one way to know for sure: to cross the road and trust that his contacts had done a good job.

Sami closed his social media accounts, put his laptop in a plastic bag and buried it outside the house. He texted his parents and siblings, without telling them what he was about to do. It had been weeks since they last talked; messages didn't use up the battery so fast. He thought about calling them now but was afraid that his voice would give him away. He then wrote to Sarah.

Bahebik kteer. I love you.

But before sending the message, he erased it. It had been too long since they had used those kinds of words and she would only get worried.

I'm thinking about u, he wrote instead.

He waited for an answer but the phone remained silent. Finally he took the SIM card out and broke it. He shook out the sofa cushions and swept the rug, even though he wasn't coming back. And at midnight he left.

The full moon hung high in the warm sky, round and so bright its craters were visible. It spread enough light to guide Sami without him needing a torch. At the same time, the moonlight made him an easier target. He stood in a doorway without a door and listened for strange sounds. Maybe in all of this destruction it was possible to see how the world had been when there were still no people in it. Once, all of this had been under water; once, there had been nothing but mountains and valleys under a scorching sun. Aside from the sound of gunfire and the airstrikes and the stones under his shoes, in the beginning there was only this: silence.

An empty tin can was being pushed along by the wind, rattling out into the road. Half an hour before the appointed time he moved to the front of the building, hiding behind a shot-up car but still able to keep an eye on the road. He had never been this close to the red line before. The car was practically in the line of fire and its metal body was scant protection – bullets would easily pierce it if anyone spotted him.

Sami stiffened. A creaking followed by a muffled curse came from diagonally behind him, up in one of the rebel positions. He hunched down behind the open car door and glanced up. He couldn't see anyone but he heard footsteps receding. It was probably a patrolling FSA soldier. He had warned them he was leaving and hoped they would honour their promise of letting him go.

While waiting for the signal from the other side, he examined the road ahead. Before the revolution it had been one of Homs' busiest thoroughfares, especially during rush hour. In the moonlit night it looked like a tsunami had crashed over it – car parts, tree limbs and blocks of concrete covered the asphalt like ancient beasts. Weeds grew out of every crack.

There were other shapes too: twisted, cramping. The bodies had reached various stages of decomposition. A few feet away lay a pile of what looked like clothes that concealed the skeleton of someone who must have been killed during the earliest days of the siege. Further on was a fresh body emitting a stench of dead flesh and excrement. Probably one of the FSA soldiers he had been told had been shot the other day, who, like Muhammed, had been unlucky or deceived in his negotiations for safe passage. Maybe the same fate awaited him.

Then he saw it: a light in the darkness. The dot was no bigger than the glowing end of a cigarette. He held his breath and stepped out.

Sami couldn't make out the faces of the bodies he stepped over but he thought he saw Muhammed's lanky frame, curled up in the foetal position, with red spatter in his dark curls and among the freckles on his forehead.

He saw the body of a fifteen-year-old boy, who he could have sworn had the same black eyes, bare feet and thin layer of dust on his downy top lip as his little brother.

There was the faint smell of fire and he saw around forty bodies belonging to men, women and children, a girl with half a head.

Further on lay an older man with a walnut walking stick, a pipe in the corner of his mouth and a red rose in the breast pocket of his suit jacket. Sami accidentally kicked a cracked gramophone. Passed a turtle with a broken shell. A grey kitten with a broken neck. He saw two schoolchildren, a boy and a girl, with a red bike between them. How could death, being so violent, give such a deceptive impression of innocence?

When Sami raised his eyes, it was as though the entire road had been transformed into a bridge under his feet. A bridge covered in blood and corpses, all turning their eyes on him. A tunnel with twelve men face down on the ground, with their hands tied behind them and bullets in the back of their heads.

With every step, he felt an overwhelming urge to stop, and with every step, he forced himself to carry on. The sound of his footsteps, creaking and crunching, was amplified and echoed in his ears, about as discreet as when the tanks rolled through the streets at the start of the siege. But if there was a sentry on duty that night, he must have dozed off.

Halfway across, he turned around. It was the first time he saw it from the other side; the houses seemed to be crouching in the darkness, turning their backs on him. In that moment, he understood why there were people who wavered and stood still one breath too long. *Freedom* – during the protests, they had shouted the word until they were hoarse, but now he no longer knew what kind of freedom he was looking for. During the siege, they had been prisoners of starvation and airstrikes, but also free to say and think whatever they wanted. Soon he would be able to eat his fill and fall asleep without hearing the distant sound of gunfire, but he would also be a prisoner once more.

There was still time to go back. The cats slunk in and out of the ruins. The snipers were on a break. He looked at his city, then turned his back on it, and as he did so the city turned its back on him. Sami would never see his home again, or what remained of it. He would never pass the playground where he once swung high on the swing and which had now been turned into a cemetery. He would no longer see the rebel soldiers play football next to his old school, divided into teams according to their battalions.

If he really did have several lives, he left one behind in Homs. Part of him continued to sleep on the cramped sofa, with his knees pulled into his chest. The glow from the stove would die out and the last heat leaving the room would be his breath.

He glanced back one last time and let his eyes linger on the house and the city that had been his home.

Then he ran fast in the direction of the glowing point.

V

Coffee and cigarettes and a never-ending stream of cars on the Champs-Élysées. You always pay. You always roll one for me first. You smile and show me a picture of kittens you put a bowl down for in a ruined house, your home. Remember?, Facebook asks. You smile and remember the kittens.

After swapping memories and stories for almost a year, we become good friends. Then more than friends. Al-tafahum. You say that's the most important thing for you in a relationship. According to the dictionary: mutual understanding. To be in agreement and exist in a context. Possibly that is the greatest kind of love: to be seen and to have your story recognized.

'Does it matter that I'm a non-believer?' I ask.

'No. I have many friends who are atheists.'

'Aren't you worried I'll go to hell?'

'I think our actions determine what happens to us after death. And you can do good or bad regardless of faith.'

Later on, you tell me you don't know what you believe. If there is a god, he's on Bashar al-Assad's side, which means he's not your god.

I used to think believers had an easier time, that they held the answers in their hands and had faith. But I was wrong; you often seem to have more questions than answers.

'Maybe you could talk to an imam,' I suggest.

You smile again and brush the crumbs on the table into a pile, shake your head.

'I'm sorry I tell you such sad stories,' you say.

'I'm sorry I ask so many questions,' I say.

'No, go on. I like it.'

'OK. What do you do when you can't sleep?'

You tell me that sometimes you imagine an old childhood friend, with freckles and a bird's nest of curly hair, who picks you up and drives you through the spring night, through the Milky Way, down a deserted Champs-Élysées. Your lips close around the filter, you inhale. Your voice rises and scatters like smoke.

37

SAMI HAD AN impulse to touch his chest to make sure it was in one piece, that he wasn't leaking from invisible bullet holes, that he hadn't been turned into a sieve and that the man in front of him wasn't the ferryman waiting to take him to the underworld. Maybe he had already crossed the black river. The regime soldier put a finger to his lips. A circus performer asking for silence, as though it were all staged, with an audience waiting on the other side, hidden behind the black velvet curtain of night. A shove in the back got him moving. The dot of light turned out to be a cigarette lighter with a built-in flashlight. That was when Sami realized he must be alive, because surely there are no lighters in the afterlife.

He was taken round the corner of a building that was almost identical to the one he had lived in for the past six months. The regime soldier led him through a doorway, gently but not particularly kindly, inside which three more soldiers were waiting. They searched him in silence, with a meticulousness that almost made Sami smile. How were they to know his most valuable possession was twelve red lentils in one of his jacket pockets.

Then began a long journey through hidden doorways and tunnels. After exiting the labyrinthine passages they stepped out on to a street, empty apart from a car with tinted windows. The night closed in around them and the moon hung over them, a fruit you could almost reach out for and pluck.

'I can get by on my own from here,' Sami whispered.

A gun was cocked and the hand on his shoulder tightened. One of the soldiers hushed him and raised his hand to calm the others. It wasn't done yet; first he had to see the general.

'Whatever you do, don't look him in the eye.'

His tongue felt coarse and swollen. This wasn't how it was supposed to happen; the deal was that he was to be released immediately. If only there had been time to think, but there wasn't. If only there had been somewhere to run, but there wasn't. He was ushered into the car with the black windows and recalled other people who had climbed into cars and disappeared. Was this the last time he, too, would be seen?

The car slowed down in front of an enormous building Sami vaguely recognized but had never looked at twice before the war. He was brought into a bare room and placed on a straight-backed wooden chair. There was a chill draught around his legs even though a radiator was steaming in the corner and the air was warm and stuffy with to-bacco, a hint of vanilla. The general greeted him and asked a few casual questions. Sami knew the type; it was the kind of politeness that people in power only deign to show when they want something in return. He straightened up and avoided looking the general in the eye, but still noticed the glass eye staring blankly at him. To his right: a short, squat man sweating profusely, his contact and the mediator of his freedom. His presence reassured Sami, but not for long.

A door opened and seven men in handcuffs were brought in and ushered to the other side of the room, which reinforced Sami's impression that this was an interrogation. Even so, a modicum of relief. He didn't recognize any of the prisoners and they didn't recognize him, so he would be able to adjust his story a little whenever prudent.

Of course, Sami said in a voice he hoped exuded calm and confidence, of course he had completed his military service. He was honourably discharged, after a couple of months' additional service.

Sure, he had sought out a media centre at the start of the revolution, he admitted it freely, but he had broken off contact with them when he realized they were traitors.

Yes, he had stayed in Homs when the shells started falling, but only to look after his gravely ill grandfather. What illness? Cancer, his lungs were black with tar, may he rest in peace. Then he had stayed in the besieged area, focusing on finding food and shelter – he only mentioned the practical, the harmless, the things that didn't have anything to do with avoiding being in places where bombs were falling.

'Mhm,' the general said sceptically. 'Fascinating story, truly.'

He looked to the left with his healthy eye and straight ahead with the glass one, then snapped his fingers at the soldier who had brought Sami in.

'That one' – the general pointed to an emaciated prisoner over by the wall, who had stuttered his way through a handful of questions – 'and that one' – the finger pointed at Sami. 'Take them to Abu Riad tomorrow morning.'

Sami was led through the long corridors and put in a grey-painted cell with a steel bed and a bucket in one corner. His contact lingered by the door, like an impatient horse waiting for lumps of sugar.

'That wasn't so bad now, was it?'

'Who's Abu Riad?' Sami asked and tried to keep his voice calm.

'The interrogator. He has quite a reputation, sorry to say.'

'This isn't what we agreed.'

'Yes, well. I'm sure it'll work out,' his contact said and wrung his hands. 'There is just one other thing, a tiny detail . . .'

He cleared his throat when Sami showed no sign of wanting to continue the conversation, running his hands over his lapels.

'Tomorrow morning, before your interrogation, a TV team will come here for an interview.'

Sami held his breath before asking: 'What interview?'

'The one where you admit to being a terrorist. A traitor. But that thanks to our benevolent leader Bashar al-Assad you have been pardoned and accepted as a citizen once more. To serve as an inspiration to your friends in the besieged area.'

Sami leaned forward and looked him in the eyes.

'So they can arrest all of us later? Over my dead body.'

'They have no other reason to let you go,' said the man and wiped his brow with a handkerchief. 'Did they let you borrow a phone? Try to sleep and we'll see how it goes.'

The cell door slammed shut and Sami called his parents. Since the call was sure to be monitored he kept it brief, but the sound of Nabil and Samira's fragile voices jogged something loose inside him.

'Why didn't you tell us you were trying to get out?'

'I didn't want you to worry. What difference would it have made?'

His parents cried quietly and asked if he had eaten; he said he was being treated well, that it was just a matter of clearing up a few routine questions.

'The battery is running low. I'll call as soon as I get out.'

Sami lay down on the cot and closed his eyes, dozed off for minutes at a time, until his body finally gave in to sleep. He was an anchor at the bottom of the sea; light danced around the dark underside of a boat, high above, out of reach. He longed for it to be over: the interrogations, the mounting fear, the walls closing in on him. He made himself a promise that if he ever got out from here, he would go to wherever he could live freely.

He was woken up by a knock on his cell door and expected to be greeted by a bright white light, blinding cameras. Instead he saw the shadow of a guard and was taken to Abu Riad.

The interrogation room looked like a normal office. Abu Riad was several inches shorter than Sami, had grey hair and was dressed in black jeans and a moss green shirt buttoned all the way up. He smoked like they do in the old western films his dad used to watch, with his cigarette between his thumb and forefinger, taking long, deep drags and blowing the smoke into Sami's face. Abu Riad seemed to consider himself a gentleman but Sami had no doubt that when he left the neat office, it was to go downstairs to the basement where the torture took place.

He stuck to his story from the night before but let slip a few seemingly important things that were useless in practice. He told him where the rebels kept their ammunition – that was no secret, since the regime attacked that particular house regularly – and he told them about the bus explosion.

The official line was that it had been an accident. Around forty rebels died when a bus exploded in one of the besieged streets. Sami told him the truth, that the bus had been filled with explosives and that the plan had been to detonate it next to a house occupied by a regime-friendly militia, right next to the red line. For whatever reason, the bus exploded too early; at least that was the rumour.

The bait seemed to work; the interrogation revolved primarily around the ammunition and the bus. Then Abu Riad changed tack. He pulled a stack of photographs from the breast pocket of his shirt.

'Tell me, do you recognize any of these people?'

Sami picked up one picture, then the next. A whirlwind swept through his stomach and he had to swallow hard not to throw up. The pictures were of dead people in prison corridors, bodies showing clear signs of torture. Infected wounds, marks from straps, blueish-black, swollen arms and legs. Even if he had known any of them when they were alive he wasn't sure he would have recognized them. The pictures could have been of anyone: a neighbour or childhood friend, his brother or sister.

'I don't recognize anyone. Can I have some water?'

'Are you sure? Absolutely sure?'

Sami went through the pile again, studying a couple of pictures more closely for show, running his finger over the sharp corners.

'Absolutely sure.'

'That's too bad for you.'

The interrogation continued with trick questions and traps designed to uncover lies. Sami listened closely for allegations he hadn't admitted to, which would become confessions if left unopposed. Like when he worked as a journalist– He hadn't worked as a journalist, Sami broke in. But he had said so in his last questioning? No. What he had said was that he had visited a media centre, but when he realized they were enemies of the country he had broken off all contact. Abu Riad mentioned the name of an international news agency.

'Did they pay you well for the pictures you sold?'

'I never worked for them.'

'So how come they were calling you so often? A nobody, an amateur who likes to snap pictures?'

After hours of questions, Abu Riad leaned forward and aimed a smoke pillar at him, making him cough.

'Your so-called information is useless. And do you know what that makes you? Useless.'

Sweat broke out around Sami's collar, curling the hair at the back of his neck. Abu Riad studied him with his chin tilted up and his nostrils flaring, as though something about Sami annoyed him but was at the same time too insignificant to waste time on – a mosquito, a pebble in his shoe.

'I have orders to let you go but we're not done with each other yet.'

Abu Riad lit another cigarette and leaned back.

'You have a week. Make sure you're less useless next time.'

Orders to let you go. That was all Sami heard.

A stack of papers was brought out. Going through it and reading it was out of the question but he skimmed a few random lines. By signing it, he would be confessing to having been a terrorist and working against his country, and making a promise never again to do anything aimed at undermining the government. Sami signed it immediately.

38

HE DRIED HIS hands on his trousers and was led out, blinking in the sunlight. Abu Riad had given him one last chance. Not out of kindness, that much was clear. No, they let him go hoping he had more information to give, or that he would talk to his friends and convince more of them to hand themselves over. Abu Riad wanted to see him in a week's time for another interrogation. One week. That was the time he had to plan his escape and leave the country.

Sami's contact drove him from the secret police headquarters to the neighbourhood where his grandmother Fatima lived and Samira had played as a young girl. It was like landing in a new world. Cars driving along unspoilt streets, people with clean clothes and faces. He saw students with school books in their arms. Women with bags of food. An old man walking his dog.

As the anxiety started to leave him, Sami fell asleep, leaning on the car window. He woke up when the car braked. A checkpoint at the end of the road.

'Let's go this way instead,' his contact mumbled and made a sharp turn.

The first thing Sami noticed was the tree. In his grandmother's garden, on a patch of green grass, stood a gnarled orange tree heavy with fruit. A similar tree had grown in the courtyard of his childhood home – before Nabil added an extra floor and before their house was hit by a missile. Samira had been sad about losing the orange tree, about chopping down something that was alive and bearing fruit.

Oranges were brought to Europe by the Moors long ago, his paternal grandfather had told him during one of their walks to the market. Sami remembered how Grandpa Faris's hands had already been full of fruit and vegetables and so he had been the one to hand over the money to the vendor. They bought five pounds of the sweetest kind and shared the sticky segments. He associated the taste of oranges with all things sweet: from the candied peel to the juice drizzled on to cakes and other pastries. The Spanish kept the Persian word for the fruit, Grandpa Faris continued.

'Your grandmother was my *media naranja*. My orange half, my soulmate.'

Sami climbed out of the car and felt an intense longing for something he couldn't define. Maybe his childhood, when it had been possible to go to the market without keeping a watchful eye on the sky. When it had been possible to lie on a stone bench and look for signs in the cloud formations. When there was time to grieve for a chopped-down orange tree.

The smell of overripe fruit was almost suffocating. Why did they let the fruit rot? There must be people who could pick and eat them. You could make preserves and jam and marmalade, squeeze them for juice . . .

'We have more than we need,' a woman's hoarse voice said behind him.

Sami turned to see his maternal grandmother, dressed in a black robe and hijab, and beaming at the sight of her long-gone grandson.

'Oh, Sami.'

She embraced him with the force and caution of someone who believed they had lost a dear object for ever and then found it again.

'You are here! You're really here.'

She laid her dry hands on his face and the tears began to fall in small streams down her wrinkled cheeks.

'Now let's go in before someone sees you.'

Sami could already see how different his and his grandmother's lives had been for the past few years. During the siege, they had suffered food shortages, power cuts and fighting too, but they had still been able to go about their lives. Sami supported his grandmother's arm, or maybe he was leaning on it, and they slowly moved towards the front steps.

'You have no idea how many times I've prayed for you and . . . Oh, Sami, your little brother . . . I'm so sorry.'

It was as if time had stood still in his grandmother's house. The same flowery curtains in the kitchen, the same furniture in the same places. Fatima made his bed with clean sheets and put out a big bath towel. Sami breathed in the smell of clean fabric with not a trace of ashes or dust. In the shower, he turned the heat up until the steam rose and his skin almost burned; brown streaks pooled around the drain. Serves you right, jinn.

The scent of the soap mingled with the smell of the food his grandmother had cooked, *kibbeh labanieh*. How did people eat again? He raised the spoon to his lips and filled his mouth with the oily yoghurt sauce, which tasted so heavenly he wanted to stick his head in the pot and drink himself full. But the moment the food touched his throat, he gagged. His body had grown used to feeling full on nothing but dreams of food – on imagining its smell, taste and appearance – and the real experience was overwhelming.

Was that how people did it? Chewed and swallowed and let it all out in a different form? It couldn't be human, this eating business. Just like it couldn't be human to sleep through an entire night without waking up to the sound of imminent death.

When darkness fell, he sat down on the edge of the bed and looked out at the orange tree, where the fruits were glowing like stars.

The next morning, his parents came to the house. He saw them from the upstairs window and found he couldn't move at first. Samira was supporting Nabil, who slowly set one foot before the other. Halfway up the path he paused and laid a hand on his chest, and the simple gesture caused the pain to rise in Sami's own breast. When they knocked on the door he finally hurried to open it.

My son, our beloved. Ya rohi. He didn't perceive all that they were saying, only felt the warmth flowing towards him.

His mum and dad embraced him at the same time, enveloping him with their arms and bodies. When he felt their wet cheeks against his, Sami didn't know if it was he who was crying or his parents, or all of them at once.

'I barely recognize you,' Samira said. 'Has Mother fed you?'

'Of course I've fed him,' his grandmother said and shook her head. 'But the poor thing doesn't eat much. I've set the table in the kitchen. Follow me.'

Their reunion was warm and tear-filled, and yet it was as though he was looking at himself from the outside. *This is how a son who has been separated from his family for two years should act*, he thought, and tried to fill out his own contours. He sat down at the table and attempted to drink and to eat, but he knew they would ask at any moment. As soon as he found his breath, he would have to tell them.

Nabil's eyes were wet and he said very little, but as they sat there he continued to kiss Sami's cheeks and stroke his hands. In the end it fell to Samira to tell Sami what their life had been like, all the things they had never been able to discuss over the phone.

His parents had been staying with a relative in the countryside since the start of the siege, and avoided the worst of the airstrikes. Instead, they had watched through their windows as their neighbour's house exploded in a sea of fire. Not even during *iftar*, when the fast was broken during Ramadan, did the regime's bombs stop falling.

And his sister and older brother? They only had sporadic contact with Ali. He was wanted by the secret police and was still in hiding. Hiba, her husband and two children had fled across an open field but had been spotted and shot at by regime soldiers. Hiba's daughter was now in a wheelchair after being hit in the back by grenade shrapnel. Hiba had tried to cross the border to Turkey to seek specialist medical care, but the aid organization they had been in contact with had told them their daughter's injuries were not considered sufficiently acute for humanitarian response.

Then his mum grew quiet and Nabil looked at her, and she looked at Sami. She folded her hands on the table and his dad moved a cloth napkin to his nose. Sami knew then that the time had come.

'We already know,' Samira said, 'but we want to hear it from you, in person. Tell us about Malik.'

And so he began to tell them how Malik, their youngest and most beloved son and his little brother, had died. He told them about his last days. He told them about his unquenchable spirit. And he told them how he had given Malik's shoes to someone who needed them more and then buried his body in the stony ground.

The next day Sarah came to visit. He heard her voice from the open window, from under the orange tree where his grandmother was collecting fruit.

'Is Sami here?'

He opened the door and there she stood. Her cheeks were slimmer. Her eyes seemed brighter. Her hair had grown out and turned black; only the ends were still red.

'Sarah.'

They hesitated on the front steps as though they were each waiting for the other to set the tone for their meeting. Sarah had already told him she wasn't leaving Syria, that she couldn't go with him. Maybe things had ended between them two years ago, the day he chose to stay in Homs, at the start of the siege. But now, were they friends or lovers? To what extent had time and circumstances made them strangers? Then Sarah leaned in and kissed him on his cheeks, gave him a brief and hard hug. Friends. Something sank down inside him.

They ignored the risk that someone might see them and sat outside on the warm stone steps with tea that Sami had made. Sami had to feel the sun on his skin, if only for a while. When he passed Sarah the cup, she smiled, and there was the dimple, the most perfect shape he had ever seen.

'You have to come with me,' he said.

'I have to stay,' Sarah answered. 'I can't leave the children I'm teaching.'

She saw them almost every day, practised grammar and spelling, blew on their scraped knees and stroked the hair out of their eyes. She was their big sister and their friend. A light breeze rustled the leaves and when he looked her in the eyes, he realized they weren't brighter but filled with a translucent darkness.

'How has it been outside Damascus?' he asked.

She folded her hands around her cup. 'Not easy.'

Their neighbours had been suspicious of the city people seeking refuge in the villages. Since when had they ever cared about the countryside? Since when had the city people taken any interest in things like drought, water shortages and the other challenges farmers faced? It served them right to have to pay through the nose for rent and food now that the countryside was suddenly good enough for them.

She talked until she was almost out of breath, then they sat in silence for a moment.

'What's the matter?' Sami asked, finally.

'Nothing, nothing at all. It's just that . . . your cheeks, and your wrists – they look like they would snap like twigs.'

Sami had changed. Of course he had changed. He had, for instance, lost twenty-five pounds, and he had been skinny before. But somehow he had managed to forget or deny it in the lead-up to her visit. He figured she wouldn't be able to tell, that it wasn't too bad.

He tried to smile but he knew it was true. He took her hands in his and felt their warmth.

'But aside from the physical I'm the same, right?'

'I don't know. It's like you're not really here.'

He looked straight ahead, beyond her and the orange tree. She was the same but moved more quickly than he remembered, and now she pulled her hair back and bit her nails. Maybe he had slowed down while her pace had increased, like two instruments playing to different beats. Maybe that was one of the more subtle effects of the war, that people lost their natural rhythm. Instead you vibrated according to external circumstances, attentive to the smallest shifts in atmosphere that might indicate danger, an approaching threat.

'How is your family? Did your dad get out?'

Sarah's dad had been arrested in one of the mass round-ups the regime performed before every round of negotiations with the opposition. They would arrest up to a thousand people in just a few days, on trifling or trumped-up charges, only to release them again as part of a deal. But Sarah's father had not been released. He was from an affluent family, which made him a perfect subject for blackmail.

'We sold everything we had,' Sarah told him.

'And they let him go?'

She nodded and took out a photo from her pocket. A picture of her father lying in a hospital bed, his ribs showing through his skin, which was transparent and as thin as rice paper.

Sami put his arms around Sarah and she leaned her head against his shoulder. He remembered the first electric feeling of her legs touching his in the university cafeteria. He remembered when they went to the festival in Palmyra and stayed up late, sharing candied nuts they had bought from the food stalls. The night sky in Palmyra had seemed bigger, starrier and a darker shade of blue than the one in Homs. It had been a different time. Everything had felt possible.

Now the echo of that previous life fluttered against the walls of his chest like a trapped butterfly looking for a way out.

When Sarah got up to leave, the only thing Sami could muster was emptiness and a feeling of futility. She kissed his cheeks and went.

Maybe he would have felt more if he hadn't been so paralysed by fear about what was going to happen next. He had taken the leap into freedom only to end up in a new kind of imprisonment. The pain in his gut made it impossible to move, to eat, to sleep. He tried to have normal conversations but all he could see was long corridors with barred doors, and all he could hear were the screams of the men dragged out into the courtyard in the military prison. He thought about the scar on Younes' forehead and the picture of Sarah's emaciated, ruined father.

That was what was waiting for him if he stayed.

39

BEFORE THE WAR began, the journey from Homs to Hermel, just over the Lebanese border, had taken thirty minutes, but with broken roads and checkpoints it was now expected to take several hours. Sami packed his backpack, put in a couple of ripe oranges and left without saying goodbye. It was safer if no one knew. It also made it easier for him to think he wasn't leaving for good.

The escape would cost him a thousand dollars, equivalent to about five months' salary before the war. Why had he spent so much on tobacco in the siege, he thought regretfully. But he had lived only from moment to moment then, with no idea whether he had a future.

A thousand dollars. Sami had brought nothing with him and his family had no money saved. However, he had the salary from the news agency he worked for. He hadn't been able to get it until now, but through a complicated transfer, which went through different hands in the activist network inside and outside Syria, he got the money together.

Sami had made enquiries with the contacts who had once smuggled computer supplies for him. He had let them know he was looking for smugglers to take him across the border to Lebanon, and he ended up with three.

The first was an Assad supporter and a member of the secret police, who was pragmatic about politics if there was money to be made.

'Climb in,' he said and held open the door of his Toyota truck.

Sami got in the passenger seat, visible to everyone. His throat seized up as they approached the first checkpoint and he found it hard to breathe. He saw the parked vehicles from afar, the soldiers with their rifles drawn. Had any of them lain on a roof and used Sami and his friends for target practice during the siege? Aiming for right arms one day. Left arms the next. An injured man or woman was a bigger drain on resources than a dead one. An injured person needed medical attention and rest and couldn't fight, even if they survived.

'Stop that,' said the driver. 'It's like nails against a blackboard.'

Sami hadn't realized he was grinding his teeth. He put his hands flat on his thighs and focused on keeping his legs still. They were getting closer; soon he would be able to see their eyes. Would his emaciated body arouse suspicion? He had shaved and had his hair cut and put on new clothes, but his trousers were held up by a belt and the double jumpers did little to conceal the emptiness inside them. He would prefer a bullet to the head to being thrown in prison. He would prefer anything to becoming an unknown name, transferred to an unknown location. The driver focused forward and slowly pressed the accelerator. When they passed the checkpoint, he smiled and casually raised his hand to the soldiers. Only around forty more to go.

Every time they came to a checkpoint, Sami thought it was over. There were the regular ones everybody knew about. And there were temporary ones, which popped up when you least expected it. On the surface they seemed random and unplanned, but the areas they covered were often negotiated between the army and regime-friendly militias. The checkpoints were like any other tradable goods – they raised money in the form of bribes, which made it possible to buy weapons.

They usually stopped in a special lane next to the civilian cars. His smuggler flashed his secret police ID and they were let through. Sometimes a soldier nodded to the washing machine strapped to the flatbed.

'Where did you get that?'

'Homs,' the driver said and held out some money.

The soldier glanced around, accepted the notes and waved the Toyota through.

'So, you want to get out of doing your military service,' the driver said. 'If you were my son, I'd give you a good beating.'

That was the story he'd been told. They didn't exchange another word for the rest of the journey. After passing abandoned and burnt-down orchards, they eventually stopped at a villa; the driver signalled to Sami to wait in the driveway while he made a call. He sought out the shade of a tree, undid his fly and tried to relieve himself, but had to give up.

His second driver was Lebanese and a member of the Shiite militia Hezbollah, al-Assad's extended arm in Lebanon. He didn't get out of the car, just waved for Sami to climb in. He had a gleaming hunting rifle between his knees, the barrel pointing diagonally up towards Sami.

'Would you mind moving that over a bit?' Sami said when they hit a bump in the road.

'Oh, this . . .'

He turned the gun out towards the window but as soon as they hit another bump, the barrel was back in Sami's face.

'So, you're from Homs?' said the Lebanese and flashed a row of yellow teeth. 'Almost all my furniture is from there. Well, not just mine, all my friends have furniture from Homs. Excellent quality – and completely free!'

The Lebanese laughed and scratched his groin; Sami felt the air in his lungs compress. He didn't feel like talking but the man seemed eager to socialize.

'Have you been to al-Qusayr before?'

Sami had, but the landscape they were driving through looked nothing like the al-Qusayr he knew. The city was about twenty miles south of Homs and had around thirty thousand inhabitants. It had been an FSA stronghold but the regime had reclaimed it with the help of Hezbollah. Now there was nothing but ghost towns, abandoned villages and bombed-out buildings. The yellow flag of Hezbollah was everywhere.

'I cut the throat of a rebel dog over there,' said the Lebanese, pointing. 'Over there, we fired missiles at those houses. You should have seen the families running out of them screaming like rats.'

Sami tried hard to seem unperturbed. They passed three checkpoints without any trouble. Sami was his cousin, the Hezbollah fighter explained, and fired his gun a few times out of the car window, straight up into the air. A pigeon landed on the ground with a thud. The soldiers lost all interest in Sami and instead admired the weapon.

On the outskirts of al-Qusayr, as they approached the border between Syria and Lebanon, the Lebanese man turned more serious. He shoved three pieces of gum in his mouth and chewed so hard his jaw creaked. The paved road meandered through mountains and vast fields.

'This is going to be the hardest one. Fingers crossed we get through.'

Sami spotted the checkpoint long before they reached it. Two armoured vehicles were parked on either side of the road, across which piles of sandbags formed a wall. Ten Syrian soldiers turned their eyes on them. The driver ran his hand across his forehead again and again; his hair was sticking to it, even though it was an overcast day and not particularly warm. The dust settled everywhere, like a second skin.

'Remember, you're my cousin.'

They stopped; the soldiers watched them in the distance without moving. The driver rolled down his window and held out a packet of cigarettes.

'Can I offer you boys a cigarette?' he called out.

His previously cocksure voice lost its authority in the wind. One of the soldiers, the youngest from the looks of him, left his post and slowly walked over to the car.

'You again,' the soldier said.

'My cousin needed a ride and you don't say no to family,' the Lebanese man said and adjusted his hunting rifle so it was visible in his lap.

'That's really nice.'

'How about a cigarette?'

The Lebanese man lit one for the soldier and one for himself, without asking Sami if he wanted one. The young soldier squinted at him with each deep drag and then flicked his ash in his direction.

'Who are you?'

'My cousin,' the Lebanese man repeated.

'I'm not talking to you. What's your name?'

'Sami.'

'I feel like I've seen you before . . . Have we met?'

The Lebanese man started coughing and beating his chest; he leaned over the steering wheel, gasping for breath.

'Damn it, my lungs,' he said with tears in his eyes. 'Here, want to try it?'

The soldier took the hunting rifle and looked through the sight. He turned it on the Lebanese man, then aimed it at Sami, caressed the trigger and finally gave it back.

'How much do you want for it?'

'Well, you know what they say, you don't sell your children.'

'All right, then I'm borrowing it.'

The Lebanese man pondered the gun, scratched his knee and nodded.

'Sure, no problem. I'll come through here tomorrow, I'll pick it up then.'

The soldier turned his back and waved them on.

'Fucking prick, thieves, the lot of them,' the Lebanese man muttered after rolling up the windows.

Then he lit another cigarette; the smoke made Sami's eyes water.

They pulled over at a petrol station where an SUV with tinted windows was already parked. How could he be sure it wasn't a trap? That they wouldn't take his money and hand him over to the regime? Why would he trust regime supporters when they were the ones who had bombed his home, killed his brother and reduced his hometown to famine and darkness? The answer was simple: because he had no choice.

The car door opened. A gangly man in tracksuit bottoms and flip-flops climbed out. Sami's heart skipped a beat when he recognized him. It was the same man he had paid to arrange this trip. The smuggler shot him a wide smile.

'Jump in,' he said and took his backpack.

They turned off on to a smaller road and the Lebanese man followed so they could split the money and the two cartons of Alhamraa cigarettes Sami had brought. Comet tails of dust swirled around the car on the dirt road. The surroundings were the same, yet everything was different. But his chest was intact and the air finally reached his lungs.

They had crossed the border into Lebanon.

40

THE YELLOW FIELDS stretched out in every direction, sandy and dry under the scorching sun. A tractor was moving over by the horizon, in front of the mountains that rose up like a wall towards the blue sky. The tractor moved back and forth, back and forth, as persistent as an ant.

Sami thought about his own cultivation on the roof in Homs, about the radishes which would have time to develop tender roots now that he wasn't harvesting them prematurely. He hoped someone else would find his rooftop garden. That someone else would treasure the vegetables and they wouldn't grow in vain. The thought of the white and pink buds and their fresh bitterness made his mouth water.

The smuggler should be back soon with food. He lived in a caravan and had invited Sami to stay with him for the first few days before he could move on. The caravan was stuffy but Sami wasn't allowed to leave it. It's too dangerous, the smuggler had told him. Hermel wasn't like the rest of Lebanon; the militant group Hezbollah had soldiers everywhere and were in cahoots with Assad. The truth was Hezbollah had extended its spiderweb to cover all of Lebanon – from being a Shiite militia it had grown into an organization with its own TV and radio channels and seats in the Lebanese parliament, and ran schools and social programmes.

Hermel was one of its strongholds. The Bekaa Valley was one of

Lebanon's most fertile areas, with fields of star-shaped leaves and the white petals of a certain type of poppy. To put it plainly, it was the ideal place to grow marijuana and opium, which made Hermel, no matter how unassuming the town was otherwise, one of the Middle East's drug capitals. Hezbollah held the monopoly on trafficking, and they used the profits to buy weapons from Iran, which were then transported via Syria with the blessing of the regime. Everything was connected in a unique ecosystem.

The view from the caravan was, however, anything but fertile. Sami contemplated disobeying instructions and heading out to scour the surroundings for green plants. Under the present circumstances, it might be a way to alleviate the tedium.

His boldness was becoming a hazard. Just because he had made it this far didn't mean he was invincible. It was tiny details that drew the invisible line between life and death. Unexpectedly finding radish seeds. An alcove in a tunnel. A sniper taking a coffee break.

No, to leave the caravan was to tempt fate. Sami remembered when one of his childhood friends quit his pharmacology studies and fled to Lebanon. He was caught almost immediately at one of Hezbollah's checkpoints in Hermel and brought back to Syria, where he was imprisoned for terrorist activities. His friend's crime: helping to smuggle medicine into the besieged parts of Homs. Two weeks later, his dismembered body was delivered to his parents.

To make matters worse, the Syrian presidential election was under way, which made Hezbollah especially interested in Syrians fleeing across the border. Their fingers were inspected for blue ink smudges from voting. If they were clean, they were driven to voting stations to give their support to Bashar al-Assad.

Sami startled at a sound. Not the tractor, which was far away, but the roaring of a car engine. He stiffened and scanned the stony road leading to the camp site. The smuggler had told him to hide if there was any sign of military vehicles or police cars. The caravan was too obvious, so his best option – his only option – was the hill behind it.

But the engine sound faded. Sami locked the door and pulled the curtains shut, curled up on the mattress and tried to slow his breathing. He had been here for almost a week. He wondered if he was becoming paranoid. Had the roar of the engine been real? A hollow sound rose from his stomach and he tried to quell his hunger with water. Then he lay down again and fell asleep.

Behind his eyelids, Homs' streets and checkpoints spread out, lifeless sparrows on their backs with their beaks pointed at the sky everywhere. The scene shifted and he was in a prison corridor full of crushed blood oranges. A whistling sound sliced through his dream, from a bomber or a thousand beating wings rising towards the sky, and he threw himself to the floor with his hands clapped to his ears.

Sami woke – this time, it really was a car engine. He got to his feet and peered out through a gap in the curtains. A military jeep was approaching at high speed. Dashing from the caravan didn't seem feasible. He would have to climb the hill and be fully visible for several seconds. Even if he got away, they would find a lit stove in the caravan and know there was a person nearby. He would be as hard to catch as a rabbit in a burrow. Yet, at the same time, was the alternative to give up? He'd rather bolt into the unknown.

Sami threw the door open and ran out with laces untied just as the military jeep turned into the sandy field. A cloud of dust rose around the car; he squinted in the harsh light. He only managed a few steps before he tripped over a detail, which is to say his laces, and felt a jolt of pain in his knee.

It was over. This was as far as he would get. After all, a person only has so many lives. He waited, on his knees, with his hands in the air, for the rifles to be aimed at him. A couple of words flashed through his mind: it was his grandmother's voice, chanting away the pain in his broken finger. Chanted verses couldn't save him now. And yet, he prayed.

When the dust cloud dissipated he heard footsteps in the sand and hoarse laughter. Then the reproachful voice of the smuggler.

'What are you doing out here? I told you to stay in the caravan.'

'I suppose this made him nervous,' said the man with the hoarse laugh, patting the bonnet of the jeep. He was dressed in a military uniform. 'Is this him?'

'Yes,' said the smuggler. 'We're going to have to do something about your appearance before we leave. Those dirty clothes and that unwashed face won't do.'

Before we leave. The smuggler had kept his promise and arranged safe passage through the checkpoints to Beirut. When Sami had composed himself and shaken the general's hand, he realized there was a woman in the driver's seat.

'Mariam, my wife,' said the general. 'They are less inclined to stop you if there's a woman in the car.'

She seemed less than happy to be there. The smuggler went into the caravan with Sami and helped him pack. Sami handed over the money and they said goodbye with a brief embrace.

The Lebanese general was friendly and didn't talk too much, but Sami didn't have the energy for long conversations anyway. The general told him it was dangerous for him to be here too, among the Hezbollah. His relative had been shot dead in Hermel a couple of years ago. This was only the second time he had been back since.

Mariam shot Sami hard looks through the rear-view mirror and said as little as possible.

'Suspicion is our biggest enemy,' the general said.

He was referring to the Lebanese and Syrian people, who had been sundered into religious and ethnic groups, but also glanced at Mariam, who frowned.

'This is when our trust is tested,' he continued, 'when you have no choice but to rely on strangers.'

It seemed like he was talking more to Mariam than to Sami. But Sami could see where she was coming from. What did she know about his past? He might be a drug trafficker or other kind of criminal. He might have fought for the jihadists, for all she knew. There was more and more talk about Islamic State now, the terror group that was growing in influence in northeastern Syria.

Sami met Mariam's eyes in the rear-view mirror and she looked away. He didn't know anything about her and the general's reasons for helping him either – other than that favours made people owe you and an extensive network was hard currency in times like these. None of them had any choice. They had to trust each other.

They were approaching Beirut. The general rolled down the windows and let the fresh Mediterranean breeze sweep in, along with the smell of car exhaust and restaurant food. There were more people than in Homs, more people than Sami had seen in years.

'Where would you like to be dropped off?'

Sami told him where Muhammed's cousin lived. Muhammed had made him repeat the address at the time and though it seemed pointless then, Sami now understood. He thought warmly of his childhood friend. Even though he was dead, he was still helping Sami. *This is for both of us*, Sami thought. *I'm finding a way out even if you couldn't.*

He didn't know what he had expected Beirut to be like, but the closer to the centre they got, the further down his seat he slid. On the way to the apartment they passed several checkpoints, where soldiers stood with heavy weapons.

'Make yourself at home,' said Muhammed's cousin when at last they arrived at the apartment. 'Stay as long as you need. Muhammed always spoke well of you.'

They shared the flat with two other Syrians. Sami was given the sofa in the living room. He unpacked his suitcase and slowly, step by tiny step, started to dare to imagine a future. But in Lebanon? He wasn't so sure. Anywhere he went the checkpoints appeared, and with them came the threat of being sent back. He wouldn't be free here either.

41

THREE HOT SUMMER months passed during which Sami mostly slept
and stayed indoors. He only went out to buy food, or to go to a café
across the street that was showing the World Cup. He followed the
tournament without any commitment to players or country. It was just
pleasant to witness the ball's journey across the field, listen to the audience's cheers and sighs, see the winners stretch their arms to the air
and think that life didn't have to be more complicated than that.

Outside the apartment in Beirut, the sea raged and the waves
crashed against the cliffs, but he went down to the beach only once for
a quick swim. He folded his clothes, placed a rock on top of them and
walked into the surge.

He enjoyed the wind and salt on his face, the frothy waves rising
towards the sun. He threw himself into the water, stood up and dived
back under. Underneath the surface, he opened his eyes and picked
up stones and shells from among the metal and plastic on the bottom.
Afterwards his eyes were red from the salt.

The water brought back a feeling he had forgotten: the feeling of
weightlessness. He soared free in the deep blue. He was part of the sea
and the sea was part of him.

It was after his short outing to the beach that Sami realized he had to
leave Beirut. He couldn't stay cooped up in the flat for ever. His money

wouldn't last long and in Beirut he couldn't work, study or lead a normal life. Even if he wasn't stopped at a checkpoint, a lot of Lebanese people looked askance at the Syrian refugees streaming across the border. Every third person in Lebanon was a refugee, primarily Palestinian and Syrian. They needed medical care, food and work and the poorest of them lived in enormous refugee camps on the outskirts of the cities. In many cases, they were people from the Syrian countryside, farmers and uneducated people, families with many children and elderly relatives, who couldn't raise the money to go any further. He had heard about Syrians being attacked for no other reason than that they were refugees.

With the help of a friend, Sami managed to get from Beirut to Tripoli in northern Lebanon. Again he travelled through the checkpoints with a military escort who called him his cousin, his nephew, his future brother-in-law – he didn't know any more. Except nameless and paperless, that was who he was.

Tripoli was a port city at the foot of Mount Lebanon. Calling it a safe place was an exaggeration but it was still easier to live there, farther from the Hezbollah. At least while he looked into the possibility of seeking asylum in another country.

Something about Tripoli reminded him of Homs. The two cities were roughly the same size, majority Sunni and had similar senses of humour. He missed his hometown, but he realized he had left in the nick of time. A couple of weeks after he crossed the six-lane motorway in the moonlight, the regime forces had reclaimed the city centre. He still hadn't heard from many of his friends that were left behind.

'You need to get out more,' said Muhammed's cousin. 'Working will take your mind off things.'

'But what work could I do?'

'Any work. You'll go crazy otherwise.'

He was right, of course. So during his autumn in Lebanon, Sami volunteered for an aid organization working in the refugee camps. The organization arranged activities and offered psychological support to women and children. Once a week he took photographs to document life in the camps.

The first time he went he had to stop for a minute to take in what he saw: the blue and white windswept tents, spreading out in their thousands. The camp was like a city, with streets and trade going on in some of the tents, and families doing what they could to gain a sense of privacy and regular everyday life.

That was where he met Leyla again. He knew she was working in one of the camps and asked if he could accompany her one day. He recognized her just from the way she walked, and when they embraced each other, neither of them wanted to let go.

'Hey, little brother,' she said and ruffled his hair. 'I've never seen it this long before.'

'The fresh saltwater winds do it good.'

'Looks like it.'

She had cut her hair short and her features seemed softer, her cheekbones less accentuated. Oddly enough, it was easier to reunite with Leyla than with his parents or with Sarah. Leyla and he had been through so much together. They understood each other without having to explain.

'How did you get out?' Sami asked.

'The same way you did, I assume.'

Like him, she preferred not to talk about herself. It was a way of avoiding having to feel. Instead, she told him about the activities in the camp.

The children painted to keep themselves busy and have fun, but also as a way of dealing with traumatic experiences. The drawings were of stickmen with weapons and aeroplanes dropping pinhead-sized bombs. The children weren't sad while they were drawing, which made Sami even more sad. Many of them had no memories of life before the war.

There was painting for adults, too. Most didn't want their picture taken or to talk about their experiences when Sami was around. But Leyla looked them in the eyes and made them relax, and some seemed to almost forget his presence.

'You can't take my picture,' said one woman. 'But I'll tell you my story.'

Then the woman turned to Leyla and began to speak. Her name was Nadine and she was from Daraa. She had joined the protests during the first few days, together with her neighbour Rasha. When people were shot, she went to the hospitals and helped wherever she could. She had no medical training but in time learnt to extract bullets and put on bandages. Soldiers visited her family home and asked: where is Nadine? And her family answered: she's not here. They came again and asked: where is Nadine? And her family cried and answered: she's not here.

Until one day, she was there.

'These are the terrorists,' said the regime soldiers when they delivered Nadine and Rasha to the detention centre.

The women were separated and Nadine was brought to an interrogation room where an officer was eating pistachio nuts and casually flicking the shells at her. After a few hours, the interrogator asked if she wanted to see her friend. Nadine heard the screaming even before the door was opened; Rasha was lying on the stone floor inside. Two men were holding her arms and legs, while a third man moved on top of her with his trousers down. Oh god, oh god, Rasha screamed fitfully.

'What do you want from me? Do you want me to confess?' Nadine asked the soldier. The door was closed and she was brought back to the interrogation room. That evening, they led her down into a basement. Finally, I'll get to sleep, Nadine thought. But then the door opened and four men entered.

'I thought about Rasha and stepped out of myself. It was as though I left my body, as though I turned into a spirit who soared up to the ceiling and watched the pain from above. The next thing I remember is waking up in the hospital. A nurse whispered and told me, shh, the doctor was going to do me a big favour and tell the soldiers I was dead.

277

It was a big surprise: apparently, I wasn't dead. For a long time, I lay on the gurney, trying to feel without feeling anything.'

Nadine showed them her painting: a white wedding dress on a bed of black blood.

'I got married the week before I was arrested. My husband left me when he found out about the rape. Rasha killed herself after a few weeks in the prison, or at least that's what I heard.'

Sami listened to the woman but was unable to fully take in her story, even less to say something that would calm her.

Later, Leyla put a hand on his shoulder. She told him some of the children had been conceived when their mothers were raped. Their trauma was double, in part caused by the war, in part by their mothers' torn feelings about them. The women's pain was double, too, caused first by the violence perpetrated by the regime soldiers and subsequently by being shunned by their families.

He didn't know when he would see Leyla again but they said good-bye that day as if it wouldn't be long. She was either going to stay in Lebanon or try to get to Turkey. In the meantime, the women and children gave her the strength to carry on. They gave her meaning amid the meaninglessness.

'If you go to Turkey, I'm sure Younes will have a place for you,' Sami said.

'So he managed to escape too?'

'Yeah, shortly after me. I heard that he crossed the northern border on foot and is reunited with his girlfriend.'

'I'm happy for them,' Leyla said. 'Maybe we'll all be reunited one day. Wouldn't that be something?'

She smiled but looked sad, and Sami gave her a long hug.

Sami continued to visit the camps, to listen and take pictures, without knowing what to do with what he heard and saw. These were not his experiences and yet they belonged to him: all these individual experiences formed part of their people's memory.

Winter was coming. A year ago, the storm had howled outside his hiding place in Homs as he lay on the sofa, worrying about how long the firewood would last. In Lebanon, the winds from the sea were milder and heavy with moisture. But it wasn't his home, it never could be. Waiting and watching were wearing on him. His friends asked him to stop jiggling his leg and pulling dry skin off his lips.

He wrote to the news agency he had worked for in Homs. Sorry, they replied, they couldn't do anything, but they sent him the name of a contact of theirs at the organization Reporters without Borders.

The shortest day of the year came and went, and afterwards he could feel the change inside. He had a reply from Reporters without Borders, asking Sami to submit papers and evidence of his journalistic work. France was his best option, they said. They couldn't fill out the paperwork for him or seek asylum on his behalf, but they could guide him through the process and attest to his being in danger on account of his work as a photographer. And so, one month after all the paperwork had been submitted, he was called to the French embassy in Beirut.

The waiting room was airy and there were only a few other people in it. There were people who had waited longer than him, months, years; there were people who applied again and again. But most of the refugees were not in the waiting room. They lived on the run in their own country, shut out of their streets and homes. A small number of Syrians, but still more numerous than the people who tried their luck at the embassy, set off on their own, primarily to neighbouring countries: Jordan, Lebanon and Turkey. Then there were some who dreamt of Europe. In France the people had risen up against a bloody regime once and declared liberty, equality and fraternity – they should understand.

Was it luck or fate, or just chance? Maybe his paperwork was enough, maybe the woman interviewing him was having a particularly good day.

Sami knew several other journalists whose applications had been denied. But not his.

He didn't have to live in a tent, hide in a lorry or climb into a leaky plastic boat to cross the Mediterranean; he was one of the lucky few who were welcomed before they even arrived. His passport was stamped and a date set for his journey. He had just enough money left to buy the ticket.

And so Sami found himself in an aeroplane for the first time. The whirling sound of the propellers, the vibrations in the body, everything was both new and familiar. Only before, the aircraft had been passing over him during the siege, leaving him in white horror.

When the plane took off, Sami felt his body press against the seat, felt it become heavier. And then came that same feeling he had had in the sea. Weightlessness.

Sami thought about the bird he and his sister had thrown from the roof, a lifetime ago. He was hurling himself out into the unknown now, and hoping his wings would carry him.

Epilogue

MARCH THE THIRTEENTH, 2015. The rain pattered against the windows as Sami looked out at a line of aeroplanes waiting to take off.

'*Bienvenue à Paris.* Welcome to Paris.' The air hostess held out a bowl of chocolate hearts wrapped in red tinfoil.

In the airport, people hurried to the baggage reclaim and Sami let the stream of muffled footsteps carry him. The speaker announced departures and delayed passengers and it struck him he wasn't one of them. He was neither late nor early, nor on his way. He had arrived, in what was to be his new home country: France.

Sami figured someone would be there to meet him. That was how it worked at airports in the movies. People came home and embraced each other with flowers and kisses. But no one knew he was coming. He picked his bag up from the belt, tried to decipher the foreign-language signs and didn't know where to go.

Reporters without Borders had reserved a hotel room for him in northern Paris for one night. They had also arranged a meeting with a refugee hostel.

He didn't know anyone, didn't speak the language and it was his first time out of Syria, not counting Lebanon. But it was going to be all right. It had to be. *What are you waiting for,* his Grandpa Faris would have said. *The Damascus of Europe is waiting for you.*

◆

That first morning Sami woke to the rising noise of morning traffic. From the narrow hotel window he saw the trains pass by on elevated tracks; under the bridge, cars and mopeds jostled for space in a busy intersection. There were two canals, lined with cafés and trees in bud. Pigeons took off in cascades and spread out across the watercolour-grey sky.

Sami walked along the streets and zigzagged between the rain puddles. He thought of Muhammed, of their walks and races to school, and he thought of other friends from his childhood and the army and all through the siege. How deep and at the same time fleeting friendships could be. You never knew who would cross your path and change your life. They just showed up one day and decided to stay by your side, until one day they were gone. Was it the nature of war or were friendships always unpredictable like that? Sami wasn't sure. He only knew that the war had separated him from his closest friends and he no longer knew where many of them were. And yet it felt like he was carrying them with him.

He moved into a refugee hostel housed in a former factory, with bare concrete rooms and windows that overlooked a cemetery. Sami unpacked his bag and studied each object in turn: the camera, the memory cards, the clothes and the miniature Quran his mother had given him when he started his military service. The first new item he purchased was a kettle so he could make himself a cup of maté when his insomnia became unbearable.

Sami was creating a context, even though everything was new and fragile. His biggest worry was that time seemed to be disintegrating. He had a hard time telling the months and days of the week apart. When people asked how long he had been in Paris, or which day he wanted to meet up, he was unable to bring himself to place the dates in his mind. Other people seemed to think of time as a straight line with fixed points for significant events, but for him everything blended together into a jumble.

When darkness fell, he listened to the monotonous ringing from his first target practice. He often found himself staring blankly at the concrete wall. Sometimes when he fell asleep, the scenes played in his dreams like in the cinema. The crackle of the projector starting up was automatic rifle fire. The red velvet curtains flowed like rivers of blood.

Sami thought about how some things here were the same as back home, and yet not. The biggest difference was the freedom: freedom to and freedom from. The freedom to act freely. The way people here embraced and kissed each other openly, and were allowed to vote and choose their leaders. And the freedom from oppression and restrictions. From worrying about arbitrarily being thrown in a dark cell and left to rot.

'Would you like to try a video call?' Samira's message said. 'We finally got hold of a new phone.'

At first his cracked screen went black, then it showed two people on a sofa. Who were these elderly people, Sami thought before recognizing his parents. Samira had deep wrinkles around her eyes. Nabil, who had been balding before, now had only a few grey tufts around his ears and new liver spots on his cheeks.

'Why don't you have a moustache, my son?'

'But, Dad, I never had a moustache.'

'Then it's about time you grew one.'

Sami asked how the family was doing and said Paris was amazing, much better than expected. Everything was good with him. He was studying French, had a place to live and was hoping to find work soon. They said the same thing: they had a roof over their heads, food on the table and the power cuts were less frequent than before. Then they fell silent, as though it took time to find the words, the right, reassuring words that wouldn't make him worry.

283

'Everything is wonderful,' Samira said. 'Hiba and her family send their love. They're good, too.'

'And Ali?'

They were evasive but said that, *inshallah*, it would be OK.

'What have you eaten today?' his mother asked to change the subject. 'And don't lie.'

'Falafel,' he said.

Sometimes Sami longed for the smell of the *kibbeh* his mum made and the *shish tawook* from Abu Karim's restaurant. He sometimes ate at a Syrian restaurant on his new block. He had made friends with the owner, a man from Aleppo who moved away long before the war broke out, and the food was good, but more than anything he felt at home in the warm kitchen. He enjoyed watching the knife slice through the big, rotating hunks of meat, the sizzling of the coriander-green chickpea balls being lowered into the hot oil. Raw, crispy onion that made his eyes water. But the smell of Karim's roasted chicken remained absorbed in a painful darkness, like the other memories of his childhood and youth.

'Just falafel, nothing else?'

There followed a series of reproaches. Samira said he had to put some meat on his bones and not go outside with wet hair, since he could catch encephalitis and die.

'Do you have to be so dramatic?' Sami sighed.

'You've survived this far, my son. Do you really think I would let you die from wet hair?'

Nabil interrupted her. 'Let me give him some pieces of advice, too.'

Nabil reminded Sami to be respectful towards strangers. In other words, to be honest, polite and just a little suspicious, yet trusting and respectful. Not envious and proud, but goodhearted, open, generous, and did he mention respectful?

When all the unimportant things had been said, Sami asked how they were again. His mother lowered her eyes and said they wouldn't be able to rebuild the house. The regime had denied their application

284

to move back, and one of the reasons was that their youngest son was wanted for evading military service.

'They don't believe us when we say Malik is dead.'

The regime was also asking for Sami and he felt a pang of guilt. Samira began to cry and Nabil took her hand. The new phones didn't crackle but Sami still imagined crackling on the line. They were so far away, or maybe he was far away from them. Yes, he was the one who had left. If something were to happen to his dad again, he wouldn't be able to take a taxi to the hospital and hold his hands, feel his warmth rise towards his face. Nabil coughed and took a deep breath.

'I have to be honest,' his father said, 'there's not much to look forward to here. But that my son is going to live a life of freedom, that is something I never thought . . .' He let the words tail off.

Sami wondered if he had heard him right. It was an admission he never expected from his father. That freedom existed, that it was worth something. And by extension: that the revolution he and his siblings had fought for had value.

'Don't forget,' his father said before they hung up.

'What?'

'Moustache.'

The exile was an involuntary loss. It was losing your linguistic, cultural and social identity. But it was first and foremost grief at having lost himself, his dreams and plans for the future. Of course it was possible to start over, but what if you didn't want to? What if you found that the weaving of your life had been torn and the wind was blowing through its warp and weft. He had been cut in two: the Sami who walked the streets of Paris and the Sami who looked up and saw the pigeons of Homs circle overhead. As though everything in his former life – all the memories associated with specific places and people – had been transformed into stories.

Longing was embedded in every memory. He could not sit in the kitchen and argue with his siblings. He could not gather up the overripe fruit under the orange tree at his grandmother's house. He couldn't walk to Clocktower Square and have a coffee with a friend. He could only tell people about it. And every time, he wondered if his memories were changing, if he was adding or subtracting, if his narrative was as fluid as he felt. Was the telling a way of keeping the memories alive, or did he lose them the moment he spoke them?

In November, two friends Sami had grown up with but not seen for many years visited him from Germany. It was a Friday night and they sat outside a bar near the Saint-Martin canal, under the patio heaters.

Their journey had been more difficult than Sami's. They had crossed the Mediterranean in a rubber dinghy that had quickly sprung a leak. At first, the boat stayed afloat, but then fuel mixed with the water and burned their skin, particularly of the women and children crowded on the floor. Only one of the two friends knew how to swim; he had to keep them both afloat. People screamed in the freezing water. One by one, the bodies sank, only to be washed up on the beach they could see in the distance. But, miraculously, the two friends made it.

'That's why my beer's always on him,' said the swimmer of the two and smiled.

They talked about childhood memories, which reminded them that they did have a past, a normal life, before everything was broken. Did they remember the theme music to *Kassandra*? Did they ever. Sami hummed its distinctive melody.

He asked the waiter for salted nuts. The bowl clattered when he put it down on their table and, in that moment, they heard the crackling bangs. The people in the bar looked around and exchanged non-plussed glances.

'Fireworks this early?'

After that, everything happened very quickly and very slowly. Phones began to ding and people were shouting that they had to leave. Chairs toppled over, glasses smashed on the ground, Sami caught the word 'shooting'. Nothing around them seemed to signal danger; maybe it was just a gang fight further down the street. They walked around the corner from the bar and had a look around before Sami dropped his friends at their hotel.

It was only on the metro back home that he realized the extent of what had happened. Normally people didn't speak to each other in the carriages but now everyone was eager to inform and warn. Sami caught snatched words and sentences and read more on his phone. Masked men had fired at several restaurants near the canal. Explosions by the football stadium, the Stade de France, where a game was being played against Germany, had been reported. He and his friends had talked about going to that game but the tickets had been too expensive. His phone dinged again; terrorists had opened fire in Bataclan, where over a thousand people had gathered for a concert.

When police helicopters began to circle above the rooftops, Sami had flashbacks to the airstrikes in Homs. He bought two large bottles of water and stocked up on candles and tinned goods. Then he paced to and fro in his room, unable to relax.

Later that night he decided to head back out for a walk around the neighbourhood. The streets were deserted but he felt like he was being watched. He turned around in the light of a streetlamp and looked into a pair of golden eyes. The cat licked its black fur, languidly stretched out its back, then jumped down from the wall and slunk into the cemetery.

The following night, to clear his head, Sami walked to the Place de la République. Marianne was standing on her stone pediment, holding an olive branch up towards the sky, surrounded by flowers and light. For the first time he felt a strong kinship with the city. They were here together and they grieved together. Perhaps the people here did have some understanding of the trauma he had been through.

The French president had declared three days of national mourning. This was not just an attack on Paris or the French people, the American president had said. This was an attack on all of humanity and our shared universal values.

Sami had passed the square many times before, had sat in its burger restaurant and gazed out of the windows on the second floor. During the day, skateboarders zigzagged across it. One time, an evangelical man had preached about sin and forgiveness through a whistling microphone. The preacher had spoken rhythmically, like a rapper, and the people had swayed around him. Sami had paused for a while, trying to decipher the French.

Now it was midnight and the mood was very different. People were gathering in groups, offering each other tissues and cigarettes. Soldiers with automatic rifles patrolled the square; Sami would have preferred it if they had kept more of a distance.

A slight cough made him jump. And when he turned around, there she was.

'Do you have a light?'

He searched his pockets.

'Thanks,' she said with an accent he couldn't place. 'You wouldn't happen to have a cigarette, too?'

He laughed and lit one; she smoked with her hand close to her chest as though she were cold. She was a journalist and there to report on the terrorist attacks.

'Stockholm,' he repeated. 'I know a couple of Syrians who live in Sweden.'

'What else do you know about Sweden?'

'There are polar bears there, right?'

'Not really.' She laughed. 'We have as many polar bears as Syria has penguins.'

'Well, it depends on how you look at it . . .'

And then he told her that his mum once knitted him a penguin jumper. That it had been his favourite. He didn't know why, but something made him want to tell her that. And tell her more, continue sharing his memories. He stopped himself in the middle of a sentence when he realized how strange he must seem.

'I guess you miss her a lot. Your mum and the rest of your family.'

Then silence, hands deep in their pockets, neither one seeming to want to leave. He nodded at the graffiti wall and asked if she knew what the words meant. *Fluctuat nec mergitur.*

'It is Paris's motto,' she said. 'She is tossed by the waves but does not sink.'

Then she took two tealights out of her coat pocket and asked if he wanted to light one with her.

Sami thought about his little brother, about the ninety people who had drawn their last breaths in the concert hall, about how death always struck out of sequence and indifferently. He cupped his hand against the wind, a flickering flame in the night.

When we were born, what did any of us know about what our lives would be like? Nothing. We knew nothing. The only thing we could do was look at the place we were in and take a step in one direction or another. Life required nothing more than that. That was freedom. One step at a time.

Sami had already started feeling at home at Charles-de-Gaulle, particularly in terminal 2F. Over a year had passed since their first meeting at the big square, where people had mourned and she had asked him for a cigarette. During the autumn, he had waited for her here every other or every third weekend. Sometimes, he had hidden behind a pillar and put his hands over her eyes and pressed his lips against the back of her neck. They took the train into Paris and forgot about time for two or three nights until they had to come back here. Charles-de-Gaulle was their passage and ritual; they met and parted under the white fluorescent lights.

But now, in December 2016, it was Sami's turn to go to her.

Sami had only been on a plane once before and had already forgotten the procedure. Did he show his passport first, or his bag? How many security checks did he have to go through? There was something about all the security guards that made his shirt cling to his back and his breathing become laboured. Martial law was still in effect over a year after the Paris terror attacks. There were reports about raids in the banlieues and Muslims being arrested in the middle of the night on the vague charge of associating with terrorists.

Her voice on the phone calmed him. Had he packed gloves and a scarf? The winter in Paris wasn't like the winter in Stockholm, even though Stockholm winters were nothing like the Arctic landscape he had dreamt of as a little boy, with penguins, seals and polar bears. The layer of powder snow that sometimes fell was usually thin enough not to settle on the asphalt, but it gathered in drifts and crept inside your collar on the faintest of breezes, or melted into sludgy patches and seeped into your shoes.

The night before his departure, he had slept poorly. He had one of his recurring nightmares, the one where he was stuck between two checkpoints. One checkpoint was on his right, and the soldiers were calling him over. Then he heard voices from the left and turned around. The soldiers at that checkpoint were waving for him to come, too. He started moving in their direction, until a round of rifle fire in the gravel made him stop dead. Come here! This way, you idiot! No, this way, or I'll shoot!

He turned left and right, increasingly unsure about which way to go. Which checkpoint was more likely to let him through, if he even managed to get to it? Then he put his hands in his pockets and realized he had lost his identity papers. He had nothing to prove who he was. Without papers, he was lost; without papers, he was no one. The bullets struck the sand, closer and closer. In that moment, he had woken up.

We fit inside a single broken ray of light that contains the echo of every spring.
One day, the people would be victorious; Sami still believed that.

The dead would never come back, but the perpetrators would be held accountable through fair trials and proportional punishment. Because that was the ultimate sign of a free society, that even the criminals benefited from democratic rules and laws.

So it's freedom you want? I'll show you freedom!

The memory was as brief as a breath. But it was possible to remember together, to turn it into a collective act. Under the regime's censorship, reading itself became a protest and spreading stories became resistance. More voices would be needed. Voices to provide wind beneath their wings.

But our bird already knows how to fly.

Exactly, it just needs to be reminded.

The plane began its final descent and everything came closer: the sea, the sun, the snow-covered city. Soon, he would see her face in the arrivals hall.

The darkness fell quickly outside her family house, the streetlights glowing like big fireflies in the winter landscape. Her parents said that he should feel at home. *Home.* No more than that. But for a moment he forgot to breathe, the pain tingling in his chest.

The night before Christmas, he gave her an early gift: a notebook bound in maroon leather. In it, he had written down details from their first weeks as a couple. The morning she had knocked on his door with breakfast. The way she walked, that her steps could be slow or fast without her getting winded. There were words in it that made her blush: about her skin, hands, the curved arc of her fingernails which left marks in his flesh. His exhilaration when their lips caught on each other. They sat in bed and Sami watched her read his scribbled notes.

To'bri albi, you bury my heart. *Tishkli assi,* you will put flowers on my grave. *Tetla'ae ala abri,* you may step on my grave.

'All your declarations of love are about death,' she said.

Perhaps the violence was buried in the language, Sami thought, and maybe that's where the change had to begin. With a new language, and new stories. Or maybe death and love really did exist in symbiosis, equally transformative and unpredictable, equally inevitable and absurd.

Sami watched her close the notebook and run her fingers over the cover.

'One day, I'm going to give you a book,' she said. 'And that book will contain your story.'

A note from the author

Dear Reader,

I call myself Eva Nour. The pseudonym is necessary to protect the main character Sami, to whom my novel is dedicated. We first met in 2015 and now share a calm life in Paris, with some stray cats in our courtyard. When we met, Sami had recently arrived in Paris as a Syrian asylum seeker and I was there as a Swedish journalist to report on the terror attacks. We became good friends and then, after a while, more than friends.

At first, Sami preferred not to talk about the war and his escape. The stories came out in fragments and flashes. Some of the things he told me were so horrifying that I had to write them down to organize my thoughts. It started as a private diary, but the narrative gradually grew and took on greater importance, while Sami encouraged me to keep making notes and asking questions.

A rule of thumb for journalists is that you should never interview people you know well. The lack of distance can be a weakness, but here, it became a strength. I dared to ask things I had never dared to ask before – and Sami dared to tell me.

Sami's story gives frightening insight into one of the world's harshest dictatorships, but it also poses universal questions about the responsibility and authority of the individual, and about the power of love. Questions that are not limited to the suffering in Syria. All major events in the novel are based on reality and are seen through Sami's eyes, but several characters and situations are fictitious. I believe fiction can often bring us closer to the truth, and in Sami's case the fiction was a necessity and prerequisite for publishing this book.

For the shape of the narrative, I have drawn inspiration from novels such as Khaled Hosseini's *The Kite Runner*, witness literature like Imre Kertész's *Fatelessness* and Samar Yazbek's brave literary journalism.

Cats have been included as a red thread in the book and the title *The Stray Cats of Homs* came after Sami showed me a picture he had taken. It showed a couple of kittens that he'd given a bowl of yogurt to. It turned out that the picture was taken in his home, shortly after the house was destroyed by the regime's missiles. *How could that be possible*, I thought. *Your home has just been destroyed and yet you feed the animals.* For me, the cats became a symbol of humanity.

It started out as a love story and turned into a novel. Which in turn is an act of love, a love of both Sami and the Syrian people. And the name? Eva is a common Swedish name that means 'life'. Nour is a common Arabic name that means 'light'. Light and life. Since this is, after all, a story about keeping hope alive.

Eva Nour
Paris, 2019

Acknowledgements

A warm thank you to my publisher Sarah Adams and her wonderful team at Transworld Publishers, who have showed tremendous support and encouragement. Also, thank you to my translator Agnes Broomé and copy-editor Mari Roberts, for an impeccable eye for details and sense of rhythm. A special thanks to my Swedish publisher Maria Såthe, editor Johan Klingborg and the other kind people at Wahlström & Widstrand, who believed in the novel right from the start. Thank you to my agent Elisabet Brännström and her team at Bonnier Rights, who have helped to share this story with more readers.

Finally, my greatest and deepest gratitude to you, Sami, and our Syrian friends, who have confided in me with your trust and testimonies. You have found a home in new parts of the world and you continue to make these places forever better.

With hope for peace and freedom.

Eva Nour is a journalist writing under a pseudonym. She was inspired to write *The Stray Cats of Homs*, her debut novel, by meeting and falling in love with the real 'Sami'. Today the couple share a life together in Paris.

Agnes Broomé is a literary translator and Preceptor in Scandinavian at Harvard University, with a PhD in Translation Studies. Her translations include August Prize winner *The Expedition* by Bea Uusma, August Prize nominee *The Gospel of Eels* by Patrik Svensson and international bestseller *For the Missing* by Lina Bengtsdotter.